To Alison.

I hope you enjoy this book as much as I enjoy working with you

Zena

When Zena Livingston introduces herself, she says she is a wife, mother and slave. She is the office manager for the podiatric practice of her husband and two sons. A City College of New York graduate with a degree in English Literature, she taught English before devoting herself to the family practice. She is also a dedicated grandmother.

An avid salt water fishing person and boater, she finds peace of mind when she is near the ocean. She lives on Long Island in New York with her husband, Leon.

'The Money God' is her first novel.

The Money God

Zena Livingston

The Money God

Vanguard Press

A CIP catalogue record for this title is
available from the British Library.

ISBN 978 1 84386 518 6

*Vanguard Press is an imprint of
Pegasus Elliot MacKenzie Publishers Ltd.*
www.pegasuspublishers.com

First Published in 2009

**Vanguard Press
Sheraton House Castle Park
Cambridge England**

Printed & Bound in Great Britain

Dedication

There is a song that says "…make someone happy, just one someone happy and you'll be happy too…" This book is dedicated to that special person in my life, my husband Leon, for whose love I am most grateful and who has done everything to make me happy.

Acknowledgements

A special thank you to Pegasus Elliot MacKenzie and especially to David Newstead and Eliza Hamilton-Kennaway for their confidence in this work. Also to Willow Thomas for her tireless proofreading.

To Douglas Livingston goes an extra special thank you for his continued support and encouragement. To Jennifer Sforzo, Douglas and Kathy Hall goes a sincere thank you for their help.

CHAPTER 1

It was a bleak, miserable day. The driving wind caused the rain to beat against the windows and the trees seemed to touch the ground with their heavy burden of wet leaves. Everything seemed to echo Ann's mood as she sat in front of the window watching the rain and feeling guilty. People are supposed to feel something when they bury a mother, but Ann felt nothing; nothing at all.

"I saw her with the feeding tubes in her nose following her stroke, and wished her dead. I've seen the casket lowered into the grave but still I feel nothing," Ann said out loud as if by uttering her thoughts, she could make herself feel something; make herself remember Celia; make herself think of something good that had happened between them during the forty-seven years they shared.

Forty-seven years is a long time to know someone and yet not really know that person. It was obvious that few people knew or cared about Cel because only Ann, her husband, Dave, their son and his girlfriend, and Dave's mother had stood in the cold rain as the Rabbi said a few brief prayers before the casket was lowered into the ground. Not even Estelle, Cel's daughter, had thought to come. Ann shuddered as she thought, "I sometimes catch glimpses of Cel when I pass a mirror or gaze at my fingers. Will it stop there or will I die alone with no one to care about me just as my mother did?" To die alone has to be the worst punishment anyone can endure. "Why was she such a failure? Oh, God where do I start?" Tears that she did not even know were buried within her began to flow, breaking the silence of the house, drowning out the sound of the rain beating against the windows.

CHAPTER 2

Cel was so beautiful at eighteen that no one was surprised when her engagement to the popular, handsome Henry was announced. Henry was twenty-five and his future in the hotel business in the Catskills was assured. He was the manager of the growing hotel owned by Cel's parents. It was there that they met and it was there that they were to be married.

For Cel, Henry Samuels was everything she ever imagined a husband to be. She was proud to stand beside him; after all he was a native American. She would never marry a "greenhorn" like so many of the men who came to the hotel. Henry's firm body and strong arms made her feel safe and when he kissed her, she felt the warmth of his mouth on hers and was excited at the tingle she felt deep within herself. She knew she would be happy sharing her life with him just like the heroines in the novels who lived happily ever after.

The preparation for the wedding kept everyone occupied. Excitement spread throughout the hotel as the day approached. Even the guests seemed happy for them. Only Sophie, Cel's mother, seemed nervous. Deep within she had a nagging feeling that something was wrong.

On her wedding day, Cel looked beautiful in her short white gown with the long veil forming a train behind her. She held one white orchid in her gloved hand, its delicate petals nearly covering her white bible. Looking into the mirror, she knew Henry would be proud of her.

"It's time to go now," Papa said as he came into her bedroom.

"Papa, do I look all right? Are you sure everything is perfect? Will Henry be pleased?"

"Everything is perfect! Come now, we mustn't keep our guests waiting."

Walking down the central staircase and entering the main dining room, Cel could hear the whispers from the guests. She and Ruben were an awesome sight. He stood so straight that his six-foot frame seemed even larger in his new suit and she was indeed a bride who looked fresh and innocent besides being so beautiful. To Cel, everyone else seemed to be far away as she focused all her attention on Henry's proud smile. She wanted to run into his arms and kiss him immediately but her father's firm arm held her back. Suddenly, she felt Henry squeeze her hand; the Rabbi was speaking to her. She said, "I do" and Henry cracked the glass. Then they were outside the dining room and everyone was kissing her and yelling "Mazel Tov". To Cel, it was all a blur.

Cel's consciousness was awakened when Henry said, "Well, Mrs. Samuels, what do you say we begin our honeymoon?" Cel anxiously agreed though she was fearful of what was to come, yet she was eager for the experience. Cel wondered what a man looked like without clothes, especially what IT would look like. She has seen little boys but could not imagine how IT grew. Her friends said IT would feel good but Cel wondered, especially after Sophie had told her she was to perform her "wifely duties, even though it is unpleasant." Cel smilingly said to herself, "I'll know soon enough."

The old Model-T Ford was started and Henry escorted Cel to the car. The last minute goodbyes and instructions came at them from all directions as they inched the car down the driveway. For a moment, they thought everyone was just going to continue yelling at them all the way down the road to Grossingers.

Grossingers was the largest hotel in the Catskills and Henry thought it would be a real treat for Cel, who had never been a guest in any hotel, to spend their first few days together in that elegant atmosphere. As they registered, Cel kept smiling acknowledgements at people whom she knew from town and they returned knowing glances. The embarrassed couple were escorted to the Honeymoon Suite, one of the few rooms with its own bathroom and a very large bed. Cel shuddered as she saw the bed. When the bellhop left, Henry took her into his arms and gently kissed her; all fear vanished.

"We don't have to do anything tonight. We can wait a while, if you want to," Henry said as he took Cel into his arms and held her tightly to his body.

"No! No! I want to be totally yours. I've always wanted to. Please let us be together."

Henry started to undo the buttons on the back of Cel's dress and helped her slip out of it, allowing the dress to fall gently to the floor. He held her away from him as he looked at her body with the slip clinging to the folds of her young firm breasts and hips. Cel pulled the straps off of her shoulders and let the slip fall onto the floor. She stepped out of the pile of clothing at her feet and stood before her handsome husband wearing only her garter belt, stockings and panties.

Her breasts were naked and Henry stepped closer and took them into his hands and kissed each one. Cel tingled from the sensation, then loosened the hooks on the garter belt and pulled the panties and stockings off in one swift action. When she looked up, Henry was standing naked before her. Cel had to fight her instinct not to open her mouth in awe when she saw his erect penis; it looked too large to fit into her body. Sensing her shock, Henry again took her into his arms and lifted her onto the bed. He lay down next to her and started to fondle her breasts, kissing her as he did so. Then he moved his hand down her body onto her clitoris and started to massage it, making her feel sensations she never believed were possible. She wanted him and he, sensing her need, moved on top of her and placed his penis into her body. After the first thrust, she felt a sharp pain and felt her body respond to his. Before she knew what was happening, her whole body contracted and released, and she felt a sense of love and well-being that seemed to be the most beautiful feeling she had ever before experienced. Henry collapsed next to her and lay there holding her tightly to him.

"Was it all right? Did I do the right things? Did I make you feel good?"

"Everything was just perfect, my love. Hush now and let me hold you a while and let our love grow," Henry replied as he stroked her long hair and enjoyed the smell of her body.

The next morning came before either of them realized it was possible. The sun snuck into the room through the heavy curtains and the birds called their morning greeting to the young lovers.

Cel stirred first and she nestled into Henry's shoulder and lay there thinking how safe she felt. It was wonderful waking up in your husband's arms.

"Are you hungry? Let's get up and go for breakfast and then we can go walking in the woods," Henry said as he stretched his body to awaken it.

"No, let's do it again. It was great last night."

Henry smiled and rolled over onto his wife's eager body, thinking how lucky he was to have married someone like Cel.

Their three days at Grossingers passed quickly. The young couple enjoyed exploring each other's body and finding ways to excite each other. During the other times, they walked in the woods around the hotel and marveled at the fall colors which made the countryside look like a fabulous painting. The food at the hotel was excellent and Cel tried to remember each dish so that she could duplicate it when she returned to the kitchen at her parents' hotel. Together they dreamed they could make the Cohen's Hotel as fabulous as Grossingers. Someday, they hoped their hotel would attract guests other than the Russian immigrants who now came. When the World War ended, everyone hoped to have greater incomes. Then the city people could look for places to go to escape the heat of the city. Of course, there were the people who thought the Catskills were the perfect place to recover from tuberculosis. No matter how great the sacrifices were, their families continued to send money for them to recuperate in the hotels in the area. In reality these were the people who provided the income at the hotels. Ruben still had connections among the Russian immigrants as he and Sophie were immigrants themselves. They left the tenements on Third Avenue several years ago because Ruben had been lucky to bring money with him, money saved by his parents to give him a start in the New Country. They used that nest egg to buy the farm and they worked the farm until they had enough saved to make it into a hotel and farm. Now it was mainly a hotel and was growing nicely as more and more guests came and enjoyed the good cooking and fresh air. People came to their place because it was cheaper than the more famous and luxurious Grossingers. However, Henry and Cel planned to upgrade it now that he was to be the manager and she was to head the kitchen. They even hoped to add a ballroom and have entertainment on Saturday nights. Someday, they would add more buildings so more guests could be accommodated and then they would be even bigger than Grossingers. Excitedly, the young couple kept making comparisons between the two places as their stay came to an end and they kept lists of things they would do when they returned to Cohen's. Together, they could conquer the world and even force Ruben and Sophie to make changes.

Cohen's looked small and dilapidated as Henry and Cel drove up the driveway. The paint was peeling from the trim on the main house and the shrubs needed trimming. Cel's stomach began to tighten as she looked around and Henry seemed to be able to read her mind.

"Don't worry. A little paint and some work will fix this place up."

"Do you really think we can make a go of it? It would be so wonderful if we could attract more native-born people. Maybe we could offer programs to keep the children busy while their parents relax. Maybe we could hire real entertainers for evening shows. We could buy more land, especially now that prices are down."

"One step at a time. We have to work to make the place look better. Then we'll have to build more guest houses so we can expand. We are fortunate to have the land and the area is certainly beautiful. City people want to come to the country. I think we can start building by offering a farm experience to our guests. The children will be able to see the animals and touch them. We can advertise that we grow our own vegetables on our own farm and the guests can watch or even help with the harvests. Many of the people who come here remember the farms they left in the old country and might enjoy playing an active part in the running of the farm as a holiday that brings back memories."

"Oh, Henry...I hope we can make my parents see things your way."

The young couple walked into the kitchen of the main house to find Sophie in a tither. Cooking for twenty people was just too much for her to handle, or so she wanted Cel to believe. All Cel could think is that things never change where her mother was concerned. Sophie was always one to complain and have everyone around do the work while she supervised. The images of her parents' bedroom floated through her mind and she could picture Sophie's clothing lying in piles on the floor. Every night, Sophie would stand in one spot and strip off her clothes, allowing them to fall to the floor in a pile. There the clothes would remain until a maid or Cel came in to straighten up the room. It was as though Sophie believed she was royalty and deserved to be catered to. If Ruben minded, he never said anything about it. Ruben always seemed timid where Sophie was concerned and never wanted to cross her and receive her ire. This was even funnier to Cel when she pictured her parents standing together; Sophie was barely five feet tall, while Ruben presented a stately image with his six-foot frame.

"I fixed the room over the kitchen for you and Henry," Sophie barked at the young couple. "Why don't you put your things in there and get down here to help me with the dinner preparations. We have guests to feed."

"Is that all you have to say? Don't you want to know if we had a good time or what we thought of Grossingers?" Cel responded.

"You'll tell me in good time. Now there is work to be done. Mac Snell!"

"Welcome home, Henry. I guess she missed us."

Cel turned and went to wash her hands and put on her apron. The flanken had to be trimmed for the beef and barley soup on the evening menu but as she began trimming the fat from the meat her thoughts turned to Sophie. "As long as we remain here, she will dominate us just as she controls Ruben and the boys. We have to get away from her and start our own place. Henry and I can buy a small farm and convert it into a hotel just as Ruben did. Now is the time, especially with the real estate prices depressed...then we'll be able to do things our own way, my way...then we'll be able to control our lives and not have to answer to Sophie and do her dirty work." The knife came down especially hard on the raw meat and Cel looked over to see Sophie staring at her as though she could read her thoughts. A shiver went down Cel's back as she wondered if she would ever be able to cross her mother.

Henry went out to the main desk in the hall and started to review the hotel's books. There was no question that hard times were ahead for the family. The census at the hotel was down and future bookings were virtually nonexistent, and several guests were late in paying their room rates. The Depression was definitely becoming a factor at Cohen's. Luckily, Sophie never believed in banks so whatever money the Cohen's had, was available in ready cash. Also, Ruben did not owe any mortgage money, so there were no monthly payments due. They would survive but they would have to cut the staff. Even the boys would have to work in the dining room besides working the farm. They should be overjoyed at the thought, but what else could be done if the hotel were to ride out the Depression? Even Henry and Ruben would have to help with the farm duties, as that looked as if it was going to be a major factor in the hotel's economic health. With the farm providing the majority of the food, costs could be kept at a minimum and they would be able to keep the rates low enough to pull people from the other hotels in the area. Cel's dreams of expansion would have to be placed on hold until the Depression was over, of that there was no doubt! Henry closed the ledger and started straightening up the desk, which had gotten cluttered while he was away; everyone just seemed to dump things on his desk. His thoughts turned to ways to approach the delinquent guests for their money due. That is always a problem because you cannot be too aggressive or they will leave, and then what?

Life became a routine of work and anxiety for the young couple. But, no matter how hard the day was, no matter how much they had to give in to Sophie's unending demands, no matter how tired they were, when evening came they were excited. At night they could go into their room over the kitchen, close the door and fall into each other's arms. Cel loved to smell Henry and feel his arms envelop her, while Henry always enjoyed the softness of Cel's body. Some nights they were too tired for sex; instead they would fall asleep holding each other and feeling each other's nakedness. From that each seemed to gain the strength needed for the next day. Of course on the nights when they found themselves exploring and touching each other, their excitement would consume them and they felt as though they would explode as Henry moved within Cel. For Cel, sex was not a wifely duty but a consuming part of life which she wanted more than she had ever wanted anything before. She loved the way Henry made her feel and she loved the power sex was giving her over her husband. The more they made love and the more she tried to please him, the more he seemed to want to do for her. She just knew she would be able to make him go out on his own; time was the only factor.

The fall foliage faded and fell, and the ground hardened as fall began to turn to winter. Inside, work consumed the time during the day, with canning going on in the kitchen and painting being done throughout the hotel. Little discussion took place about future plans as even Cel realized the time was not right to spend money. Thanksgiving came and the family was grateful they were in a better position than the immigrants in the city. During the holiday, there were a few guests who came, as they had for several years. Henry treated them as if they were royalty in hopes of encouraging them to return. Only Sophie remained her same biting self with her sharp tongue and ever-present demands for attention.

Preparations for Chanukah were simple; few gifts were to be exchanged as the family put their money back into the hotel. However, Cel was radiant as her birthday approached on New Year's Eve. She just knew Henry would be extra attentive to make the evening special, even if Sophie ignored her birthday. On the day, she dressed in her best house dress and set about preparing an extra special dinner for the family. Sophie caught the glee in Cel's eyes and turned to her and said in a tone that sent ice water through Cel's blood, "Don't become pregnant, whatever you do. We do not need you to be throwing up and slowed up this spring when things have to be done around here. Remember, you have to work!"

"Oh, Momma, don't start that. I can't worry about becoming pregnant. Anyway, it hasn't happened yet."

"Just remember, let him keep his pecker in his pants and you stop looking at him like a love-starved puppy, or you'll mess things up. You had better learn what to do to stop a pregnancy. Only do it when it's your safe time. It is up to you, men don't think."

Cel just turned her back on her mother and wondered when Sophie would not try to meddle in her life. How could she believe she had the right to tell her when she could or could not have sex, when she could have a child, or anything else as far as that is concerned. After all, she was old enough to marry; now it was between her and Henry, not Sophie.

That night the family enjoyed their dinner and then Cel and Henry went for a walk in the crisp night air. There was a light snow on the ground and their footprints could be seen as they walked with their arms around each other's waists.

"A new year is about to begin and with it our love will grow," Henry whispered into Cel's ear.

"How can it grow when it is already all-consuming?"

"Love must continue to grow if it is to continue. As we know each other better and better, you'll see that what we feel today will be paled by what tomorrow will bring."

They turned to the house with frost on their clothes and eyes just for each other. "Good nights" were said and the couple went to their room, their haven over the kitchen. Henry wrapped his arms around Cel and held her to him, kissing her so that his lips enveloped hers. Hastily he removed her clothes and she removed his. Still wrapped in each other's arms they fell onto the bed and began running their hands over each other's bodies. While Henry touched her, he entered her with a thrust that made her quiver. Kissing her, he moved to a rhythm that seemed theirs alone and she began to respond to his movements as if they had rehearsed the scene. Together they climaxed as though they were indeed one. Still in her, they fell asleep feeling that they were in heaven. What a way to start 1932.

January passed into February and then it was March. Preparations were underway for the spring both on the farm and in the hotel. Everyone was busy preparing for the upcoming planting and the newly arriving guests, several of whom had made reservations. The hotel smelled from the fresh paint and there was an air of excitement permeating the atmosphere. Early one morning, Cel awoke feeling a gush of nausea as she opened her eyes. Darting to the bathroom, she threw up the meager contents from her stomach and looked bewildered as Henry rushed to her side.

"What's the matter? You are never sick."

"I must have a stomach virus...it'll pass. Just give me a few minutes to get myself together."

"I'll go tell Sophie you will not be down to help prepare breakfast. Just go back to bed and rest for a while."

"No... don't do that. She'll be angry and we don't need her yelling at us."

"Why will she be angry? Everyone gets sick."

"No, Henry, do not say anything to her. I think I could be pregnant. She definitely does not want me to become pregnant and there will be a scene."

"Pregnant! Cel, that's wonderful! What a way to start the spring. Don't you worry about anything; I'll take care of Sophie. You just take care of yourself and our baby. Oh, Cel, I have loved you since I first saw you when you were still in pigtails. All those years I spent in New York City going to school, I thought about you, never expecting you to care about me. Now you are having my baby. It is a gift from God and we must cherish it. No one has the right to dampen our joy. This child is a symbol of our love and with it our lives will be all the more beautiful."

"Does this mean you will consider starting a place of our own and getting away from Sophie's domination?"

"Time, Cel, give me time. Right now the time is not right to start a new place. We will continue here and help Sophie and Ruben make a go of this hotel. When this place is on its own feet, then we can consider starting a new place. By then the baby will be older and we can save up for a proper nest egg."

"I hope so. I really cannot imagine staying under Sophie's roof forever. She feels she can control everything and that everyone must do things her way or no way. She did not have her children because she loved them, she had them so that they can work for her. I hope my child never feels that way about me."

"Our child is born of love and will know that love every day of his or her life. You are not your mother and you will never treat our child the way she has treated her children. Too bad your father could not have been a greater influence in your upbringing. He is really an unusual human being with a great deal of love to share."

"He cannot stand up to Sophie. What she says is what has to be. Pop has always been totally controlled by her and I have always wondered why."

"He is too good, that's why. Now go lie down and rest, and let me handle Sophie and see that the kitchen gets started with the day's duties. There are only three guests, so it really is not a big burden on anyone if you rest in."

He bent down and kissed Cel's forehead and smiled. The joy of being a prospective father shone in his eyes. Cel thought that the baby would indeed be lucky to have him as its father. Now, could she be the type of mother Henry wanted her to be? That was a question she would have to wait to answer. She hoped she could love the child the way Henry would but there was the possibility she could turn into a mother like her own; after all, that was her only model to follow. She shuddered at the thought and lay back on her pillow to rest.

Cel came down to the kitchen around ten that morning, only to find Sophie refusing to speak to her.

"Momma, don't be angry. Henry and I are overjoyed and we can't wait to see this baby."

"You should have an abortion. I told you, we don't need a baby around here."

"Momma, don't be ridiculous. I could never have an abortion. This child is a product of our love and will be loved."

"That child is a product of your lust."

"Momma! Don't you ever speak to me that way again. Maybe you did not have your children because you loved Pop, but I love Henry and this child is going to be very special to both of us. I hope you and Pop will also love it and treat it with love or you will never see it."

Cel turned and ran out of the kitchen with tears flowing from her eyes. Why did Sophie have to turn joy into heartache at every turn?

"Dear God, please help me to get away from that woman so that she does not ruin my life."

The pregnancy advanced without incident. As Cel's body began to become rounded, Henry became increasingly excited. He loved to touch the swollen belly and to feel the baby move within her. Sometimes at night they would lie in bed and watch an arm or leg kick and protrude through the roundness. They continued to enjoy sex, though with greater care so as not to harm the growing child. To Cel, life was perfect. Even Sophie left her alone. Ruben seemed genuinely pleased about becoming a grandfather and started helping with the plans for the nursery which was to be added onto their bedroom.

That summer there was a steady flow of guests at the hotel. Many people brought their children and Cel helped to entertain the youngsters by playing games and reading to them. The parents seemed to enjoy the time they had to walk around the grounds without the children and often complimented Cel on her ability to relate to the youngsters. They thought her pregnancy gave her the needed instincts. Cel squirreled away the tip money the parents gave to her and continued to hope that it could go towards her own place some day.

The nights were the best time of all. Cel and Henry seemed to lose themselves in their own world, a world away from the hotel, the farm and the family. Henry would wrap his arms around her belly and hold their unborn child as if he hoped to give it his strength. One night he approached Cel.

"You should really see a doctor and let him make sure everything is going all right."

"Sophie says that is not necessary. She did not have any doctor when we were born and feels I will not need one either. Mrs. Weidman has promised to come over and help when my time comes. She has experience as a midwife and Sophie says she is better than any doctor."

"Cel, this is 1932. Women have doctors and you should have one too. No one knows what can happen and I would feel better knowing a doctor is taking care of you and our baby."

"I can't go against Sophie."

"I will never understand the hold that woman has on the entire family. Everyone keeps saying they cannot go against Sophie. Why do you all believe she knows everything?"

"If we cross her, her anger is horrible and she stays mad forever. Life around here becomes unbearable. She has run this family ever since I can remember. Pop never has spoken up to her and none of us have either."

"Someone has to end this! She is not always right. Don't you see that the model she has set can influence you with our child? She probably treats you as her mother treated her. It's a cycle that must be broken or you will treat our child the same way."

"Never! I will never treat our child the way Sophie has treated me. Our child will know love and will know that she or he is not my servant but the recipient of our love. That's one of the reasons I so want us to get a place of our own and get out from under Sophie's control. She will try to control you and our child if we stay here. The only reason she has left you alone is that she respects your education and knows that you understand the books better than she does."

"You must promise me that no matter what happens in the future, you will always love this child, who will be a symbol of our love. Always remember that the child's feelings must be considered and not manipulated. This child will grow up knowing it has merit and worth and that it comes first in our lives. Before Sophie, even before you and me."

"I will try. I understand what you are saying about having to break the model set for me. I will never be like my mother. But this doctor thing is one I think will work out Sophie's way. Our baby will be born in the same bed in which it was conceived with you and me together. If I have it here, you can stay in the room with me, but if I go to a hospital, you can't be with me. I want you here to help me. Everything will be fine."

Henry had no answer; his only thought was that Sophie was about to win out again. Again things were going to be done her way, just as everything else was done. Maybe she could dominate Ruben and the boys, but she was not going to rule his life with his family. Someday things were going to be different and she would respect him for what he would accomplish.

September came and the fall foliage was more brilliant than ever. Walking around the farm was like walking into a painting, with colors all around. The mountains seemed to be alive with life and beckoning all to see their glory, Every step sang its own music as the leaves rustled underfoot and the air was crisp and fresh. Henry kept saying that the beauty was Nature's way of preparing to welcome his child while Cel giggled at his romantic nonsense and began to wish for the end of her pregnancy. It was definitely becoming harder to do her work in the kitchen; her feet were constantly swollen and her belly seemed forever in her way. She felt so top heavy whenever she had to bend down for something that she was constantly in fear of falling and then wondered if she would be able to get up if she did fall. However, the canning had to be finished, the kitchen had to be prepared for the holidays and the work never seemed to end; nor did Sophie's complaints. No matter how much was done in a day, it was never enough to make that woman happy. With every demand Sophie made, Cel's resolve to move out and get a place of her own seemed to become stronger. Cel knew she and Henry and their child would be happier away from Sophie's constant nagging and attempting to control their every move.

The hotel was busy for the Jewish holidays as was to be expected. Many new guests came to enjoy the traditional foods and to worship with their friends. A Rabbi came to conduct services right in the hotel and some of the guests from neighboring hotels came for the services as well. Hearing the Shofar welcome in the New Year made Cel smile because she just knew it was going to be a joyous year for her and Henry. She kept thinking "a New Year and a new beginning." Yom Kippur passed with Cel busy preparing the breakfast meal for the family and guests. She did not attempt to fast because Henry felt it would not be good for the baby.

After dinner was finished and the kitchen was placed back in order, Cel went to their room and waited for Henry. He looked so handsome in his holiday suit and she enjoyed watching him undress and longed for his tender touch. Sex was an impossibility at this stage of her pregnancy, but they still enjoyed holding and touching each other and feeling each other's warmth and tenderness. Henry rubbed her tired back and gave her an ever-so-gentle massage which seemed to relax her muscles and make her so sleepy. Despite her efforts to stay awake and prolong their tenderness, Cel fell asleep in the crook of Henry's arm.

At six in the morning Cel awoke and felt a sharp pain cutting her abdomen in half. Her groan woke Henry instantly. "Cel, what is it? Is the baby coming!"

"I don't know! Maybe I just have to get to the bathroom."

"Cel, it doesn't take a genius to know you are in labor. I'm going to get the doctor."

"No! Please, I want you to stay with me!"

Henry was just about to argue with Cel when another gripping pain pierced her and she doubled over, grabbing him.

"Okay, I'll go and ask Sophie to send Sam or Abe for Dr. Bergman," Henry said, knowing that Sophie would not send for the doctor but for Mrs. Weidman, the local midwife instead. Again, his will would not be had and Sophie would do as she pleased.

Day passed slowly into dusk and Henry sat at Cel's bedside, mopping her brow which would become soaked with perspiration as the labor pain increased in intensity. The shadows of evening fell on the surrounding mountains and the stars appeared in the sky while the living quarters echoed with Cel's moans. Ruben and the boys kept checking but still the baby had not appeared. Henry's concerns were repeatedly put aside by assurances from Mrs. Weidman that the first birth is often arduous and everything was normal. Henry was consumed with guilt that he had caused Cel to experience such tremendous pain and Sophie kept reinforcing his feelings by reminding Cel that this was the payment for enjoying sex. She kept saying, "Remember this the next time he comes to you and wants you. Remember this will happen again."

"Oh, mother, please keep quiet. I don't need this now! You had three children!" Cel replied, gripping Henry's hands and trying to let him know she did not blame him.

The night sky was beautiful and Cel could see it through the window across from her bed. Just as she was about to comment on its beauty, a pain greater than any before it encompassed her and she pushed her daughter out from her body. The child cried as she entered this world and was placed on her mother's chest. Henry and Cel looked at their daughter, whose dark hair resembled the night and whose fair skin looked like the stars in the heavens above.

"She's beautiful; almost as beautiful as her mother," Henry said as he held both his daughter and his wife in his strong arms. "What shall we name her?"

"We'll name her after your father, Edwin, and call her Estelle."

"It almost sounds like the stars under which she was born. I like your choice and thanks for naming her after my father. I know he will always look down from heaven and take care of her."

After Mrs. Weidman left, the three of them fell asleep together, exhausted from the day's trauma but happy.

CHAPTER 3

Life for Cel and Henry continued along the same path after Estelle was born. They remained busy during the day with the tasks of running the hotel and in the evening returned to their quarters, where they played with the baby and fell into each other's arms. At first Henry hesitated to take Cel to bed for fear of causing another pregnancy and more pain. But Cel longed to feel Henry inside her and soon convinced him that there was no reason to fear hurting her as she needed him as much as he needed her. The intensity of their love prevailed and they each enjoyed the closeness they experienced. If anything, their sex life was better than before, as Cel was less inhibited and more willing to experiment with new positions and even began to read about new ways to please her man. One night Henry was shocked when Cel undressed him and went down on her knees and started to kiss his member before taking it into her mouth. He was about to stop her when she placed her hand on his and continued moving her mouth along his penis until he felt he was about to explode. Quickly, he moved away and lifted her onto the bed and entered her, knowing he would never forget this moment.

When Henry lay next to her, Cel snuggled against him and ran her hand over his chest.

"You know how much I love you. Now you must think about moving out of here and getting a place of our own. We're a family now and we need to get away from Sophie or she will forever dominate our lives, just as she has dominated Papa's and the boys."

"If that is what you really want we will start looking for a place this spring. I'll do anything you want, anything."

Cel smiled and knew she had won a major battle. Soon she would be the master of her own life instead of working to Sophie's drummer. She thought to herself, "This was easier than even I had hoped it would be! Now we'll be able to start our own hotel and we'll be more successful than Sophie will ever be."

As the snow began to melt and the trees started to bud, Cel's mood became increasingly excited. She kept asking in town about who was selling their property and would drag Estelle and Henry with her to look at the various farms that were put up for sale. None were exactly right but she never gave up hope that they would find the perfect place.

It was early June when Henry started coughing. At first they thought he had caught a cold but when the cough did not go away they decided to go to Dr. Bergman. After examining Henry and listening to his chest, Dr. Bergman took them into his office and sat them down.

"Henry, I think you should go to see a specialist in New York City. I know him well and he just specializes in chest problems. I want his opinion because I do not like the way your chest sounds."

"I don't understand. I have a cold, pure and simple. I thought you would give me some cough medicine."

"I don't think it is that simple. I hear rales in your chest. It could be just from chronic congestion but I think we should check it out completely."

"Do you think he has TB?" Cel questioned with a worried look on her face.

"That is a possibility. You people work with and live with many TB patients and it is possible to catch the disease. I just cannot say what it is without further testing and Dr. Cohen is the man to do that testing. I can tell you I would not let this go."

"How do I get an appointment with Dr. Cohen?"

"I will call his office for you."

Henry and Cel sat holding each other's hands as Dr. Bergman made the call to New York City. All Cel could think was that nothing must happen to Henry; her entire life was based around him and if anything happened to him she would have nothing and no one. She began to shake with fear.

The appointment was for the following week. During the wait, Henry stayed away from Cel and Estelle for fear of passing whatever it was on to them. Cel felt as if he had distanced himself from them and longed for good news from the doctor that would put an end to the isolation. Even Estelle seemed more cranky than usual as though she too missed being with her father. Cel insisted on going with Henry to the City and left Estelle with Sophie, hoping they would be returning with good news which would allow them to put their lives back on track.

Dr. Cohen's office was on Park Avenue in Manhattan, an area Cel had never seen before. The building seemed to glitter in the sun and everyone in the street was dressed in what appeared to her to be their finest clothing. There were no immigrants in this part of the city. The office itself was decorated as if it were a living room, with seating arrangements instead of the bench seats that dominated Dr. Bergman's simple country office. When the nurse called Henry into the examining room, Cel was instructed to wait in the reception area until after the doctor had seen him. Sitting alone on one of the couches, Cel's fear began to take over and she felt as if she would lose control. Without Henry she would never be able to live like these people whom she saw in the streets of this affluent area; she would forever be Sophie's kitchen slave. If anything happened to Henry, who would hold her, love her, and make her feel special? "Please, dear God, let him be all right."

It seemed as if Henry was in the doctor's office for hours before the nurse asked Cel to join her husband in the consultation room. When she entered the paneled office, which was dominated by a huge desk, Henry seemed smaller and more vulnerable than ever before. Cel quickly walked to his side and took his cold hand. A shiver went through her as they waited for Dr. Cohen to come in and speak with them.

Dr. Cohen came into the room and took his seat behind the huge desk. He cleared his throat as if he needed to gain their attention. Both Cel and Henry had their eyes glued on the man whom they felt held their fate in his hands. He began to speak in a monotone which only increased their anxiety.

"It is not TB but the x-rays do reveal a large tumor in the right lung which, in my opinion, based on the sound of the lungs and the short duration of the problem, is probably a malignant tumor. Further testing is necessary to determine if other organs are involved," he continued over Cel's gasp and Henry's sigh. "I cannot, at this time, recommend surgery because I do not think there is any purpose in subjecting you to the procedure which would probably just hasten the final outcome. However, we will know more after all the tests come back."

"Are you telling me that there is no hope and that I should just go home to die?" Henry questioned unbelievingly.

"Unfortunately, we have not had great success with cases such as yours. Lung cancer is a terminal illness. I cannot say how long you have as no one knows how fast the cancer will spread. I can tell you that you will continue to be able to function normally for a period of time, then you will become increasingly weak. Eventually you will be bedridden and there will be considerable pain. We can give you medications that will control the pain, but there is little else we can do."

"You're wrong. You have to be wrong!" Cel screamed. "Henry is too young to die. We have a baby and our whole lives are ahead of us."

"I wish I were wrong. This is an unpleasant experience for me. Believe me, I feel totally helpless. The fact that Henry is young and strong may help him survive longer than the next person. My advice is that you both go home and enjoy being with each other for as long as you can."

"Do you think it would be beneficial to get another opinion?" Henry questioned.

"By all means get another opinion. I will forward your test results to whomever you wish. Unfortunately, I do not think the end prognosis will change. Some doctors will recommend the removal of the affected lung. I have not found that helpful. As of this point in time, we do not have anything that can kill the cancer cells and unless they are killed, they just pop up somewhere else in the body. I have found that once surgery is performed, the cancer seems to grow more rapidly than it would have done without surgery."

"You are giving me a death sentence at age thirty-two. This is very hard to accept."

"I realize that; believe me when I say I wish the news were different. We just do not know very much about cancer. It is very unusual to see it in someone your age, but I have seen it before and I am sure that I will see it again. I feel I have to be honest with you despite the harshness of these findings because I want you to be able to enjoy what is left of your life and to be able to put your affairs in order. I am a realist and I would want someone to tell me the truth, if the positions were reversed."

"I agree with you there," Henry replied, shaking his head and feeling as though his world had come to a virtual stop.

Slowly the young couple rose from their seats and left the doctor's office clinging to each other. Each was totally lost in thought as they made their way back to the Catskills; each knowing life as they had known it before was to be forever changed.

Ruben was devastated by the news when they told him what had transpired. He immediately told Henry that he should not worry about Cel and Estelle, as they would always have a place in his home and that they would all do whatever they could to make him comfortable. Sophie for once seemed speechless as tears welled in her eyes and she felt genuinely sorry for her daughter and granddaughter. She looked at the handsome young man before her and could not visualize him dead. Only Estelle seemed unchanged by the dire news that had cast a black cloud over the entire family.

That night, after everyone had retired, Cel and Sophie met in the kitchen. Cel's tears fell as Sophie took her daughter into her arms and held her with a tenderness that Cel had never experienced before this.

"What am I to do, Momma?"

"There is nothing, my kinda. You will take care of him, love him and try to enjoy every moment you have left together. That is all you can do."

"Oh, Momma, I love him so."

"I know, I know. Life is sometimes hard for us to understand. Sometimes it does not seem that we are dealt a fair hand."

"Why Henry? He never hurt a fly. He is such a good person. So smart, so loving, so understanding."

"The why's and the wherefore's have no answers."

"What will become of us?"

"You'll survive!"

"How?"

"You'll find a way. You're young and smart and beautiful. Somehow you will find a way. Now is not the time for long-range plans. Now you must be strong and you must take care of him and the baby. Later, we'll plan. Now dry your tears and go to your husband; he, too, has his fears. He needs you and he needs you to be strong."

"I'll try, Momma. I'll try!"

"Oh, Cel, don't forget tomorrow there is work to be done around here. We are expecting six new guests on Friday."

"Good night, Momma. Don't worry. I'll be up early and I'll get the work done."

Cel went to their quarters only to find Henry fast asleep. Knowing that he was exhausted from the trip to New York, she silently undressed and got into their bed. She was overcome with a hunger to be close to Henry, to try and give him her strength and she snuggled next to him, pressing her body into his body folds, and holding him tightly, she too fell asleep. The next morning, she felt him stir and held him, stroking his private parts, and she felt him become aroused. He turned and held her and they came together, feeling their love and knowing their bliss was doomed by fate. Later, while still in each other's arms, Henry began to speak.

"No matter what happens, our love will always be with you. You will always have Estelle to remind you of our love and she will be a comfort to you."

"This whole thing is something I cannot accept. You are too young to die. Without you, I have nothing."

"Cel, someday you will remarry. Hopefully you will find someone who will love you as I do, and will also love our child and help you to bring her up so that she will be a credit to you and to the love we have shared."

"I only want you. No one will ever take your place! Please don't talk about my finding someone else. I will never love another man as I love you."

"Love takes many forms. Maybe you will not love someone in the same way as you love me, but you will need someone to provide for you and for Estelle. Right now, this whole thing is a terrible shock to both of us, but we have to be realistic. I will not be able to see our child grow up. Believe me, I will fight with everything in me to remain by your side for as long as God allows.

"Just hold me and let's not talk about the future. Estelle needs her breakfast and we both must get some work done," Henry said, as he patted Cel on the behind and got out of bed, coughing as he did so.

Three days passed before Dr. Cohen called with the news that the tests had confirmed his suspicions. Henry indeed had cancer and the disease had spread to his liver as well as his lungs. He told Cel that prescriptions were being sent to help keep Henry comfortable but there was little else they could do for him.

Tearfully, Cel asked, "How long do you think he has?"

"He is a young man and he appears relatively strong, so I would say he should be able to function for approximately six months to a year. Then I would expect him to become bedridden. The cough will become worse and he will experience severe pain as the cancer spreads throughout his body. I am sincerely sorry to have to tell you this news, but honesty is best. You both have to make your plans accordingly."

After the phone call, Cel was too shaken to continue working in the kitchen. She went to their bed and fell sobbing onto the pillows. Why was this happening to her? Why was God so mean that he was taking her Henry from her? Answers were not there and in her misery all that Cel wanted to do was to die before her beloved Henry, but she knew she would not be that lucky.

Spring passed into summer and the hotel was busier than ever before. Both Cel and Henry were caught up in the activities around them and could have forgotten the sentence hovering over them if Henry's persistent cough had not served as a constant reminder. While his body tanned from the warm summer sun, he became thinner with each passing week. Fatigue was becoming a companion to his every movement and often he was too tired at the end of the day even to hold Cel as they fell asleep. Her body craved his more than ever before and she was insatiable when it came to sex, but she felt him slipping away as his weakness was making him less able to respond to her advances.

October came and with it came extremely heavy rains. The roads leading to town were being washed out by the floods from the mountains. Few guests were able to come to the hotel because of the bad weather and the family could not even prepare properly for the winter ahead. One particularly rainy night, Cel and Henry were in the kitchen having dinner when Ruben came in. His face was drawn and white, and Cel immediately knew he was not feeling well.

"What is it, Pappa?"

"I don't know. I feel very strange." With those words he turned and fell to the floor.

Henry rushed to his father-in-law and felt for the pulse in his neck. It was weak. All the color was drained from Ruben's face and his skin was clammy and damp.

"Call Dr. Bergman."

"The phone is dead."

"You had better send one of the boys for him."

Cel ran from the room and yelled for Sam to get the doctor. Without asking any questions, Sam ran out of the door, only to return a short time later with news that he could not get through to town. The bridge was washed away and even their neighbors down the road did not have any phone service.

Helplessly, the family stood over Ruben as life slipped out of his body. His pulse stilled and his breathing stopped without anyone being able to do anything for him. It was incredible that one minute he was there standing before his family like a pillar of strength and the next he was laying dead on the kitchen floor. No one knew anything was wrong with him. He never complained about anything. Now they would have to wait for the storm to end to even find out why he had died. They all stood around him in utter shock.

It was three days before the bridge was restored and the family could contact Dr. Bergman. They were told that Ruben had known he was a diabetic for some time but had made the doctor promise that he would not tell the family as they were under too much stress because of Henry's illness. Dr. Bergman guessed that Ruben died as a result of a diabetic coma.

The funeral was subdued, with only the immediate family and close neighbors present to say their final farewells to a truly gentle man. Sophie stood alone during the burial, knowing that she would have to continue to find a way for the family to survive. Their lives were now her sole responsibility and she knew she would find a way. Ruben had often said to her that the family should move to the city if anything ever happened to him. They could sell the farm and the boys could find work as mechanics. Automobiles were becoming ever more common on the streets and people needed mechanics. In her heart, she knew that Henry would not last past the following summer, and she would see to it that Cel remarried and that she would be taken care of by her new husband. As for herself, Sophie was sure she could live off the sale of the farm for a long time. Maybe she would move in with her sister in Brighton Beach. There she would be with others from Russia and she could be happier than she was working day and night at the farm. But for now, things would have to wait. There was no point in uprooting Henry. They could keep the place going as long as he was there to help administer the hotel's affairs. Then there would be time for her to do what she had to do. One step at a time. Of course, she knew it was going to be hard to attract guests to the hotel. Only Ruben seemed to have the personality necessary to bring the city people out to the mountains. He never lost contact with the immigrants in the city; they seemed to follow him like sheep following the shepherd. Sam and Abe lacked the personality to bring in new business and Henry was too sick to make the necessary trips to New York.

As the casket was lowered into the ground, Sophie thought back upon her life with Ruben. She and Bella had come to America as young girls and had moved in with Aunt Frieda, who lived with her family in Brooklyn. One night, Aunt Frieda invited the tall and handsome Ruben to come for dinner. As soon as he entered the living room, Sophie knew she was in love with a man who looked to be a knight in shining armor. He was so tall, so straight and so kindly. The fact that he had saved some money and could afford to plan to buy a farm in the country made him all the more appealing to the young girl who had nothing and whose only hope appeared to be for her to become a domestic in the home of some wealthy businessman in Manhattan. Ruben was a gentleman whose manner prevented him from refusing anyone anything, so their relationship developed, with Sophie being the business person and Ruben being the one with the personality. He brought the people to the hotel and she got them to pay their bills. But to her, her gentle giant was the sun around which her world rotated and now he was gone forever. A tear ran down her check as Sam threw the first shovel full of earth over his father's casket. Sophie glanced over at her family and knew that as of that moment her leadership would be ever so much more in need and she would have to do it alone, without the gentle guidance of the man who had always been there for her.

The neighbors were wonderful and, when the family returned home, food and drink were there for everyone. All the mirrors were covered so that the family would not see the face of grief and the shiva benches were in place. Henry excused himself and went to bed; he was physically and emotionally drained. Cel took her seat and stared blankly at those assembled, knowing that this would not be the only time she would be sitting on the hard wooden bench of mourning. Only Estelle seemed to enjoy the company because she was too young to understand the sorrow that had befallen the household. The baby's laughter was like a counterbalance for the grief.

Cold is the word that best described the winter. The days were bitter cold with wind driving against the farmhouse and snow forming mountains in the courtyard. But as cold as the days were, the nights were even colder for Cel. Henry no longer had the strength for sex. He either coughed all night or wheezed and gasped for air so that he could no longer even hold her in his arms. Cel's body ached for his touch; she dreamed of feeling his penis in her, of feeling her nipples harden with the excitement of feeling his strong arms holding her during the afterglow of lovemaking. Sometimes the dreams were so real that she would awaken to find herself wet with anticipation but the wetness quickly dried as she heard Henry fighting to breathe; she knew he was losing the battle and she was losing him.

As the crocuses began to bloom and the mountains started to awaken from their winter's sleep, the angel of death again visited the Cohen farm. Henry died in his sleep and Cel needed no one to tell her that he was dead when she awoke to silence in their room. No coughing, no wheezing, no moaning; only peace. Henry was at last at peace. Cel was almost relieved that his suffering was over at last. She kissed his lips and held his body to hers, knowing this was to be the last time she would ever be able to put her arms around him.

"I will love you always. No one will ever take your place in my heart; every hour we spent together was a precious gift. Oh my God, why did you have to die?" Cel sobbed, the tears falling on Henry's still chest. She stayed holding him and sobbing for what seemed like hours before she could go and face the family. As she rose, she saw paper on the night stand beside Henry's side of the bed. She picked up the paper, saw Henry's handwriting and started to shake; he had written to say goodbye.

My beloved Celia,

These few pages are to contain my last words and my last thoughts and wishes. I would like very much that you save these pages, for perhaps some years later in reading them over they will recall the short life we had together and the few moments of happiness we enjoyed. Perhaps a word of advice, a note of courage or an incident related here may help you or cheer you in the years to come.

Probably in after years you will show our Estelle what her daddy thought of her and how her daddy longed and struggled to make her happy and how I prayed to be with her always.

It is almost useless to say that all my dreams and all my plans and hopes are shattered. My body refuses to go on. Tho' my mind and heart and my will urge me yet to carry on, still my body refuses and my arms and legs are heavy as tho' they were made of lead.

I never pictured that my end would come as it is now coming. I never dreamed that God would call me before my time, taking me away from loved ones and ending my life just when I thought it had only begun. Happiness with you and our child was just around the corner, but I had not the strength nor the power to manage to get around that corner.

Some may say I did not rightfully prepare myself for the struggle of life, but they were wrong. From boyhood on I have realized my responsibilities to life and have always striven to build up a good foundation in every respect – educated myself, built myself up physically, belonged to social, literary and athletic clubs, was well represented in all my classes both academically and athletically, belonged for years to Y.M.H.A., and always had medical examinations. And most important of all, I have prided myself on always living a clean, wholesome life; I always hoped for that day when I would be married, when I could give what I would demand in my mate; a clean and faithful companion.

Yet somewhere along the road of my short life something slipped, something went wrong and the beautiful monument I was building to the Goddess of Happiness came tumbling down about my ears. And now, amidst the ruins, there remains only the memories of the things we had, and might have had...

Honestly, Celia, I am not sorry one bit for my own self. My life with you, tho' short, meant so much to me; the little bits of joy and happiness we had together to me were huge chunks of gold. I loved you so, and realized how wonderful you were, how good and fine, that to me the littlest thing was wonderful. And then our struggles together welded our hearts so that there could be no truer understanding. And that was not all. Our Estelle was our treasure. She made life brighter, more promising, more beautiful.

That is what I am sorry for; sorry to be unable to see or hear you two around. No more to see the wonderful smiles, nor to wipe away the tears. No more to play with Estelle and to hear her ringing childish laughter. No more to kiss her perfumed cheek nor to caress her silken hair.

That is what I'll miss, dear. That is what I'll miss. And God knows and only you know that I shall miss you ever, ever so much. If life were longer I would have struggled on so that someday I could have been able to repay you for all you have done, for all you have given up, for all you have sacrificed for me. Our love could have been the world's most beautiful thing because I believe your love was as holy, as fine and as true as my own love was for you.

My only wish is that after I am gone, God will see that you get your share of happiness, that you and our Estelle will never more have trouble or heartache, and that for the rest of your lives you may be happy and cheerful. And may your lives be long and healthy, and may you spread cheer and joyfulness wherever you may go, because real happiness comes from making others happy, too.

One of the main problems I wish to mention, dear, is the fact that you will want to marry again. It is no crime and it is perfectly proper, providing you marry a worthy man and one whom you will like. Do not marry anyone unless you believe you like him. Naturally your experiences in life will find you now more fully equipped to know what is best and proper. You must not forget to keep in mind that your future mate must also love Estelle. These conditions, the fact you were married to me, and possibly other conditions which I cannot think of just now, and some conditions that may arise after I am gone, will make it important you decide honestly and properly.

I want to help you decide. I pray you will not make a mistake. I hope you will do the right thing at the right time. I don't believe your fine character will change after I am gone. I believe your high ideals, and your fairness and squareness with all whom you come in contact with, will be the same later as now. In other words, I don't think you will accept any man later, if he is not the proper mate for one like you. I feel that what you would demand before you married me, you will demand again before marrying anyone else. Because I know you, and know how beautiful your heart is, because I feel that any man getting you gets just the same kind of wonderful woman I got when I married you. Do not feel yourself one bit lower than you were six years ago. In fact you should feel more valuable, have just as much pride and honesty as ever. To me you were always as ever faithful as I was to you. You kept your marriage vows to man and God. To your future mate you must also remain faithful and true, and you must demand of him the same condition. Only with fairness and openness and truthfulness can you and he be happy with each other. You must, I think, seek someone about your age or somewhat older. A youngster would never live up to your ideals, I fear. It would be nice if you would meet a man established in life, a type who loves a good home and loves the companionship of a pretty and lovable wife. Forget not, he must protect Estelle and if he cannot love her, he must at least like her. You must build your health up to the mark, and I believe you will have at least one more child.

I cannot put on paper my inner feelings as I write the above because in my heart I never, never dreamed that someday you would belong to another. As I write the tears blind my eyes, my throat chokes me and my heart is bleeding and hurting. If I had ever known that God would separate us before our time, I swear I would never have married. If I ever had the tiniest suspicion that I was sick or unfit in any way for you, I would have gone on my way by myself. Yet wasn't it Destiny or Fate that brought us together? I was hundreds of miles away in Montana, where I expected to spend all my life. Doctors not caring to assume responsibility for an appendicitis operation made me come to New York. Then Fate saw to it that I moved next door to you. You were in pigtails and I was just a book-reading kid. Then you go to Monticello, a hundred miles away from Third Avenue and for ten years we forget each other. In fact, there was nothing to forget.

Then I come to Monticello and we get married. The sun shines, the flowers bloom, the trees wave in splendor, the green grass like velvet rugs spread under our feet, the birds sing madly, life is sweet and gay, youth is in love, and we were married...

Then Fate took a vacation. Left us. Gave us a year of unhappiness and trouble. Hounded us and beat us at every step, cursed us and broke us as if we had violated every law of God! The birds ceased their singing, the flowers died, the trees dropped their leaves like big drops of blood, and everything started to wither and drop – and my life was ending...

It is a bitter dose to drink but I must drink it. After all I've gone through and suffered and sacrificed. Crawling to work when every muscle in my body shrieked with pain. On! On! there must be no stop. Loved ones are waiting for bread, dear ones are hungry for joy, onward!

Yet, with all my bitterness and sorrow, I have one happy thought and that is that maybe now when I've gone you will at last find your happiness. After all I have done to ruin your dear life, after all the terrible hardship you have gone through on account of me, maybe now your luck will turn and God will reward your faithfulness and your efforts.

Would that my last act on earth, the last thing I could do, would be to make you happy. But I can only wish and pray that from now on you will have the happiness you deserve, and that I was unable to give to you. That's why I fervently hope that the man you will take will be worthy of you and your love. That he will respect and honor you as I did. Only he who respects and honors you can ever love you truly. He who marries you merely for material things or for mere physical possession will quickly tire of you. Likewise, if you accept a man only for material advantage you cannot hope for true love again. That's why I say, be careful and think what you are about before you choose another mate. If I could talk to that fortunate man who will eventually be your mate and companion, I would shake his hand and say, "Be good to her, be true and respect her, and in turn she will be ever a faithful and wonderful pal."

I will not impose a time limit as to when you should remarry. When the wound in your dear heart will have healed then you are free to go ahead and continue onward through life with our dear Estelle, and with you always will be my sincere blessings and wishes for your happiness and success.

A few words about our Estelle. I certainly hope you will not let her forget her daddy completely. I would like her to always remember the love I had for her, the hopes I treasured in my heart for her future. It was my greatest wish to live to see her grown to womanhood and to be able to teach her the many, many things my father was unable to teach me. Especially was it my dearest wish to help her through school, when many problems come up and a child feels lost and hopeless unless a helping hand is near to assist and encourage and cheer up. Those are the wonderful things I dreamed of and hoped for but will be beyond my power to do. So that duty will be yours dear and may it give you a great happiness.

Dear Estelle, oh! how I shall miss her. And if there is such a thing as a life after death and if I can look down from God's beautiful blue sky, then I shall do so, and I shall bless her (and you, too) wherever you be. That is why I asked that you remind her of her daddy sometimes and teach her to remember my memory by some fitting token on each anniversary of my departure.

And, Celia dear, don't fear death. For I don't. Sorry, yes, for the many things I will leave behind and the loved ones I must say "Goodbye" to. But I fear nothing. I was brave enough to undergo so much torture in my life, that death can hold no such terror for me.

After you have lived your life to the fullest, had the happiness you deserve, and when your hair has turned gray, and your step has lost its spring and you feel tired – then we will meet again, dear heart, and once more our lips will meet and then you will tell me what you did and what Estelle did and where she is. We then will laugh joyfully over our olden troubles. Oh! 'twill be a lovely meeting of old hearts that long, long ago loved in a glorious way.

What more can I say, Celia dear, except I hope you will not forget me entirely. When and if you do think of me, don't think of me in sorrow, but in happiness. Shed no tears from your dear eyes, except tears of gladness. Yes, dear, be happy. Happy that we loved even tho' we lost. Be happy for the golden moments God gave us. Be happy because you have Estelle for a companion, make her a real pal. It's up to you. Also be happy that your troubles are over, that my troubles are over forever. Be happy and proud in the everlasting thought that I loved you truly and faithfully unto the end. Remember those last words of the marriage vows? "Unto death do we part." And so goodbye my dear, be kind to our Estelle, and firm when necessary. Remember I have always loved you and that God is Supreme and his will cannot be changed. He will keep you well and bless you from now on. Goodbye, sweetheart, goodbye forever and ever, until we meet again in Another World.

With sweetest memories and also bitter ones.

Yours,
Henry C. Samuels

CHAPTER 4

Cel was a different person following Henry's death. It was as if she had created a shell around herself and no one, with the exception of Estelle, was allowed to penetrate that shell. She performed her daily chores as if she were a robot and rarely spoke to the other members of the family or the few guests who still came to Cohen's. Her weight dropped below her normal 120 pounds and her clothing seemed to hang on her bony frame; her face was drawn and showed her lack of sleep. Only when it came to Estelle did Cel seem to be alive. The child became the focus of her world and she would not let her out of her sight even for short periods of time during the day. At night, the child slept in Cel's bed. It was as though Cel feared the child would be snatched from her just as Henry was snatched away.

Sophie repeatedly tried to get Cel to stop being so overprotective and overindulgent with the child. She could see that Estelle would be excessively spoiled by Cel and would not be able to develop normally. Estelle, for her part, was becoming increasingly demanding and would throw temper tantrums whenever anyone tried to discipline her or refuse to give her what she demanded. At such times, Cel would rush to her daughter and calm her down by giving into her and by being angry with the others involved. Sophie tried to account for her daughter's behavior by blaming it on her grief but in her heart she knew something had to be done to permanently correct the situation; that something would have to be a new man in Cel's life, someone who would care about her, understand her needs and help her bring up her daughter. Of course, every time she tried to mention the idea to Cel,

Cel would clam up and walk away without letting her mother even finish her thought. The tension in the household was stifling and even the guests were aware of it; few ever returned and most shortened their expected stays. Cohen's was becoming known as a hotel of grief, gloom and tension.

The anniversary of Henry's death passed and the flicker of the memorial candle seemed to set Sophie's mind that action had to be taken. It was then that she decided to sell the farm and move to the city. First, she would have to find a new husband for Cel; that would be no easy matter, but she was sure there had to be a widower in the Russian community who would want her for a wife. Sophie decided to speak to Mrs. Bergman and Mrs. Weidman; surely they would know if a young wife had recently died. Maybe the man would have been left with young children and would need someone to help raise them. Surely Cel would feel sorry for such a person and would marry him out of pity. If that would not be reason enough, Sophie would make Cel realize that she needed someone to support her and Estelle, and that she would also need a place to live. After all, Henry did not leave her financially secure and with the farm sold, Cel would have to find a place for herself and Estelle. Sophie knew one thing for sure: Cel would never go to work and leave the child with someone during the day. She also knew that there was no point in hoping that Cel would fall in love with any other man. As Sophie closed the door and shut out the light of the candle, she resolved that she would be the one who would be tough and cold-hearted; she would be the one who would force Cel to return to the world of the living for her own sake and for the sake of the child. Then, and only then, would she herself be able to go forward with her own life. After all, she wasn't too old to start a new life with a new man who would be able to provide for her old age. What did she need with this farm and the emotional drain of having guests to prepare for and cater to. Ruben was the one who had loved this place, not her.

"Yes, it is time to change things around here, and I'm going to be the one who does the changing," Sophie said to herself with new resolve as she mounted the stairs to her sleeping quarters. Shaking her head, she heard herself say, "Children are little problems when they are young and bigger problems as they get older." She stopped and smiled, remembering that it was Ruben who had always made that statement in the past.

While Sophie was having her thoughts, Cel too was deep in thought as she lay in her bed staring into the night's darkness. She felt empty and cold as she thought how she missed being held and feeling a man's hardness within her. Sure, she could play with herself and feel a release of the tensions within her, but it was an empty release. She felt that her juices were drying up and she yearned for the comfort only a man could give.

"Oh, to be held and to feel strong arms surrounding me; to snuggle against a strong chest and rest my head on a comfortable shoulder," Cel thought to herself. "I miss a man trying to please me and make me feel like a woman. I miss running my hands down a warm chest and feeling his hardness aroused in response to me. God! I miss being a woman! My life is not worth living this way. All I do is work and take care of Estelle. There has to be more to living. Henry died, not me!"

Anger choked Cel as she reflected on the dismayed life she was living. She was too young to be among the living dead so many widows resembled. For her it was even worse than it was for the older widows who used to come to the hotel. She had a baby to raise, no income, no inheritance, no life. Most of the widows had older children to whom they could turn for support; she had no one.

"Henry, how could you do this to me? We had dreams to live, plans to fulfill. You abandoned me! God has abandoned me! WHY? WHY me? I am not a bad person; I deserve a life!"

Just then the child sleeping next to her stirred in her sleep as though Cel's thoughts were disturbing her. Cel reached over and took the small figure into her arms and held her, hoping to give and get some comfort. Feeling the warmth from the small body did reassure Cel that she was indeed alive and she relaxed enough to fall into a light sleep, knowing that she still had a part of Henry beside her.

It did not take long for the word to get around the immigrant community that Sophie was looking to make a match for her daughter. Cel's beauty was well known and there was no doubt that she was a ball buster. Of course she could only expect to get a widower... used is used. Most likely she would have to settle for a man with children; after all, she has a child. Everyone also realized that Cel would be picky. She would never settle for just any man; he would have to be clean, relatively good-looking, a good provider, and would have to be somewhat assertive to be able to handle that headstrong girl. Cel was always the one with the big dreams.

Sophie was sure that a match for Cel would be found before too long. Her only problems were to arrange for the sale of the farm and to convince Cel once someone was found. Convincing Cel could be a big problem since she always refused to entertain the idea of remarrying. Every time Sophie broached the subject, Cel would refuse to discuss it or simply leave the room. There was no doubt that Cel could be stubborn but Sophie was sure that she would, in time, convince her that there was simply no other way around the situation. Cel needed a place to live and someone to support her and Estelle, and Sophie was not going to be that person. Cel would have to consent to marrying.

The next morning, Sophie went into town with Sam. She went directly to the General Store and spoke with Mr. Weiss, letting him know the farm was to be sold as soon as a buyer could be found. She also stopped at the bank and spoke with the president there. There was little doubt that between these two contacts, someone would be directed to her, as most newcomers stopped in these places looking for land. On the way home, Sophie spoke to Sam.

"I know you think it's wrong of me to sell Papa's dream but there really is no choice. We cannot keep the place going without him and Henry."

"What is to become of us?"

"You and Abe will have to find work in the city. You are both good with engines and you can be mechanics. Everyone needs someone to fix their cars."

"I don't know, Momma. I'm not one to work for someone else and Abe is very lazy."

"You're both grown now and it's time for you to move on with your lives."

"What about Cel and the baby?"

"She'll have to remarry and make a life for herself too."

"I think that is easier said than done."

"You'll see. It will all work out. Just leave it to me."

Sam looked at his mother and knew there was no point in arguing. Once her mind was set on a course, there was no changing it. He just wondered how much of a sacrifice she expected them to make. It seemed to him that it was really she who wanted to move on with her own life. He smiled to himself, as he thought it would not be too long before she remarried and moved on. Sophie was not a woman to be without a man in her life. As for himself, he knew someday he would have to leave the farm and go out on his own.

Maybe he could find someone to marry and start his own family. His needs were small; he could do it. As for Abe, that would be a different story. He really had no skills and was so sickly that it was hard to imagine him as a self-sufficient person.

When they came home, Cel refused to speak to either of them. She knew in her heart that Sophie would force her to take an action that would not be her own choice. Time would be a factor. In her heart she just knew the farm would not sell overnight. Maybe she could work something out to find a job so that she could support herself and Estelle without having to marry some stranger Sophie would find. Maybe she could even find someone on her own. Yes, that would be better than just accepting Sophie's choice. She could start going to some socials at the other hotels and she could start to make herself look nicer and be a better conversationalist. Something would break for her, she just knew it.

That night, Cel came down for dinner dressed in a fresh dress and looking more radiant than she had since Henry's death. Sophie smiled to herself and knew a new beginning was starting for her family. She was more convinced than ever before that she had chosen the right course of action. After all, any course was better than living in the no man's land they had been in for too long already.

"You look nice tonight. Any special plans?" Sophie questioned.

"Yes, I thought I would go over to the social at Grossingers. I thought it would be nice to see some of my friends. That is, if you do not mind watching Estelle."

"Go and have a good time. I'll put her to bed on time. You needn't worry. It is about time that you rejoined the living. It'll be good for you to be among young people."

"Do you think Sam will be able to drive me over and I'll call when I want to come home?"

"Of course he'll drive you. Sam wants you to rejoin the living world as much as I do."

"Oh, Momma, stop that. I am just going to the social to see some of my old friends."

They drove to Grossingers in silence. Sam was never a great conversationalist and tonight was no exception. Cel was grateful for the silence as it gave her time to compose herself. This was a difficult step for her to take, one she would not be doing if she did not feel the pressure from Sophie.

Walking into the large dining room, Cel could feel the silence as the others saw her for the first time. She felt like an outsider among her former friends. Her widowhood made her different, a difference she keenly felt as Sadie came over to greet her.

"It's good to see you. It has really been too long since you have joined us. Come and help dish out the punch."

"Thanks, I would like to help. How have things been going for you?"

"The same as always. I'm still waiting for Prince Charming to fall out of the sky and rescue me from all of this. Who knows, maybe tonight he'll appear!"

"There are no Prince Charmings in the Catskills. But Sophie is also searching for one to come and sweep me off my feet and save the family. She'd marry me off to the first man with a possibility to make a living if she had her way."

"Oh, I heard she is putting the farm up for sale. I thought she wants to move everyone to the City to start a new life there."

"She wants to start a life for herself but wants me and Estelle to be taken care of by someone else. She seems pretty desperate and I don't want any part of it. I just know she will find some greenhorn who needs a housekeeper and will force me to marry him."

"No one can force you to do anything. We both know that."

"Don't be so sure. I have no skills except housekeeping and there is no way I can support Estelle and myself, especially since I would have to find a babysitter even if I did manage to get a job in the City. I just do not see myself leaving Estelle with a stranger."

"Didn't Henry leave you some insurance money?"

"With the Depression and Henry's illness, we used up all the money we had just to pay the bills and keep the farm going. Everything Poppa and Henry saved is just about gone. Now the guests are not coming and we are not making ends meet."

"Well, let's go and join the others. Now is the time for you to forget about everything for a little while and have some fun."

People came over to say hello as Cel dished out the punch and small talk filled the evening. It was fun dancing with some of the guys who Cel remembered from her single days and she did begin to have a good time despite herself. Sadie was right, it was fun to be there and the evening flew by.

At midnight, Cel was about to go and call Sam to come and pick her up as Jack came over to her. His farm was down the road from the Cohen's and she had known him since she was a child.

"What's up?"

"I was just going to call Sam to come and pick me up."

"I'll take you home. I have to go that way anyway. Why bother Sam?"

"That'll be great. Thanks."

They left the social together after a quick round of goodbyes and got into Jack's car.

"I bet things have been hard for you now that Henry is gone."

"Yes, I really miss him."

"It's rotten to be without a man after you've gotten used to having one. I bet you really miss having a man's attention."

"Jack, let's not even get into that. I really do not want to discuss it now or ever."

Jack stopped the car and before Cel even knew what was happening, he had his hands on her breast and his hot, wet lips over hers.

"Stop it!"

"Don't be a child; you need it as much as I do. It has been a long time for you and you need a man. Come on, you know what's up. Stop acting like some type of virgin who has never felt it," he said, as he reached under her dress and caressed her pubic hair through her panties.

Cel pushed his hand away and reached for the door handle, throwing the door open and jumping out of the car in one quick movement.

"Jack, you are an animal, not a man who I would want near me. Just get out of my sight and never speak to me again. I know what a real man is and you could not even share his footsteps."

With that Cel started walking towards home. She felt her whole body shaking but was even more alarmed by the wetness she felt on her panties. Did she want it? Did her body crave a man's attention, even an animal like Jack? No... no matter how much she wanted sex, she would never allow herself to be reduced to that level. Someday she would find a man whom she craved and she would commit herself to him and him alone. One-night stands would never be a part of her life. After all, even Henry had said that she had worth and she would live up to his vision of her.

On the road behind her, she saw the headlights of an approaching car. It had to be Jack following her route. As the car neared, she huddled on the side of the road, hoping it would just pass her by. But as it pulled up alongside of her, it stopped and the door opened.

"Get in! I'll drive you home. I promise, no more advances."

"Promise?"

"Yeah! I promise. Listen, I'm sorry if I was out of hand; but you can't blame a guy for trying."

Cel got into the back seat of the car and sat in silence for the remainder of the trip to her house. There was just nothing to say, but she knew this was the way it was going to be if she continued going to local socials. The guys would always view her as used merchandise and would expect free samples.

That night she could not wait to get into the shower and to wash away the horrors of the evening. Cel felt dirtied by it, most of all because she realized how much she longed for sex, longed to feel a man's hardness in her and to be caressed by his hands. In the shower her nipples hardened as she allowed her feeling to surface in her mind. She resolved not to put herself into a position of temptation again. She would stay away from socials and men who only wanted one thing from her. There is just no way that she would let someone like Jack dirty her. Once again, she felt angry at Henry for leaving her like this. If only he had lived, their life together would be perfect; their sex together would be perfect. If only he had lived, Sophie would not have to sell the farm and life could have continued just the way it always had been.

"Oh well, there is no use thinking about the 'if onlys'," Cel said out loud as she tried to rub her hair dry. "'If onlys' 'and 'could have beens' are as much of a dead end as my life!"

She wrapped herself in a large dry towel and curled into bed to wait for sunrise. It was comforting to listen to Estelle's gentle breathing as she slept soundly in their bed. "At least I have something tangible to remind me of Henry," Cel thought as she reached over to touch the sleeping child. "All of my love will always go to this symbol of Henry."

The gentle breezes of summer floated through the kitchen where once there was always great activity preparing meals for the guests. Now there were no guests at Cohens. The house was dilapidated, with paint peeling off the outside walls, and the shutters were all loose. Sam had taken a job in town helping the mechanic fix cars, while Abe continued to complain about his fragile health and Sophie lamented their financial condition on a daily basis. The livestock which had amused the visiting children had been sold and now only old Betsy remained, and she seemed to be kept alive by God's will alone. Betsy was too old to produce milk so no one wanted her. Abe was unable to maintain the fields which had previously provided produce for the farm and now the weeds had taken over to add to the desolate appearance of the property. Few prospective buyers came and those who did wanted to pay so little for the property that Sophie took offense at their offers. The only living thing that seemed to prosper was Estelle, on whom Cel bestowed all of her attention. When she was not playing mindless games with the child, she was sewing clothes so that Estelle was always dressed like a little doll. The child seemed endlessly demanding and Cel gave into each demand, while Sophie complained that she was spoiling the child and making her into a little devil. But Cel refused to pay any heed to her mother. The tension between the two women was so thick that often days would pass without them sharing a word. Even Cel realized something had to be done to break away from this oppressive life, but the question was, what could be done? She lacked any skills that would make her employable and there definitely was no money to finance a change.

It was at this low point that Bella, Sophie's sister from Brighton Beach, came to the Catskills to visit. Bella had married a Russian immigrant and had two children of her own. While the family was not wealthy they made ends meet. Bella's husband worked in the garment center as a cutter of ladies clothing and his salary was adequate for their quiet lifestyle. Bella had come because she knew of a dress designer who had recently lost his wife and desperately needed to marry so that his two small boys would have a home. His wife had died in childbirth, leaving him with a five-year-old and a newborn, who now were living with relatives while their father worked.

"He's a clean man who would make few demands on a woman and who would be grateful to have his children living with him again. He makes a good living and probably someday will own his own factory," Bella told Sophie.

"Is he American?" asked Sophie. "You know how Cel feels about greenhorns."

"No, he is not American. He came here when he was thirteen with only a sewing machine to his name. His parents sent him to America during the Cossack raids in Russia. It turns out he was the only member of his family to escape. The others were all killed before he could save enough money to send for them. He is a good man, a religious man, who holds his family as being extremely important. It is said that he treated his wife very well and was heartbroken when she died."

"What happened to her?"

"I heard that she had a heart condition and was told not to have any more children, but she wanted another child and became pregnant against doctor's orders. Labor was just too much for her and her heart gave out just before the little one was born. Unfortunately, the baby survived and now he grows without a mother to love him. It's so sad."

"What does this man look like? Have you seen him yourself?"

"I've met him several times – Sol often brings him home for a home cooked meal. He is average height, somewhat stocky and balding but he had strong features and a very pleasant but sad-looking face. He is always grateful for the meal and has very fine manners. This is a smart man who can speak and read five languages. His father was a Rabbi in Russia."

"Does he want to meet Cel?"

"I think I can arrange for him to come up here for a weekend to meet her if you can arrange for her to be receptive to him."

"That could be easier said than done but I will try. Lord knows we have to do something. If she is married off, I can move to the city and start a new life too."

"What about this place?"

"I will sell it for whatever I can get and say good riddance to it."

"The boys..."

"They will have to make their own ways. Sam is learning to be a mechanic; he'll always be able to make a living. As for Abe, well, it is time he did something. Maybe in the city he can find work that will not be too demanding on his health. Here the work is too hard for him and he gets short of breath easily. He is seeing a woman, an older woman who talks about opening some sort of store with him. Who knows, maybe they will marry; then she can take care of him. I'm tired of taking care of him. I don't view him as a problem. Cel and Estelle are the problem. I cannot just turn them out."

"Well, you work on Cel and let me know when to arrange a visit. Then I will come up with Morris and introduce them. I just don't want to be embarrassed by Cel openly rejecting him. You and I know she can be mean if she wants to be."

"Cel has been hurt. She continues to miss Henry and is just miserable with her life as it now is. She is not mean, she is just extremely unhappy."

"You call it what you want, I'll call it what I want. She gives the impression that she is above everyone and it is hard to take. She isn't even nice to Helen and Issie when they try to reach out to her. My children think she is stuck up and they wonder what she has to be stuck up about."

"This is just a cover for her unhappiness. But I do not understand why you want to help her if you feel this way about her."

"You are my sister. I cannot stand to see you this way. I know if I help her find a husband, it will free you from this bondage. That is why!"

After Bella left to return to the city, Sophie asked Cel to join her in the kitchen. As they sat at the table drinking tea, Sophie brought up the subject of Morris and the proposal that Bella had made. She expected that anger would ensue and that was why she waited for Bella to leave before broaching the subject. It was better not to add fuel to Bella's resentment of Cel. At first, Cel glared at her mother with daggers in her eyes.

"How can you even suggest such a thing?"

"Just in case you fail to realize it, we are in a desperate situation. We can no longer afford to keep the farm. It means that we must make changes and move to the city. You cannot afford to support yourself and Estelle, and I cannot afford to either. The only solution is for you to remarry and let your husband support you both. This is a golden opportunity. Here is a man who needs a wife as desperately as you need a husband. Okay, he is not your Prince Charming. You married for love once and look where it has gotten you. Now you must marry to improve your situation and provide a home for your child. This man needs someone to take care of his children; you can do that. Look at it as a job."

"But he will want more than just that."

"More...do you mean sex? Of course he will expect that of you; it is part of your job. But who knows. This is a man who lost a woman he loved because of sex, so maybe his guilt will keep that part of the relationship in control. Besides, he is eighteen years older than you so I am sure sex is less important to him."

"You don't know men!"

"You do?"

"But he is a greenhorn and you know how I hate them."

"He is smarter than you. Bella says he reads and speaks five languages. You can barely manage one."

"You told me Bella said he is religious. I don't want to keep kosher and have to deal with all of that crap."

"In a job you do what you have to do. That's all there is to that."

"Oh, Momma, I don't think I can do it! I don't want to marry and look at it as a job. I want what I had with Henry."

"Henry is dead and buried. You are alive and you must do whatever is necessary to remain alive and to take care of that child you hold so precious. If you marry this man, she will have children to play with immediately. It would be good for her to be with other children. Now she is spoiled rotten. If she continues to grow up the way she is now, she will be a miserable adult."

"Stop picking on Estelle; she is perfect!"

"Look, I do not want to argue about Estelle. Now I want you to think about meeting this man. Who knows, maybe he will not like you and this will all be for nothing. Maybe, just maybe, you will like him and find him appealing. It all could be for nothing. But if you never meet him, you will never know. Think about it and give me an answer. Bella thinks she can arrange for the two of you to meet here in about two weeks. I just have to call her. At least she is your aunt and looking out for your best interests. She is not a matchmaker who wants to make a match just to get paid. But if this does not work out, we might have to call a matchmaker. Get it through your head, we are desperate."

With tears rolling down her cheeks, Cel stood and without a word left the kitchen. She ran into the shower so that her sobs would not wake Estelle and her sobs rocked her body as she thought about her options. Options that did not exist. As she dried her body, she knew she would agree to meet this man and, if she pleased him, she knew she would marry him just to get away from Sophie and to ensure that she and Estelle would have a home. She vowed that Estelle would always come first no matter what because she would always be a symbol of her real love. That night she held the child in her arms as she waited for the sleep that would not come. All night her life flashed before her and the desperation of her situation became ever so much clearer. The next morning she told Sophie to call Bella and arrange the meeting. There was no more fight remaining in her.

CHAPTER 5

Two weeks later, Bella called to say that she and Morris would be coming up to the Catskills the following weekend. Sophie told Cel of Bella's plans in a matter-of-fact manner, much as if she was telling her to go to the store or to wash the kitchen floor. Cel's only response was equally non-emotional as she nodded to acknowledge Sophie's comment, but in her heart she dreaded the meeting. What if he expected something sexual from her? What if he repulsed her? Could she go through with this arrangement despite her true feelings? These were questions that flashed through her mind. She knew that the Europeans that used to come to the hotel did not believe it was necessary to bathe frequently. Oh, how she hated the way they smelled! What if this man was like that? She shuddered but knew she had to go ahead with the meeting, if for no other reason, than to satisfy Sophie so that she would not just go ahead and arrange a marriage to some old man for whom she would have to be a nursemaid.

On Sunday morning, Cel awoke, showered and dressed in one of her better garments. She carefully applied her makeup so that she could look her best and was pleased with her image as she looked at herself in the mirror. She dressed Estelle with equal care, as she wanted to make an immediate statement that the child was important and had to be considered in any possible plans. As she heard the old car pull into the driveway in front of the house, she went to the window and watched as her aunt and the man with her emerged from the back seat. He was short and somewhat stocky but appeared well dressed. That was all Cel could make out from her window.

"Well, here goes nothing," she said, as she prepared to take Estelle downstairs with her. She had decided they would appear as a pair so that she could make a statement from the start that her child was of paramount importance.

Bella and Morris were in the living room when Cel came down and the introductions were made. Cel was immediately relieved to see that he was as nervous as she and the two of them just stood looking at each other without being able to find any words to utter. Bella sensed their awkwardness and started telling Cel about the trip up from Brighton Beach, and then suggested they go for a walk and that Cel show Morris the area while Sophie and she prepared lunch.

"Let Estelle stay here with us and help set the table," Sophie said. "That way the two of you can get to know each other while you go for a walk."

"I guess we have no choice," replied Cel as she looked over at Morris, who seemed afraid to say anything with all of the overbearing women around him. "Come, Mr. Beckman, and I'll show you around the farm. It is not as nice as it used to be when we had guests up here but you can get the idea of what it was like."

"I understand that things have been difficult for you since your husband died," was his reply.

Cel was touched by his statement and looked more closely at the man who was here looking for a wife. She knew he was older than she and his face showed that he too had suffered. Cel knew he was a widower with two small boys but she knew nothing else about him. She decided to try to get to know him a little before they came back in for lunch.

As the two of them walked outside into the brisk autumn air, the silence hung heavily around them. Neither felt comfortable starting a conversation. They walked back toward the barn and Cel began telling him about the animals that used to be housed within it and how the children from the city used to love to touch them. He smiled as he thought of how his older son would love that too.

"My son would love to see animals. He only knows city life and now that he is living with his grandparents, his world is even smaller than it used to be."

"Do you also live with your parents?" Cel inquired.

"No, I have an apartment in Manhattan so that I can be near my factory. The boys are with my wife's parents but it is hard on them to take care of two small children. That is why I am considering remarrying."

"I see."

"Please let me explain. I never thought I would be in this situation. I loved my wife dearly and we had a good life together. It was a tragedy that she died in childbirth and now I am in a desperate situation. I need someone to look after my sons and help bring them up. I do not want to hire someone and have that person leave in the future. That would be hard on the children. I have decided that I have to find a lady who would be a good mother to my sons and who would be able to offer them a stable family life. Your aunt has told me that you are in an equally desperate situation and, while I never thought I would consider an arrangement such as she proposed, I think it has merit. She has told me you loved your husband dearly and that you are a dedicated mother to your daughter. I would not expect you to have the same feelings toward me as you did for your husband, just as I know I can never have the same feelings I had for my Lilly. But if we find we like each other, and if we feel, in time, we can give the children the feeling that we are a family, maybe this can work out. Right now, I can only say that I am obviously willing to try."

"I am relieved that your feelings are similar to my own. I, too, never thought I would consider meeting anyone through an arrangement. I only consented to this meeting because my mother wants to sell the farm and then I would not have a place to live. I cannot see myself allowing Estelle to be cared for by a stranger while I go to work and Sophie refused to take care of the child once she leaves the farm."

"I can understand her position. It is very difficult for someone who is older to take care of an active child. I see the toll it is taking on my wife's mother. She has neither the energy nor the patience to run after a five-year-old."

"How old is your other child?"

"Norman is one year old now. He is a quiet baby and is not much trouble for his grandmother."

"It is a shame that he never knew his mother. Does the other boy remember his mother?"

"He has some memories of her but they are not really clear ones. She had a difficult pregnancy and was unable to spend much time with Joseph prior to her death, so most of his memories of her are of a lady in bed."

"That is the same way that Estelle remembers her father. He had been ill with cancer for over a year prior to his death and she was too young to have ever done anything with him before he became ill. It is such a shame they were robbed of a parent at such young ages."

"I know. That is why I want my boys to know a stable family life now. Unfortunately, not too many women are willing to marry a man with two young children. It is not the most romantic way to start a marriage, especially as I am still in love with my wife."

"I understand what you are saying. I never thought I could remarry after Henry died. But ..."

"Your aunt explained all of this to me before I agreed to come up here. We are both in equally desperate situations and we do not have to pretend with each other. It could be a comfortable way to start a relationship. You know my feelings and I can accept yours."

"Time is what we both need. Time to see if we can really accept each other. It is nice not to have to pretend, but I could never agree to any relationship unless I really feel I like the other person. Despite everything, we have to at least like one another or the children will suffer."

"I agree, and I am willing to come here and even bring the boys up so that we can all get to know each other. You are a pretty woman and there is no denying that you deserve a husband who can love you. I wish it could be different but I do not want to foster any false pretenses. That is why I am being so honest so quickly."

"I respect you for your honesty. The love I had with Henry was a beautiful experience, one which I know will never be equaled."

"It is very pretty up here. I never appreciated the beauty of fall as much."

"Nature really paints the countryside this time of year with the most magnificent colors. The fall and spring are the two most beautiful seasons. Winter is a time that is hard on those of us who live here. It is really difficult to get around when the roads are loaded with snow. Summers are too crowded up here. The people come to the hotels and everything seems cluttered."

"Have you ever lived in the city?"

"Before my father bought this place we lived in Brooklyn. It was nice because I could travel around without having my brothers drive me and it was fun always having other girls around. Up here the neighbors are too far away to just drop in and chat. I do not think I will mind living in the city. Of course, it will be a big adjustment for Estelle. She has never known an apartment and will miss the freedom of being able to go out and play in the yard by herself. But I am sure she will adjust. She has no choice once the farm is sold."

"My boys are also used to living in a private house. Before Lilly died we had a nice house with a yard in Brooklyn and now they are still living in the same neighborhood. It is impossible for me to keep up a house and do everything I have to do at the factory so I prefer apartment living."

"What kind of factory do you have?"

"Excuse me, I thought your aunt told you. I manufacture ladies' dresses. My factory is in downtown Manhattan in the garment district."

"I think we should start back to the house. They probably have lunch on the table and you must be hungry after the trip up here."

"Okay, but before we go back please let me say something. I do not want you to feel pressured by your aunt or your mother. We both need time and we will take the time needed to see if we like each other. I am willing to come back up here and you can even come to Manhattan if you want to."

"Morris, may I call you that?"

"Of course."

"I want you to know I really appreciate your attitude. I feel like a piece of merchandise that is up for sale right now and I cannot consent to anything unless I feel comfortable."

"Come, let's rejoin the women."

They came back into the house to find the dining room table set and the family waiting for them. At the table they were joined by Sam and Abe, as well as Estelle, who seemed proud to be joining the grown-ups for lunch. After polite inquiries about Uncle Saul and cousins Helen and Herbie, Cel sat back and observed the man Aunt Bella had brought up for her. She listened while Sophie pumped him about his life. She learned he had come to America from Russia at the age of thirteen with only a sewing machine to his name. He had worked in the sweat shops of Manhattan and had saved his money in hopes of bringing the remaining members of his family to America. Unfortunately, he believed that they had all been killed by the Cossacks before he could help them. He then used his savings to start his own factory, where he made the patterns for dresses and then produced them for the lower-cost outlets in New York. He impressed Cel as a man who was cultured in an old world manner and she was pleased to see he was clean and neat, even if he was balding and spoke with a soft accent that reflected his European background. He was a religious man who kept the Sabbath and seemed well mannered. He was very patient with the women as they continued to ask him questions, which he answered modestly but directly. Whenever they asked about his sons, his responses were touched with pain, a pain of separation that Cel could relate to and be touched by. She kept thinking that here was a man willing to do just about anything to see his family reunited. But she kept thinking and wondering if she could stand being with him, if she could ever feel anything for this stranger. She concluded that only time would tell and wondered if they would have enough time.

Lunch ended and Sam and Abe left to return to their chores. Bella and Sophie refused Cel's offer to help do the dishes. Once again she was left with Morris. As they sat in the living room, they quietly watched Estelle play with her doll. While the silence was strained, neither of them seemed able to break it. Before long, Bella came into the room and announced that they had to leave shortly if they were going to catch the last train back to New York. Morris stood and shook hands with Cel and Sophie before taking his hat and preparing to leave with Bella.

"I will call and possibly we can set a date for another visit in the near future," he said.

"That would be nice; just let me know when you can come up. I'll be here."

"Maybe next time I come, I'll bring Joseph, and he and Estelle can play together."

"That would be nice. I would like to meet him."

Just then they heard the horn indicating that Sam had the car out front and was ready to drive them to the train station. Goodbyes were quickly affected and Cel watched the car go down the driveway, knowing that she would hear from him again.

What followed was a barrage of questions from Sophie. What did she think of him? Would she marry him? Sophie went on and on about what a good provider he was and how Cel's life would be so much better if she married him.

Finally, Cel felt she could take no more.

"Momma, please stop. I only just met the man. I do not know if he will ever call again and neither do you. After all, this is not as if we are buying a new dress; this is my life we are dealing with. I need time and he needs time."

"Time... what do you need time for? You have to marry and he at least can take care of you and the child. What is there to think about?"

"Momma! He is a stranger and you want me to just hop into his bed and live with him without really knowing him. That's ridiculous and you know it."

"I don't care about his bed. I just want you to marry him and have a place to live. Whether you hop into his bed or not is up to you."

"Then what you are saying is that you want me to be like a hired person. To just go and take care of him and his family in exchange for a place to live."

"That's reality."

"Whose reality?"

"Look, Cel, we have to make changes. We are selling this farm and it will not be long before we have to move. You have to do something and this is something. I don't care if you love him. All I care is that you and the child have a place to live. He needs someone to take care of his children and he seems willing to marry. What more is there?"

"There is a lot more. Both of us must like each other if we are going to make this work out and right now we don't even know each other. I am not going to jump and marry anyone just to please you or to accommodate your demands. Please stop trying to run my life."

Finally, Cel was alone with her thoughts in the comfort of the darkness of her room. Estelle was peacefully asleep in the bed they had come to believe belonged to them both. In her heart she knew she would hear from Morris and, if she wanted, he would marry her. What did she want? That was the question she pondered. True, her situation was desperate and, true, Sophie would force her into a marriage whether or not she wanted to remarry. Now the question was merely whether this man could satisfy her needs. He was clean and neat, well-spoken and appeared to be a good provider. From his conversation, she was reasonably sure he would not make sexual demands of her. At least she would be spared that indignity! But did she want to be spared? Well, that was a question remaining to be answered. For her part, she would keep a clean apartment, take care of his children and appear to the world as his wife. She thought of ways to save money so that she would never again be placed in this situation. Every week she could put away part of the weekly money and if there was not enough she would merely ask for more. He would never know what she saved. Maybe if the nest egg became large enough she could even leave him and start a real life with Estelle. Yes, that was a possibility! Best of all, she would be away from Sophie's domination. Sophie would not be able to prevent her from indulging Estelle the way she wanted to. She would be free of her mother's endless nagging about how spoiled the child was becoming. As Cel's eyelids became heavy with sleep, her final thought was that things could be worse; this man definitely had the ability to solve her immediate problems.

A few days passed without any call from Morris. Sophie kept asking but Cel seemed nonchalant. In her heart she knew he would call and she would arrange another visit. In the meantime, a buyer materialized for the farm. The price was lower than Sophie wanted but the condition of the place made her accept his offer. She told the children that in one month they would have to move as the new person wanted to take title of the property by the beginning of November. For Sam and Abe this presented little trouble as they were anxious to leave the farm and start their new lives in the city. Sam had a job lined up as a mechanic-in-training in a service station in Newark. Abe planned to marry Martha, his long-term girlfriend and move into her apartment on Long Island. Since her family had a store in the same town, it was assumed he would work there. Only Cel did not have a place to go. Sophie realized that the time frame was too short to complete the marriage, so she told Cel that she would have to move into whatever apartment she took in Brighton Beach... on a temporary basis, of course.

Toward the end of the week, Morris called and told Cel he would like to come up for another visit. This time he would come without Bella. Cel was quick to suggest that he come for the weekend and bring his children.

"I'll bring Joseph, as he is not as much trouble as the baby and he can play with your daughter," Morris replied.

"That sounds good. It will give the children a chance to get to know each other. Please plan to stay with us at the house. There is plenty of room and it would be no trouble at all."

"I can leave the factory early on Friday. We should be there by dinner, if that is all right with you."

"That will be fine. We will look forward to having Sabbath dinner together."

When she hung up the phone, Cel decided she would show Joey a good time. She quickly called a neighbor and arranged to have the children go over to that farm and play with the animals. A city child never has enough contact with cows and horses; she was sure this would excite the child. She then called to find out what activities were planned for Saturday night at the local hotels. Sophie certainly could watch the children while she and Morris went out, especially since there was a dance at a nearby hotel. The farm visit and the dance would take care of Saturday, and Friday night would center around dinner and small talk, Cel thought as she mentally checked off the weekend. Sunday would have to be an early train back to the city, so she knew she would not have to worry about any amusements.

Friday seemed to come with unusual haste. Before she knew it, Estelle and she were standing on the porch watching the car approach. To her surprise, Cel felt nervous about meeting Joey. Children can be very hard to please and she knew in her heart that if the child did not take to her, the relationship would be over before it had a chance to begin. Estelle was unusually excited at the prospect of meeting "that nice man's son". She was looking forward to showing the boy around the farm and playing with him. Her excitement made Cel realize the child needed other children. Their isolation was beginning to appear unnatural, even to Cel.

As Sam drove up the driveway, Cel and Estelle waved. The car stopped and the little boy jumped out and stood at the steps of the porch staring at Cel. When his father came up beside him Cel heard him say, "Oh, Daddy, she is a pretty lady!"

"Welcome, Joey," Cel responded, smiling at the child whose big brown eyes stared at her with a look of longing in them. She could not help but think this was a child who was hurting and who needed someone to love him.

"Please excuse my son's forwardness. He is very excited about meeting you and Estelle and does tend to say whatever crosses his mind. I think I should add that children do tell the truth."

"It is nice to see you again. Please come into the house and freshen up before dinner."

The two children ran ahead as Estelle anxiously started telling Joey about their plans for the next day and about all the toys she wanted to show him. Morris and Cel followed, content just to watch the children's excitement.

Dinner passed with conversation being superficial and with Sophie dominating most of it, explaining the plans for the upcoming move and the changes that were about to take place in their lives. After dinner, Cel and Morris went for a walk while the children continued playing in the living room.

"It is nice the two children seem to have hit it off," Cel said, hoping to provide a common ground for conversation.

"Yes; Joey craves being with other children. His grandparents do not have friends with young children."

"The same is true for Estelle; however, I can say I had no idea how much she needed to play with other children until I saw how excited she was to have you come. She could hardly contain herself waiting for you to arrive. I guess I have been so wrapped up in myself these days that I did not think about having her play with other children. Up here we have to arrange things like that, at least until the children start school, and I never thought about it."

"It is an advantage living in the city. At least there are other children in the same building and they can all play together in one apartment or the other."

"Are there children in your building?"

"I would assume so. I have had little contact with my neighbors because I come home late from the factory and on the weekends I go to see the children."

"It must really be hard on you not having the children with you during the week."

"What would I do with them? It is not practical to even think about it now. At least their grandmother takes good care of them, better than any hired woman would."

"It's a nice evening. I like this time of year; the air is crisp, but it's not as cold as it is in the winter and we can still go walking without feeling our noses are going to fall off," Cel said trying to turn the conversation away from Morris' plight and, talk about hiring a woman to take care of the children.

"Will you miss the mountains when you move to the city?"

"Of course. I'll miss many aspects of my life up here. But I doubt whether I'll miss the hard work that went into this place. When we had guests, there was always so much to be done that I never seemed to have any time to enjoy the scenery or the fresh air. Now just keeping the place in reasonable order has been very difficult for us. Life up here has been very lonely since Henry and my dad died, so I am looking forward to a change and to being among people. This life can be very isolated."

"Under our circumstances, we can feel alone even in a crowd."

"I relate to what you are saying, but I think I am ready to reach out and to start rejoining the human race, so to speak."

"I guess I am ready too or I would not be here."

They walked along in silence, each engulfed in thought, each finding a degree of comfort in being with the other one.

"Are you getting cold? The wind seems to be picking up a bit," Morris asked.

"Evenings are like this up here. I am going to miss this breeze when we move to the city. It always seems as if the breeze cleans the air and makes it ready for a new day."

"The city air never seems to clear. One day goes into the next with little change. Eventually they all seem to blend together. I find that to be especially true since my life has changed. Now I go to work, rush to see the children, and get home just in time to go to bed. I miss waking up and hearing Joey. This may sound strange, but I even miss the smells that go with having children in the house. His bad breath in the morning, his bathroom odors; they should be a part of my life. Now I am a visitor in his life; I'm not truly his father. It is even worse with Norman. I do not know that child. He is being brought up by a stranger his grandmother hired to help with the children. Who knows what values she is instilling in him. These early years are important and they are just fleeing without any input from me."

"I guess it is harder for a man to raise children when he is alone. After all, you have to earn a living and you can't be with the children all day. At least I have been able to remain with Estelle, even though money is getting tighter each day."

"Well, should we join forces – so to say? We could make a home for the children. You would be able to stay home and raise them together while I bring in the money. Money will not be a problem for us. I do make a decent living. Rich, no, but comfortable! I would not make any demands on you except that the children be taken care of."

"Let me move to New York. I'm sure Sophie will let us stay with her for a while and you and I can get to know each other better. Marriage is a serious commitment and I want to be sure we can live together in harmony. It would be disruptive for the children to live in a home where the parents argue all the time. I also would want to get to know both of the boys and to have them like me before I become their mother. Joey and Estelle seem to relate to each other. Now we have to bring Norman into the picture too. For Estelle this will be a major adjustment as she is used to having me all to herself. I want her to be comfortable."

"That's very fair and very true. The children will all need time to adjust. Children have a way of working things out as long as their needs are taken care of; they seem to adjust to new things better than adults. These children, in particular, are familiar with making adjustments in their lives. They have learned to live under different conditions and, in the boys case, they have had to accept different people as their care-givers. I am sure the children will be all right. The big question is if we can adjust. We each had loving relationships and are now considering one that is accommodative. I fear that in itself will put a huge burden on us."

"Time will have to tell. Sometimes relationships have strange ways of developing. I cannot deny that I crave a man and hopefully, in time, we can grow to feel something for each other. I know that I can never take your first wife's place in your heart, just as you could never replace Henry in mine. But I would like to hope that a different relationship will form and that we could have feelings for each other. Otherwise I would have a hard time marrying you."

"Are you saying you would want to live as man and wife?"

"Look, Morris, I am a young woman. I have needs that go beyond financial ones. I do not plan to live the rest of my life as a celibate."

"I am surprised. I had thought that a physical relationship was out of the question."

"Do you find me unattractive?"

"Of course not! You are a very pretty woman. It is just that I thought you were looking for a different arrangement and I certainly had no plans of pushing you into anything different."

"I'll be honest. Nights are horrible for me. Every night I crave a man's touch. I want to be held and loved and made to feel like a woman. That may sound cheap to you but that is the way I feel. Sex was wonderful with Henry, and I want more. I am not the type for one-night stands, nor can I throw myself at men, but if I were to remarry, I want a husband. That's why I think we have to get to know each other better. We have to court and develop a hunger for each other."

"I am surprised. I never expected this conversation to take this turn."

"I know – women are supposed to endure sex, not to enjoy it. Well, please understand, this woman wants to enjoy it again."

"To be honest, I had hoped that in time you might consider such a relationship, but I never thought it would be a priority. The thought is exciting and I am willing if you are. You will have to be aware that it has been a long time since I have been with a woman and there are ghosts that have to be buried. I feel it is my fault that Lilly died. If she had not become pregnant, her heart would have lasted many more years."

"She became pregnant because she wanted to. You cannot go on blaming yourself. I am sure she wanted the physical aspects of your relationship as much as you did. She was unlucky, that's all."

"That is easier to say than to accept. Wouldn't you always compare any man with Henry? Wouldn't he always be in your bed?"

"Henry will always be in my heart. No one can ever remove him from my feelings. To be realistic, I never expect to feel for any man the way I felt for him. I do expect to feel differently and intensely for a man who is my husband. I expect to love that person, in a different way maybe, but I do want to love him nevertheless. I want to give myself to a man and, while there may be memories in my bed, there will be no ghosts to get in our way."

"Cel, you are indeed a different type of woman. I am not used to such honesty. You shock me, but at the same time you excite me. I wonder if I can be man enough to satisfy you."

"Time will tell. I am willing to change my life, to take care of additional children, to keep a good Jewish home. I am willing to do all those things but in return I want a man. I am not willing to live in a house and pretend I am living with my brother; I can do that without a marriage. Sam or Abe would be happy to have me take care of them and to be their housekeeper. I want a man who will be a man in my house and in my bed."

"I am willing to try if you are."

"If I were not willing to try, I would not have spoken out and been so open with you."

"Do you want more children?"

"That is something I have not thought about. Having more children will depend on the circumstances in the future. If we were to marry, we would have three children to feed and clothe. In my present financial condition, I cannot imagine doing that without sacrifice and I cannot picture adding to my problems. I believe children should come into this world by choice and I know how to have my pleasure without conceiving. I do not see myself as the perpetually pregnant wife."

"I cannot imagine having more children."

They walked along in silence as the mountain breeze picked up and the air chilled even more. Cel was lost in her own thoughts, amazed at what had come out of her mouth and yet happy to have cleared the air. Right up to this point she had no idea that she would be making these demands. Morris was shocked. He never expected someone as beautiful as Cel to desire him. He wondered if he could physically satisfy her. She seemed so hungry for sex and so demanding. He could not help wondering what she would be like in bed. Would she demand a trial performance before consenting to marry him? He cleared his throat to break the silence that seemed to hang heavily between them.

"Let's go back to the house now. It is really getting cold," he said, gently taking her arm.

"I have a busy day planned for tomorrow. I thought Joey might like to visit a farm and to play with the cows and horses. City children all love to see the animals up close. Many of them have never touched a cow or a horse."

"I doubt if he ever has been close to a cow. He has seen horses in the park. I am sure he'll love to visit a farm. That boy is like a sponge when it comes to new experiences. He always has a million questions."

Before they knew it, the lights of the house were upon them. They both knew they would have little chance to talk once they entered and they both wondered how the other was receiving the conversation they had. As they entered the house, children's voices could be heard as they played a game Sophie had found on the shelf. Both Cel and Morris smiled as they watched the children and they both thought these two could certainly adjust if they were to marry.

The remainder of the visit passed quickly, with the children dominating their attention. Saturday night came and went with their being too tired to go to the hotel for the dance. Instead, they spent the evening telling stories with the children and enjoying their excitement after visiting the farm and petting the animals. Even Estelle seemed to find new amusement in the animals as she shared her experiences with Joey.

Sunday seemed to come too quickly for all the parties involved and before they knew it Morris was saying goodbye. Cel and he made plans to meet in the city once she moved. He gave her his phone number at the factory and at home so she could call him and let him know exactly when she would be arriving. They seemed comfortable with this arrangement, even though Sophie seemed disappointed. She wanted a commitment now. As Morris left the driveway in Sam's car, she turned to Cel and said, "Neu...what's the story?"

"There is no story yet. We will have to get to know each other before any decisions are made."

"What's to know? He is a good man, a clean man, and a good provider. You should kiss your lucky star that Aunt Bella introduced you to him."

"Oh, Momma, this is another time. Marriages cannot just be arranged. The involved people have to have some feelings for each other. We need time to get to know each other to make sure this is the right thing."

"Oh, now you are going to tell me you want to be in love. Love, my child, is for the first time around; not for second marriages. This time you have to look at other things, and this man has those qualities."

"Momma, I want more. I feel that I am young enough to want to feel something towards the man I live with. If you cannot understand that, it is too bad. This is my life and I have to live it my way."

"On whose money?"

"Money, money is all I hear from you. Money is not my god."

"Money is a necessary fact of life. Stop being such an idealist and start thinking about how you will support yourself and that child. I do not have enough money to support you indefinitely. Do you understand me?"

"I hear you. Maybe once we get to the city I can get a job."

"Yes, and who will take care of the child?"

"You will until things work out differently."

"Wrong! I want to live my life, whatever is left of it. I will not be saddled with your child. I raised my children, now you have to raise your child. Get thee to the altar and do it quickly."

"Oh, Momma, you are unreasonable."

"No, I am practical. I am too old to raise a five-year-old and the sooner you understand that, the better. You can just make up your mind and you will marry this man and he can support you and Estelle. Then you will be able to stay at home and raise your child. It could be worse. He is at least a clean man and seems to be a man of character. Open your eyes, my child, and stop dreaming of love."

Cel just turned her back on Sophie and walked into the house. All she could think was that she hated her mother. How could this woman be so selfish? Someday she would return the same treatment. How and when would remain to be answered, but she knew she would never forget this conversation and she would never, ever be able to love her mother again. She felt chilled by the hatred that was going through her body and by the feeling of isolation and desperation she was experiencing.

CHAPTER 6

The next month passed quickly as the family prepared for the big move, belongings had to be separated into groups that would be taken. Items that would be discarded and those that would be sold. Their neighbors came and purchased whatever farm equipment that was usable and the boys took the tools they thought they might need. Cel took whatever kitchen equipment she wanted and Sophie took the rest. Before long the boxes were all over the place awaiting the movers.

Arrangements were made for Sophie to rent an apartment in Aunt Bella's building in Brighton Beach. It was a one-bedroom apartment and Cel and Estelle were going to sleep in the living room until Cel made other arrangements. Some of their belongings were to be kept in Aunt Bella's apartment as there would not be room for everything in Sophie's small place. It was clear that the pressure was on Cel, and she would have to marry if she wanted any type of life. Sophie had no plans to let her decision take too much time.

The day of the move came. With sorrow in her heart and tears in her eyes, Cel walked through the farmhouse that had always been her home. Memories of the good times with Papa and Henry flooded her thoughts as she closed the door to each room. She tried to remember the good times, the happy moments she had spent in that house. The hardest door to close was her bedroom, where once her life had been so full and so happy. She stood in the center of the room and remembered how it felt to have Henry's arms around her. She imagined that she could smell him and feel his presence in the empty room. Their love had indeed been special and their life had held so much promise. If only...but there was no finishing the thought. Cel walked out of the room and slammed the door. She would survive!

Both Cel and Estelle were especially quiet during the trip to the city. Estelle, as young as she was, seemed to realize that her life was to radically change and seemed to fear the unknown. For Cel, the trip was an additional time to come to grips with Sophie's demands. Only Sophie seemed excited. In her heart, she knew she was doing the right thing. It was time to move on and start a new life. After all, there was no one to say she would not meet a nice man and remarry. She may be getting older, but dead she wasn't. Some man just might want her. Who knows? After all, the area where Bella lives is full of Russians who have no one. But first things first. She had to get Cel married off so that her future would have some security, and Morris was certainly a distinct possibility.

They arrived just before dinner and Bella greeted them outside the apartment building.

"Why don't you come upstairs and we'll have dinner together before the men start unloading the truck?"

"No," Cel replied. "I want to see the apartment and get everything set up so that Estelle can go to bed before it's too late. You and Sophie can help out by taking her upstairs and I'll stay and direct the men."

Sophie quickly agreed as she was dreading the work ahead. Even though they had taken just what was essential, moving was hard work. She replied, "You can get started. Just remember that the bedroom will be mine and you and Estelle can set your things in the living room."

"Yes, Momma, you have made yourself clear too many times."

As she walked into the apartment for the first time, she was struck by its smallness. It was going to be a challenge to make the place appear homey and uncluttered, especially since the first room you see when you enter is the living room. Cel quickly decided to create groupings with the furniture. One group would be the living room furniture, and behind that she decided to place her bed and Estelle's in an L-shaped arrangement with their dresser between them. She knew she would be able to make them look like day-beds during the day, so at least the place would be livable. They would just have to share the closets in Sophie's room for now, whether or not she liked it. She created a mental picture of how she wanted the furniture placed before the men started bringing it up. Before she knew it, the apartment was set up enough to allow them to go to sleep for the night. The kitchen and everything else would have to wait for the morning.

When Sophie and Estelle finally came to the apartment, Cel felt pleased with herself. Of course, Sophie had some comments to make about the set-up, but Cel ignored her. There was no sense in getting into an argument. They would just have to tolerate each other until things could be changed.

That night, Estelle wanted to share Cel's narrow bed with her. But that was not going to be possible. It was not the same as the nice double bed they had shared on the farm. Despite the child's cries, Cel made her sleep in her own bed, only to lie awake most of the night feeling her own loneliness. Sleeping with the child had given her comfort, a comfort that was part of the past.

The next few days flew by without notice. They shopped to stock the kitchen and tried to find everything they needed in this very foreign environment. Many of the shopkeepers did not speak English and Cel found it difficult to communicate in Yiddish, but Sophie seemed to enjoy herself. She loved being with all of the new people and set about making friends with her neighbors, while Cel seemed more and more withdrawn. She hated being among foreigners and greenhorns. It seemed to her that she had been transported to another country, not just to a new city. Estelle also felt the strangeness and became more demanding of Cel's attention. It rapidly became even more evident that they would have to make changes and get out of this area. If they were going to be able to live a near normal life, Morris was going to have to be called and made to marry her.

One week after arriving in New York City, Cel called Morris at the factory. He seemed pleasant but distracted. There was no small talk and Morris just said he would call that evening. Cel did not know what to think. Had she scared him with physical demands or was it just that he was busy at work?

The evening passed without any calls. The next evening also passed in the same manner. Cel now was really becoming concerned. What if he did not call? Sophie would surely find another greenhorn for her to marry. She hated the people she was meeting. They all seemed to have body odor...What would she do? She wondered if she should call Morris again. But she decided to just wait longer. After all, if she appeared too anxious, she would have less bargaining power. Maybe Aunt Bella could find out his intentions. No – that just might give Sophie reason to doubt that he was interested. She shuddered at the thought that any doubts would just propel Sophie into action. No – just wait it out; that is the only conclusion that seemed feasible.

Days passed and soon it was a week since she had placed the call. The passage of time had not escaped Sophie's attention and that night after dinner she started harping at Cel.

"Did you call Morris yet? You know its hard living like this. You have to do something."

"I need a little more time to get settled."

"Time for nothing – that's what you need. Go call him now."

"Okay, okay – maybe tomorrow."

"Not tomorrow – now. I know you have his home phone number. Use it!"

"But –"

"No buts – go do it or I'll do it for you."

"You wouldn't do that!"

"Watch and see. I'll do it right now. Things have to change and we cannot start making new lives for ourselves this way. You have to start your own life so I can start mine. The way we're living now is exactly the same as we lived on the farm, only now we are doing it in smaller quarters and getting on each other's nerves faster."

"Push, push – that's all you know. What if I do not want to marry Morris?"

"Then you'll have to marry someone else. There are several men here who would love to marry an American citizen and guarantee their ability to remain in this country. If they marry an American, they can be granted citizenship."

"Wonderful – now it is like you want me to marry the highest bidder."

"That's not a bad idea. We could make a little by arranging the right shidak."

"You disgust me."

"Then go and call him. Enough waiting."

"I'll call later."

"Not later – now!"

Cel starred at her mother with hatred in her eyes. This woman was just horrid. She always had to manage everyone's life and there was no winning an argument once she decided what she wanted done. Cel never doubted for a minute that Sophie would enjoy auctioning her off to the highest bidder. Well, in reality, she had nothing to lose by calling Morris again. If he was no longer interested, it would be best to know that now so that she could make other plans before Sophie completely took over. She pushed herself away from the kitchen table and got the phone number from her dresser drawer.

"You win. I'll call him, but I want to do it without you listening in."

"Why? You hiding something?"

"No. I just want some privacy. So please take Estelle and go up to Bella's. Then I'll call him."

"Promise to tell me the truth. I have to know if he's not interested in you."

"You sound like you have an alternative ready to propose."

"Possibly. Only the next time I'll make sure the arrangements are made, sealed and delivered before you even meet him. No more ridiculous talk about love."

"Sophie, please go up to Bella's. I need time by myself."

"I'll go if you promise to call Morris. Make sure you know his intentions or I'll just go ahead and arrange for you to meet someone else. Am I making myself clear?"

"Clear as can be..."

Anger gripped Cel's heart and she watched Sophie and Estelle leave the apartment. It was beyond her imagination that Sophie would be so ruthless. How could she even threaten to force her into an arranged marriage? It was inconceivable that this could be happening to her in this day and age. After all, this was the 1930s in America and not the 1800s in Russia. Cel tried to take deep breaths to control her rage; she tried to reach deeply within herself to think of a solution – any solution except Morris. There was none. Work was out of the question because she had no one to watch Estelle. She could not afford to move into an apartment by herself. Sam and Abe were just getting started themselves and certainly could not afford two more mouths to feed. Desperation drove her to the phone. While she was dialing Morris' home number, she prayed he would not answer. On the third ring, she heard his voice.

"Hello, Morris, it's Cel."

"Cel, it's good to hear from you. I had been meaning to call but Norman has been sick and I am forever running out there to see him."

"What's the matter?"

"I really do not know. He has been having convulsions and the doctors think it might be the result of an infection that is in his system."

"Poor baby. Why don't I go out with you next time and see if there is anything I can do."

"That is very kind of you. I hate to impose on you."

"It's not an imposition. It would give me a chance to meet the baby and allow us to see each other as well. That is if you are still interested in a relationship for us."

"Of course I am interested – it's just…"

"Please forgive my boldness. I understand you have many things on your mind that should and do come first. It is just that Sophie is pressuring me. She wants to force me to meet some man who needs an American citizenship. I guess I am desperate now. I cannot face her. Now I have to get out of this apartment. I am sorry to burden you with my problems, especially when you have your own worries on your mind. It is just I do find you attractive and a union of the two of us could solve things for both of us."

"Cel, I have been thinking about us and you are right. If we married, my children could be here with me and I am sure you would do a better job with the baby than the sitter. I'll come over tomorrow night and speak to Sophie. Then we can spend time together and I promise she will leave you alone."

"How will you accomplish that?"

"Don't you worry. All that Sophie needs is a man to tell her what to do and she will listen."

"You do not know Sophie. She was always the manager in our household. No man can ever make her stop once she decides what she wants."

"You will see tomorrow. Shall I be there at seven?"

"That's fine. I will have dinner for you here."

"You are living in Bella's building. Is that right?"

"Yes, apartment 31."

"See you at seven and then we will make plans to go out to see Norman."

"I will look forward to both and thank you for understanding. I really hate being so aggressive."

"Say no more."

Cel replaced the receiver on the cradle and sat looking at the telephone but seeing nothing. She hoped that she had done the right thing and that her future and Estelle's would be protected by the stranger on the other end. So much was riding on him and she knew so little about the man. At least he did not disgust her like the people she was meeting in the neighborhood.

Cel was still sitting and starring at the phone when she heard Sophie's key in the door.

"Neu?"

"Morris will be here for dinner tomorrow. Now, please, no more talk; just let me put the child to bed."

"You know, my kinda, I only want what is best for you."

"Momma, you want what is best for you."

The next day was spent in preparation for the evening meal. Sophie and Cel worked together to make the meal a perfect one. Before they knew it, it was seven o'clock and they were awaiting the doorbell. Cel was dressed in a tailored suit that showed her figure off to its best advantage. Even Estelle was wearing her party dress and looked adorable.

When the doorbell rang just ten minutes after the appointed time, Cel's heart started beating extra fast. There was no denying that her future was on the line and she hoped the evening would go well.

Dinner passed with the usual small talk about the weather, the children and the relocation. Sophie did not hesitate to mention that they were living in tight quarters and it was inconvenient to have Cel and Estelle sleeping in the living room. Morris tried to just ignore her as though she was not present and quickly changed the subject every time. Finally, he could take no more of Sophie's badgering.

"Look, Mrs. Cohen, I know that you are anxious to have Cel married and living in her own place. Everything happens in good time. Right now Cel and I need some time to get to know each other. I will not allow her to marry me unless she at least cares deeply for me. She is too nice a person to marry just to get out of your apartment. Please allow us a courtship and allow our feelings to come together. I want to make your daughter happy, as I am sure you do."

"A courtship? How long does it take to have a courtship?"

"Time is a relevant thing. Some people develop sincere feelings quickly while others need additional time to cultivate their feelings. We are both adults and we perceive things in an adult manner. However, we need some time and you have to grant us that opportunity. I want it that way and so does Cel, so please honor our wishes and stop making demands."

"You know, you are not the only man in the world who is interested in my Cel."

"As I said before, Cel is a beautiful woman and I am sure she must have many men who would be interested in marrying her. But she has told me she desires a relationship with me and that relationship has to be on our terms, not yours."

"No one speaks to me this way."

"I am not trying to be disrespectful. I just want you to understand our position. We want time to get to know each other before any commitment is made. That is all there is to it. I am not talking about an unreasonable length of time, but we want it this way. That is all there is to it. Now, if you don't mind, Cel and I would like to go for a walk on the beach."

"Go and have a good time. Just go."

The two of them left the apartment without another word being spoken. Cel was amazed at how Morris had handled her mother and respected him for not allowing Sophie to push him around. She knew she would have to be equally firm later when she and Sophie were alone.

Once they were outside Morris turned to her.

"Well, I hope that will keep your mother in her place for a while. You are right; she is a woman who is used to having her own way. If we allowed it, she would have us in front of a Justice of the Peace in three days."

"She is too anxious to have me married off. I would not put it past her if she were to have found a man who wants to marry her or something."

"Well, I want you to be happy and to want to marry me. After all, I realize that it will not be easy for you to take on the responsibility of two young boys in addition to a new husband and everything else. By the way, I have given some thought about our conversation at the farm. I do want a wife, not a housekeeper, and I hope we will be able to have a physical relationship."

"Morris, you are a strong man. Any man who can stand up to my mother is a man who should be admired. I know I will desire you."

With those words, Morris stopped and took Cel into his arms. She shuddered at the feel of the strong arms around her and leaned into his body in an effort to feel it against hers. It was too long since she was held like that – much too long. As he lowered his lips to touch hers, she gave into it and kissed him back. When it was over, she touched her lips as though to hold the kiss there a little longer.

"I did not know how much I missed that until this moment," Cel said in earnest.

"That is only the beginning," he replied, putting his arm around her narrow waist as they continued to walk to the beach.

"Let's plan to go out to visit Norman on Sunday. You can bring Estelle if you want. The doctors assure me that whatever he has is not contagious. The other children in the house are all well."

"What time do you want us to be ready?"

"We'll leave at ten and take the train out to Long Island. That way we can have a full day with him and still get back early enough to have dinner around here. The restaurants near where he is are not much."

"Estelle has never been on a train. She'll love it. We'll be ready at ten. Can Joseph come as well?"

"Not this time. If he were to come, it would be too hectic and we would not be able to give the baby any attention. Joseph is very demanding of my time. I guess it is because I do not get to see very much of him."

"You know what is best. I just did not want him to feel left out."

"He needn't know anything about our trip. We'll arrange to see him next week and have dinner with him."

"Yes, but I cannot guarantee that Estelle will not tell him about the train ride and seeing the baby. Wouldn't it make him feel bad?"

"I had not thought of that. I'll deal with it when it happens."

They walked along the water's edge in silence for a few minutes. Each seemed content to just feel the closeness of the other and conversation seemed unnecessary. For Cel it was wonderful to have a man's arms around her waist. It was the first time she really felt like a woman since Henry. She tried to shake the thought of Henry away.

"Are you cold?" asked Morris.

"No, not at all. I am just enjoying having your arm around my waist. It makes me feel whole again."

"I was also thinking how nice it feels to have a woman so close to me. It has been too long since I walked along like this. You know, Lilly was not able to do very much while she was pregnant. She spent most of the time in bed. I too have forgotten how wonderful it is to smell a woman, to feel her body close to mine, and to hold her and kiss her."

They stopped walking and he again took her into his arms and kissed her tenderly. Cel hungrily reached up and returned the embrace, feeling his chest across her breasts and his manhood harden as she pressed her body into his. She almost wished they could go back to the apartment and really experience each other. But that was an impossibility, so she pushed the thought from her mind. Looking up at him, she said, "This is some way to begin a courtship. I feel as though I want to begin a marriage."

They both laughed. There was no need for further words. They turned and started walking back towards the apartment, each enjoying holding the other and each feeling somewhat like a teenager trying to steal a few moments of intimacy away from the gaze of their parents.

That evening, after Morris left, Cel refused to discuss their plans with Sophie. All she would say was that she was going to see him again on Sunday and that they would be taking Estelle away with them for the day. Sophie seemed to accept that and agreed to leave her alone, for the time being at least. For Cel, the evening left her somewhat unnerved. She had not expected to have her female juices awakened so quickly and she knew she wanted more, more physical contact with this man. She wanted to feel his penis in her and she knew she would not wait until they were married to do so. She also knew in her heart that she could satisfy him and guarantee her marriage as well as her future happiness. He would do anything she wanted if she pulled the right strings and she would do just that. But would he satisfy her? That was a question she wanted answered. There was no denying she wanted a man; a man who could make her feel good and feel like a woman; a man who could make her jump with excitement from touching her and rubbing her private parts in just the right way. She quivered as she felt the wetness in her crotch.

"Cel, you are one wicked bitch," she said out loud.

The week passed quickly as Cel caught Estelle's excitement about the upcoming train ride. On Sunday, Estelle insisted on wearing her best dress, so that the baby would like her. Cel decided on wearing a conservative suit. She applied her makeup with care so that she would look attractive, but not cheap, and made sure they were both ready before ten o'clock so as not to keep Morris waiting.

The doorbell rang precisely at ten and she was amazed at how nice Morris looked dressed in casual attire. It was obvious he too wanted to make a positive impression. He greeted Estelle with enthusiasm as she ran to him to make sure they were indeed taking a train. Taking the child's hand, he asked if Cel was ready as he reached for the doorknob, never even asking if Sophie were at home.

Walking down the street, Cel felt good about the image they projected with Estelle skipping along between them. It would be nice to have a man around again and complete the family image. Hopefully, the boys would get along well with Estelle.

Morris broke her thoughts.

"Cel, I hope you will not be disappointed with Norman. He is just a baby and has never known anything but the home he is in."

"Disappointed? How could I be disappointed? I expect nothing from him. My only hope is that he and I can develop a relationship and maybe I can be the mother he has never had."

"You are really thinking positively about us and the family."

"Yes, I am."

Estelle was amazed when the train pulled into the station. It seemed huge and the noise was overwhelming. She pulled back as Morris tried to help her up the high steps. Once in her seat, she stared out of the window as the world seemed to fly by. Both Cel and Morris laughed as they watched her mouth open in awe.

"A child's enthusiasm can be catching," Cel commented.

"I love to see the world through a child's eye. It seems so much purer and new."

"Next time we do something like this we have to bring Joey along, too. That way the children can really get to know each other."

"He just cannot understand about the baby and always makes a scene about leaving him when it is time to go."

"He is old enough to understand that he has a brother and probably wants his brother with him."

"I agree, but the grandparents cannot possibly take care of the two of them. That brings up another question which we have to deal with. I can never turn my back on Lil's parents. They are particularly close to Joseph and want to continue seeing him even if I were to remarry."

"That is not an issue. My only thought is that I would expect them to treat Estelle nicely so that she would not feel left out. I know I would demand that Sophie treat the boys as if they were her grandchildren."

"I am sure they would do the same, but it would be normal for them to be distant with you."

"Why? I had no part in their daughter's death and am not responsible for anything that happened. I would hope they will be civil towards me, especially if they see that I am taking good care of their grandchildren."

"What type of relationship do you have with Henry's parents?"

"Henry's father is dead and his mother never liked me or wanted to have anything to do with me. I never see her and unfortunately neither does Estelle. Before Henry died he would take Estelle to see her, but the woman never wanted to be close to the child."

"How unfortunate for everyone."

"Hannah is a cold person. She rarely allowed anyone to break through her ice barrier. Even Henry was always kept at a distance and that distance seemed even greater after her husband died. It appeared as though she did not want to be hurt by anyone and the way to guarantee that was by not letting anyone get too close."

"You seem very understanding."

"I do not believe in wasting energy trying to do the impossible. The way I see it, she missed out on everything. She did not see her son enough and now he is gone; she never tried to really get to know her only grandchild, and now she is too far away to get to see her and I could not care less. She made her own bed and now she can sleep in it."

"Now you sound bitter."

"I guess I am to a degree. It is hard to like someone who never wanted to like you."

"Maybe I was just lucky with my in-laws, because they always went out of their way to make me feel welcomed. Even when Lil died, they never blamed me."

"You didn't kill her!"

"In a way I feel as though I did. If she hadn't become pregnant, her heart would not have given out."

"That is a ghost you have to let die."

"It is easier said than done."

"Morris, we cannot have that guilt between us. It will poison our relationship."

"How?"

"How what? How will you let it die, or how will it poison our relationship?"

"How will it ruin our relationship?"

"You will fear being a man."

"I have thought about that. I will not fear a physical relationship, but I will fear another pregnancy."

"Right now I cannot picture wanting another child. There are ways to prevent it and I plan on using a diaphragm. Margaret Sanger just invented it to help women prevent unwanted pregnancy and it is very successful."

"I know nothing about it."

"It is very simple. A woman just inserts it before having sex and uses a jelly in it to kill the sperm. The diaphragm remains in place for something like ten or twelve hours and then it can be removed. They say you do not feel it during the act and it is more reliable than the condoms."

"Very interesting."

"Anyway, I plan on going to her clinic and being fitted for one. If we marry, three children are enough."

"Do you think it is good to have this type of conversation in front of the child?"

"She is too busy looking out of the window to think about what we are saying. Don't worry about her."

"Well, we're almost there. Let's get everything together."

They took a taxi to the simple house where Norman was staying. The yard was nicely kept and the place appeared clean and neat on the outside. Cel took Estelle's hand as Morris knocked on the front door. The woman who opened the door seemed pleasant but a little surprised at the sight of Cel and the child. Morris quickly made the necessary introductions and they all went into the living room, where the baby was propped up on the couch. He was small and appeared no more than six months old. Cel was taken aback by him and could not help but think that something was wrong with the child. After all, he was over a year old and seemed to barely be able to sit up by himself.

"Doesn't he crawl?" Cel asked.

"No, not yet. The doctor assures me that he is only a little slow in development, possibly because he was premature, and he needs a little longer to develop than other children."

"What is being done to help him along?"

"There is not a whole lot that can be done. He will get there when he is ready."

"Come, Estelle, and play with the baby," Morris urged as he drew closer to the infant.

"Oh, Mommy, look, he is so cute."

"Yes, he is like a little doll. Why don't we get a toy and see if he can hold it?"

"Look, he can hold the rattle."

"Let's put him on the floor and see if he will try to get the rattle. Here, you hold it, and let's see what he does."

Cel quickly picked the child up and placed him on his stomach on the carpet. He was able to hold his head up and look around but seemed bewildered by everyone standing around him. Estelle got down onto her stomach and started playing with the rattle, trying to entice Norman to move towards it. He started to reach out but became frightened and began to cry. Morris picked him up and held him to his chest as if to give the child his strength.

"This little guy has had a hard time in his short life."

"You know, Mr. B., I do everything I can for him. He is kept clean and well fed and I do take him to the doctor and all."

"Lisa, no one is saying you don't. But Cel is right, Norman is definitely behind in development."

"The doctor assures me that he is normal, just a little slow, that's all."

"Hopefully, he's right. I know Joey was running around by the time he was a year old."

"So was Estelle..."

The rest of the afternoon passed with little conversation. The adults took turns holding the baby and Estelle kept trying to play with him. She was like a little mother with him, and both Cel and Morris were impressed with her patience. She helped feed him and change his diaper, and tickled him until he laughed. It was cute to watch and before they knew it, it was time to leave.

In the taxi going back to the train, Cel turned to Morris and said, "That child needs special attention if he is ever to develop normally. I do not blame Lisa, she is doing everything she can, but he needs more."

"He will be a burden to anyone and probably will be that way for a long time, if he ever develops normally. That is why I wanted you to meet him before we got any further into our relationship. I want to be fair with you."

"Yes, he is a challenge, but love can go a great distance. I think I will be able to help that child and I know I will be willing to try."

"That is very big of you. I fear it is asking too much."

"Morris, let's be honest. You are helping me out of a difficult situation. In a sense, you are rescuing me. I, in turn, am willing to help you. If it ever became too much for me to bear, I will tell you and then we can do whatever is necessary. But, we cannot write that child off without giving him a chance."

"You are too good."

They rode in silence for the remainder of the trip. Cel was sure she had guaranteed her position and hoped she could live up to the bargain. Taking care of a slow child would be a challenge even if there were not other children to tend to. She knew one thing: no way would that child ever take over and leave Estelle out. She would always give her daughter the best and the others would have to get by with what was left. Estelle would always be first and last!

Morris, for his part, kept thinking how lucky he was to have found someone like Cel. Not every woman would be willing to try and help a child like Norman. Most would not even want to try. He knew in his heart that he would be forever grateful to Cel, even if they could not help the child. Joey would be all right no matter what. He was a bright child who could adapt to change and he would always blossom. But Norman, that was another story. Morris knew his mind was made up and that he would marry Cel. All that he hoped was that she would still want him and his children.

During the weeks that followed, Cel felt like a princess. Morris took her out to dinner, to Broadway shows, to the Jewish theater, and helped her get to know Manhattan, a borough that seemed full of life and excitement. People never seemed to sleep. No matter how late in the evening, the streets were full of bustle, the restaurants had patrons and the subways had riders. This was so different from the country that Cel felt overwhelmed. Together they explored the Cloisters and walked around the tranquil Fort Tryon Park.

Other days they walked along the Hudson River and watched the boats slowly making their way upstream. It was a different world than Brooklyn and the people whom they passed seemed more sophisticated and worldly than the immigrants in Brighton Beach. Cel knew she wanted to live in Manhattan some day.

The only cloud was that Morris remained the perfect gentleman. He made no advances and no demands of Cel. Sometimes they held hands and there was always a good night kiss, but nothing more. Cel was hesitant to make the first move, but in her heart she knew they had to cross the barrier if they were ever to marry. He had to want her in every sense of the word or they would have nothing together. She knew the romantic walks and beautiful dinners would end once they were married and the children all lived with them. Then what? She did not want to be the housekeeper; she wanted to be his wife and be treated as such. Only then would she be able to get whatever she wanted.

One day, as they walked along the river's edge, she turned to Morris and suggested he take her to see his apartment in Washington Heights.

"We are really close to where you live, aren't we?" she asked.

"Yes, as a matter of fact we are only a few blocks away from the apartment. Unfortunately, I do not have a view of the river. The apartments with a view are just too expensive. But the building is nice and clean, and there are three bedrooms so the children can stay."

"I would like to see it."

"Do you think that would be proper? After all, what would the neighbors think of a young woman coming to my apartment when we are alone?"

"Morris, we are both adults. Who cares what the neighbors think? Let their tongues wag if that gives them pleasure."

"Well – the place is really not ready for company."

"Obviously, you do not have the time to keep it the way you would like, but I do not care about that. Let's go."

Her stomach was tight as they walked along the city blocks towards Morris' home. She knew what she was about to force and hoped against hope she would be able to go through with her plan. Part of her dreaded this time. She felt as though she was about to be unfaithful to Henry and she was dirty. But she knew she had to live in the present, not in the past, and this was necessary if she was to get Morris to marry her and to provide a place of her own where she and Estelle could live and have security for the future.

Morris also walked along in silence. He knew what Cel was planning and was worried whether he was going to be able to perform the way she expected. He had never been with any woman other than Lil and she was not a demanding wife. Sex had always been just an act that required little on his part, as she never seemed to demand much of him. Cel, on the other hand, seemed to know what she wanted and seemed to have a hunger that he had never experienced before. How would he be able to satisfy her? What if he failed, would that mean the end of their relationship? They seemed to get along so well and she seemed to be the perfect woman to help him out of his untenable situation. He wished they could just marry and then face this problem, but he knew that was an impossibility with Cel. Their physical relationship had to be addressed before she would consent to marriage and he had to face that fact now. She was no shy virgin fearing her wedding night.

Forty one Bennett Avenue was one of three identical buildings along a neatly hilled street. The area was clean and quiet despite it being late afternoon. As they approached the entry, Cel was impressed with the double glass doors that opened into the tiled lobby. The stairway was wide and curved, and the marble tiles on the steps gave an impression of elegance as they climbed them toward the third-floor apartment.

"There are plans to install an elevator and that will make life much easier."

"I would imagine the rents are high."

"Not too bad, considering everything. I am not far from the factory and the subway station is only two blocks away. The convenience is something I considered when I took this place. Also, it is a large apartment and the rooms are airy and light, especially the living room which faces the front. The bedrooms face the courtyard so they are really quiet at night."

All the doors were painted the same color and the hallway was remarkably clean, much cleaner than the hallways in Brighton Beach. Cel was happy no one opened their door as Morris put the key in the lock and stood back to allow Cel to enter first. In front of her was a bedroom and to her left was a long hallway from which she could see the other two bedrooms. As she walked up the hallway, she passed the bathroom and then entered the kitchen which had a large window that provided ample light. Another doorway from the kitchen led to what was obviously a dining room and French doors opened to a modest living room where there were double windows that allowed the afternoon sun to flood the room with a golden glow.

"This is a lovely apartment," she said when she walked to the couch and put her bag down.

"Yes, I think a woman could make this place into a home. Right now it seems lacking, but adequate."

She walked over to him, put her arms around his neck and kissed him.

"Come, let's start making this place a home," she replied, and she rubbed his back and held him close, pressing her breasts into his chest.

"Oh, Cel, part of me has dreaded this moment and part has craved it since I first saw you. I only hope I will not disappoint you."

"Fear not. I too have wanted you and I know that we can make this work. Let me go into the bathroom and freshen up. Why don't you get more comfortable?"

She took her purse and went into the bathroom, which was clean but devoid of any personality. Once the door was closed she undressed and fumbled with the diaphragm she had gotten at the clinic. She had practiced inserting it but she found now that she was nervous, the thing just did not slide in correctly. It seemed like an eternity before she felt it was properly in place. There was no way she was going to take any chances that she might become pregnant.

She looked at herself in the mirror and felt pleased with her image as she put her loosely fitting blouse over her ample breasts and applied some fresh lipstick. She knew a man could not help but be aroused as she left the bathroom and walked towards where Morris was sitting on the couch. He was still dressed in his slacks and shirt, and seemed to hold his breath as she walked towards him wearing nothing but the loose fitting blouse that went down past her hips. She kneeled in front of him and started opening his shirt. Once he stood, she helped him remove his pants and his underwear. She noticed at once that he was amply endowed as he reached down and pulled her to her feet, holding her close to his chest, so close that she could feel the hair on his chest through her blouse. His hands were under her shirt on her naked back and as he stroked her back she shivered, excited by the touch of a man. He stroked her breast and her nipple hardened as she reached and rubbed her hand along his leg and felt his hardness. Lying back on the couch, he entered her and she was excited by the firm penis within her. Moments later she felt his pulsation as she contracted around him. It was wonderful having a man, but she knew immediately she would have to teach him how to satisfy her.

They remained on the couch, holding each other as if they were afraid to lose each other, until she said, "Come, Morris, let us go into the bedroom where we can be more comfortable."

"You weren't satisfied. I'm sorry."

"No, no – please do not misunderstand. It felt wonderful but I want more."

"Cel, I don't think I can."

"Don't think! Come."

The bed was neatly made as she threw the covers back and pulled him down onto the mattress. Lying beside her, he just watched as she removed her blouse and placed her breasts over his face. He could not help but reach up and try to cup them in his palms. As he did so, she lay on her side and allowed him to cuddle her. Then she began to stroke his penis, helping it to harden once more. Slowly, she took his hand and brought it to her clitoris and indicated that she wanted him to massage it. He groaned as he became excited by her touch and by touching her. As she started to become aroused, she pushed his head down onto her breast and made him suck on her firm nipple. Beads of perspiration formed on his forehead as he buried his face in her breast and tried to pull the goodness from it. This time when he entered her and felt her wetness, they both came with such force that they felt their bodies arch before the ultimate release. Exhausted, they held each other closely as they fell into a perfect post-coital sleep.

When Cel awoke, she smiled to herself. She knew immediately she had him just where she wanted him and that he would do anything for her. There were no more questions about her security. Everything was going to work out just the way she wanted it, maybe even better. At least he was a willing lover. She knew she had missed having sex, but until this very moment, she did not know exactly how much she had missed it. In time, she was now sure he would be a more than adequate partner and she was relieved by that knowledge.

Morris awoke to find her staring at him and her smile assured him that he had indeed pleased her. His relief was evident as he took her in his arms and caressed her, holding her as closely as humanly possible. She was more woman than he had ever had and the fact that she wanted him was flattering, to say the least.

"I am sorry that I have to take you home."

"I wish, too, I could just stay here with you just as we are right now. But Sophie would have a fit if I were not to come back."

"Let's get married right away so that we no longer have to answer to her."

"That sounds like a plan to me."

"Tomorrow let's go and get our blood tests. Then we can get the license and be married by the Justice of the Peace. We do not need a wedding as I think we just had that."

"I think I would prefer a rabbi to marry us instead of a Justice of the Peace. We can be married in the rabbi's study and have the children there to share the moment. It would be more special that way."

"So be it. Do you know a rabbi?"

"We can use your rabbi."

"Oh, Cel, I feel so lucky to have met you. I will forever be indebted to Bella for introducing us," he said, as he rolled over onto her body and kissed her deeply.

114

"Come, let's get dressed and we can get a bite to eat before I take you home."

"Just one more thing. Come kiss me here," she said, indicating a spot in the cleavage between her breasts.

Morris put his head down and kissed her, burying his face as he did so and inhaling her smell as if to keep it with him until he could enjoy her body again.

Shortly afterwards, Morris took Cel back to Brighton Beach. Once she was alone in the safety of her bed, she gave in to her feelings. She felt dirty, as if she had used her body, giving it as payment for something. She knew she had also used Morris, used him as a means of escape. The only question was, what was she escaping to. Certainly it was not to love, because she did not feel that way towards him.

CHAPTER 7

Three weeks later they were married in a simple ceremony in the rabbi's study. Joey and Estelle were there, along with Sophie and Aunt Bella. Cel looked radiant in a silk suit that Morris had designed especially for the occasion. He told her the suit would be the center of his new line for the spring and hoped it would bring double luck for them: happiness and profit.

Following the wedding they went to Atlantic City for a long weekend honeymoon. There they walked the boardwalk, despite the chill in the winter air, and watched the waves hit the beach. Cel was amazed at the beauty of the ocean and the peacefulness of its sounds. This was so foreign to her after the years in the mountains.

Physically, their relationship was satisfying. Morris was willing to try to please his beautiful bride and Cel was more than willing to guide him. It was obvious to her that sex had been a routine exercise for him previously and that his first wife had never made demands for her own pleasure. Cel's attitude was different. If she was going to submit to sex, it should at the very least be pleasurable to her. She was going to make sure that all her needs were taken care of by this man, both physically and financially. She knew she would never again be placed in a situation whereby she would have to compromise herself.

Once home from their honeymoon, life became increasingly complicated. The children had to be moved into the apartment and everything had to be set up for the family. Norman presented the greatest problem because everything had to be done for him. He could not even sit up by himself.

Obviously, this was a backward child who was going to tax Cel's physical and emotional strength. Joey and Estelle presented few problems, as they were each excited by the other's presence and enjoyed playing together. Of course, Estelle was given a room to herself and whenever food was served, Cel always made sure the choicest pieces were placed on Estelle's dish. Cel swore to herself that her child would always come first, before Morris or his children.

Every week Morris would give Cel her weekly money and every week she would take a part of it and put it away for herself. If she found that she did not have enough money as the end of the week approached, she would merely ask for more. Morris was a generous man; he never questioned her about how she spent the money and Cel was careful not to take too much so as to raise any suspicions. However, she really liked acquiring her own money; it reminded her of the days when she would save her tip money, except then she was saving for herself and Henry and now she was saving for herself and Estelle.

Sophie presented the only other problem. She continued to butt in and to try and control Cel's life. She even demanded a weekly allowance, telling Morris that she needed money to keep herself in her own apartment and threatening to give it up and move in with them. This was not an option for Cel. She had married to get away from Sophie and kept reminding her mother that she had pushed Cel into marriage because she wanted to make a life for herself without being saddled with Cel and Estelle. At first Morris agreed to send Sophie money each week but he too refused to have her live with them. The apartment was crowded with the three children and all the paraphernalia needed for the baby, and he just could not see himself being told what to do by that woman. Whenever she came to visit, arguments erupted because of her demands and meddling, and Morris quickly became tired of them.

"Look, Sophie," he told her on one of her more bossy visits, "I know you are used to telling everyone what to do and how to do it. I am not going to permit it in my house. Cel will do things my way, not yours, and you will keep your opinions to yourself."

"You have too much nerve, young man. Who do you think you are, speaking to me like that?"

"You cannot come here and think you can dictate to us."

"I am not dictating, I am suggesting. My suggestions are made on the basis of experience. I know what is best for my daughter."

"She is my wife."

"She is my daughter and will always be my daughter first."

"Yes, I know how much you cared for her. You were willing to marry her off to just about anyone just to get her out of your apartment."

"I wanted her to have security and to be taken care of. That's not wrong."

"Look, Sophie, all I have to say to you is that you have to mind your own business and leave us alone. If you cannot do that, please do not come here any more."

Sophie just sat with her mouth opened. No one ever had spoken to her like that and she just did not know how to respond. There was something in Morris' tone that indicated he was not going to soften his approach and for the moment she was speechless. She had hoped to come and live with them and to benefit from Cel's good marriage. In her heart she knew not to push Morris; she would just have to find another way to get what she wanted, security and an easier life. After all, she was the mother and they were the children and they should show her proper respect. She had to make sure that she would continue getting money, and more of it. Just what buttons she had to push to achieve this was the question, and she decided to bide her time and to try to keep her mouth shut for now.

"Okay, have it your way. I only want to help make things easier for you."

"You can do that by minding your own business. We will make mistakes, but they will be ours. Let us live our lives our way, then we will all be happier," Morris replied, walking out of the room.

Cel stood there with her mouth opened. No one ever spoke to her mother like that. How often she wanted to say just that but never had the courage to stand up to Sophie. She could not help but think how much happier her years with Henry could have been if they were on their own and away from Sophie. She shook her head just as she heard Sophie say, "You are my kinda. You must make him understand that he has to take care of me."

"Momma, you can take care of yourself. You wanted to make a new life for yourself. That is what you repeatedly said when you wanted to marry me off. Now you are free to do just that, do it. Why don't you go find a nice Russian husband like you wanted me to do?"

"I'm too old for that. They want young women, not old hags like me. You have to take care of me. You can afford it, your brothers can't."

"Take care of yourself. We cannot do any more for you than we are now doing. Stop badgering me – if you don't Morris will cut you off completely. He has been generous but you are pushing him too hard. He is not a man you can manipulate like you did Papa and Henry."

"Maybe I can't, but you can."

Yes, I can, Cel thought to herself, but I wouldn't do it for you. I have myself to think about and I have to make sure

Estelle is taken care of, not you. But her reply out loud was simply, "Momma, let it rest!" In her heart she knew she would make sure that Sophie's visits were spread out more and that she and Morris would not be together unless it served her own purposes, and if Sophie continued pushing her, her purpose would be to end the visits altogether. No one, not Sophie and not Morris, was going to control her life from now on.

CHAPTER 8

Time seemed to pass quickly for Cel. She was ever so busy taking care of the child and trying to teach Norman the simplest of tasks. His progress seemed painstakingly slow. At a year-and-a-half, he was finally able to sit up by himself and play with his hand-held toys. He showed no desire to crawl and did not even reach for his feeding spoon. Cel took him to the doctor and got little encouragement from him. The doctor could only tell her that he appeared retarded and time would tell how far he would go with his development. The circumstances of his birth were definitely against the child and, since no one really knew how he was handled at birth or thereafter, it was impossible to gauge if his brain were damaged.

When Cel told Morris about her conversation with the doctor, he merely shook his head and closed his eyes.

"You realize he is not a child we should keep at home. He belongs in an institution where they can take care of him."

"No, Cel, he is my son and he stays right here. We can take better care of him than any institution and he will learn, give him time."

"That's easier for you to say than it is for me. I have two other children who need my time and I cannot do it all."

"You can and you will."

I can't and I won't, were her thoughts but she lacked the courage to say them at this time. She knew instantly that she would have to work on him until he accepted the idea. After all, it is a shunda to have a child like Norman and she did not want to be embarrassed in front of the neighbors. Someone might even think he and Estelle were related and then no one would ever want to have anything to do with her. She knew how to change his mind and she welcomed the idea. She would complain about how tired she is and withhold sexual attention.

Night after night when Morris came to bed, she complained of her fatigue and refused his advances. Night after night, he said nothing. He knew exactly what she was up to and he knew he would not succumb to her demands. After all, he married to provide his children with a home and a mother, and that meant both of his children. He was willing to overlook the favoritism Cel displayed towards Estelle. He was even willing to put up with Sophie, but he was not willing to give up his son, no matter how much of an embarrassment he was.

Finally, after several months of being treated as if he had no rights to have any wifely attentions, Morris had had it. Late one night when he came to bed and saw Cel feigning sleep, he decided to have it out with her. She would not use this method to get her own way. Cel had to know he was the boss in his own house and he had the right to demand certain things of her. She had to be good to his sons and she had to be a wife to him.

"Cel, we have to talk."

"Not now, you know I'm too tired after taking care of that child all day."

"That child is my son and you knew when you married me you would have to take care of him. You saw him and you even spoke about how slow he was. His condition is not a surprise to you, but I have a surprise for you. I am not the fool that you think I am. I know exactly what you are trying to do. Let me tell you something. Withholding your attentions will not convince me to put Norman into an institution. I know that has been your objective and it won't work. Let me tell you something else. I am well aware that you are putting money away each week and that you are always looking for ways to favor Estelle. None of these things have escaped me. You just think I am stupid. Well think again. If you believe for one minute you can manipulate me the way Sophie manipulated the men in her life, you had better think again."

"I'm not trying to manipulate anyone—"

"Don't even finish that statement. We both know it's a lie. Just think about what I have said. Think long and hard and decide what kind of life you want. I can give you everything you will ever desire or I can give you nothing. Either way, my children will be taken care of for as long as you remain under my roof. The decision is yours."

With that he walked out of the bedroom and closed the door just as he closed the conversation. Cel lay there staring at the ceiling and felt a fear she had never felt before. If she were to leave Morris, there was nowhere for her to go. Sure she had saved some money, but not nearly enough to support herself and Estelle. Sophie would not take her back, not after she refused to allow her to live with them and even discouraged her visits. She had no one, no one except Morris, and he had not left any doubts about his feelings. The lump in her throat felt so large she felt as though she could not breathe. She was stupid to push him so hard so soon. She knew she had not played her cards properly. She definitely had misjudged him. Now what to do was an even greater problem. She could not just run to him and throw herself at him. She realized that sex alone would not satisfy this man. For the first time since they met, she understood that he was not a man governed by his male organ, nor was he a stupid man. How did he know she was taking money out for herself? She had thought she was so careful. What was she to do? What?

The night passed so very slowly. Morris never opened the bedroom door and Cel was too shaken to go out and see where he was. As daybreak peeked through the window shade, she decided to just get up and start making breakfast for everyone. Her best option was to continue as though nothing had been said and to try to stop complaining about Norman. She would even be better towards Joey, though that child could drive a person crazy with his constant activity. Maybe if she showed she was a better mother to the children, Morris would soften towards her. One thing was for sure, she would never again turn him away from her bed, not if she wanted to stay. With the new day she knew Morris was the man in his house and not one that could be easily managed. Cel knew she was the fool to have thought differently. Maybe someday she would have enough money to be independent, but that day was too far away now and she had better mend her ways for sure.

Cel got up and made her way into the kitchen to start breakfast, trying to act as though nothing had occurred the night before. Morris came into the kitchen and seemed extremely cold and formal. He refused anything to eat except some black coffee and told her he would be home late that evening as he had to get the new line of dresses ready for the cutters. Nothing else was said, much to Cel's relief.

The day passed ever so slowly as Cel tried her best to take care of Norman despite her fatigue. Luckily Joey and Estelle had school so they were gone most of the day and she was able to get a little rest when Norman was not crying. She kept wondering if she could hide her dislike for this helpless child. She kept telling herself it was not his fault but every time she lifted his now heavy body, she felt her heart turn cold. There was so little hope for him and now for her.

Evening finally came and the children were in bed before Morris came home. She gave him a reheated meal and their conversation was kept at a minimum. She thought of trying to apologize but thought better of it. What could she say to make things better? She simply had to let her actions speak for her. After dinner they went to bed and the tension between them seemed like a wall which neither could cross. They merely lay next to each other, not speaking, not touching, not sleeping. Cel realized she must have fallen asleep finally when the daybreak again peeked through the shade and signaled the beginning of a new day, hopefully a better day for her.

Hearing the shower running, she decided to get up and make breakfast. When Morris came into the kitchen, she went to him and put her arms around him.

"We must put this tension behind us. The way things are is not good for anyone in this house."

"Cel, there are things that just must be my way. The boys will always come first. They are my obligation and one that I take quite seriously. Norman cannot help the way he is. It's not his fault that he needs extra attention. Just remember, no matter what, he is my son."

"I know...I was wrong."

"That I can accept...but your tactics are hurtful."

"I am sorry. Please let's go back to the way things were before."

"Do you care about me at all?"

"Oh, Morris, of course I care dearly about you. Why else would I have married you?"

"Cel, we both know the possible answer to that question."

"If you are accusing me of having sold myself, you are wrong. I married you because you are a special man, a man whom I want to be with."

"Well, that's good to hear. Now start acting that way and things will be better in this household. I don't like all of the tension either. Just understand one thing. I will not be manipulated when it comes to the boys. You can manipulate the money, you can send whatever you want to Sophie...all of that is something I really don't care about. I expect the boys to be well cared for and I expect you to give Norman whatever time and energy he needs. Promise me, right now, you will never mistreat him because if you do it will be the end of us."

"I promise. But understand he is a problem and at times it is beyond my ability to deal with his constant crying and helplessness. The other children also need my attention."

"Let them help with him. It is good for them to understand there are people in this world who need extra attention. This will make them less selfish."

"What if he just never develops past the level he is now at?"

""We'll deal with that if it happens. Right now he is still a baby and maybe he can start to develop other skills. Time will tell. I know of others like him who become self-sufficient. It just takes more time. Time and attention are what he needs and what we as a family are going to give him."

"I'll try but you must be there too. You have to give me some relief when you are home. It is impossible for me to deal with him day and night. I must be able to leave him with you and go out with Joey and Estelle and do things just with them, let alone do things for myself."

"I will arrange to have someone come in for a few hours each week so that you can get out more. I know a woman who is looking for some work and she can even do some cleaning for you. Your request is not unreasonable."

"Let's try that. It would be good to escape from the crying."

"Settled."

"No, not settled. What about us? Is there still going to be a wall in our bed?"

"You put it there. Now it is up to you to take it down."

"Consider it down!"

She turned away from his glance, knowing that she would have to change her ways and show him tenderness. She knew she would have to keep her bargain or everything would be lost.

CHAPTER 9

Life fell into a pattern of sameness; sameness, but different than before. During the day, Cel took care of the children; attentive, but never with tenderness, except where Estelle was concerned and then she was extremely tender. Morris went to the factory and usually arrived home by dinner time. Joey and Estelle were in school all day and when they came home, Cel made sure homework was completed before they could see their friends or listen to the radio. The only break was when Stephanie came to watch Norman. Then Cel would leave to go shopping and occasionally meet the few neighbors she had befriended. At night Morris would let it be known when he wanted sex and Cel never refused, though she stopped feigning excitement. She would respond only enough to show interest; never would she initiate or direct. This was fine with Morris as it was what he was used to, but he too felt the lack of excitement that was there in the beginning. He just accepted what was too difficult to change, though he could not help but notice that Cel was definitely not the woman he had married. Her figure was now plump and matronly. It was no longer as much fun to bring home pretty dresses for her, so he brought home the ones that best suited her rounded figure, only to have her complain that his clothes were for old ladies.

Norman remained a problem. At four his mental development remained that of a one-year-old. He could barely walk unassisted and his verbal ability was non-existent. Obviously, he would not be accepted into regular school, so some arrangement had to be addressed. Morris still would not entertain any mention of a residential school and

Cel would never broach the subject. She did inquire at the local public school and was told they did have one class for all the retarded children. This was unacceptable because there were twelve-year-olds in the same room and clearly Norman would be victimized. The only alternative would be a private day school and Cel explained this to Morris, who was receptive to the idea. The advantage to her was that Norman would not be in the daily sight of the other mothers and at least she would be spared that shame. A special bus would pick him up each morning and return him at five each evening. Cel viewed this as a clemency; she could hardly wait. It would be wonderful not to have a baby pulling on her skirt and screaming for her attention. What she would do with her time was not a question she addressed. She was merely looking forward to doing nothing. She even considered asking Morris to continue having the housekeeper come to clean. After all, it was a busy house with the three children and they were certainly messy.

Of the neighbors she met in Washington Heights, one in particular became a close friend. Sadie Glassman knew all the right places to get everything from meat to fine gifts at wholesale. Her husband, Sam, was a salesman; for what Cel never knew, but he was gone for a week at a time, leaving Sadie free to do her own thing. Their two sons were the same ages as Joey and Estelle, so the children played together while their mothers gossiped about everyone in the three sister buildings on Bennett Avenue. In fact, it was Sadie who found a way to end Cel's problems with Sophie. She introduced Sophie to a widower whom she knew from the neighborhood. The two of them became fast friends and before anyone could take a breath, they were married and off to Miami Beach to live. What a break for Cel: not only was her mother married, but she was two days away by train and could no longer just pop in. Mr. Richman, Sophie's new husband, was financially secure and so Cel was able to pocket the money she always sent to Sophie. Of course, she allowed Morris to continue to believe Sophie needed the funds. Cel's nest egg was growing and so was her delight.

Summer was a time when most of the neighborhood left the city and took bungalows in the Catskills or Berkshire mountains or down along the New Jersey shore. Cel favored the Catskills because she was so familiar with the area and it did not take her long to find a bungalow colony on a lake. She convinced Morris it was the best thing for the children because they had so much to do and there would be many others their ages for them to play with. The colony she chose was in the Catskills, closer to New York than Middletown so that Morris could come for the weekends but too far from the city for a daily commute. The lake had row-boats for the children and there was a raft for swimming and a basketball court. Most importantly it was cooler than the city and there were several other mothers who liked to play cards and pass the hot days of summer doing very little else. The Colony, as it was called, was perfect even for Norman, who spent his day in the kiddie pool or just sitting on the grass watching insects. Cel would make sure that Joey took his brother for a walk and insisted that he play with Norman for a few hours each day. If he complied, he was free to do his own thing for the rest of the time. If he refused, he had to spend the day in his room. Surprisingly, Joey did not seem to resent spending time with Norman, because he realized how special his brother was to his father. Estelle, on the other hand, wanted nothing to do with Norman and refused to even talk to him. Cel never made an issue of her daughter's behavior and allowed her to go about her day without restriction; after all, Norman was no relation to her and why should she have to give him any time?

Norman, for his part, made exceptional progress during that first summer at the Colony. His walking improved and he was able to express himself in broken sentences. Every once in a while he would attempt to do the same things Joey did, only to get hurt while trying. Cel would ignore the hurts, and so would Norman after a while and he would continue to keep trying to do things. Little by little, he was able to execute more tasks and become more self-sufficient.

One day, as he was walking with his feet on Joey's, he lost his grip on Joey's hands and fell backwards, hitting his head on the corner of a metal cabinet in the kitchen. The child seemed to be unconscious, but then Cel witnessed the worst sight she had even seen. Suddenly, Norman's entire body convulsed in a wild seizure. Every part of his body seemed to jerk in a different direction; his tongue was larger than life and protruded from his mouth so far that it looked like he would bite it off. Cel tried to hold his flaying arms and keep him from continuing to hit his head, but she was not strong enough to do so. Joey seemed frozen in fear as he watched his brother's twisted body. Finally, the movement stopped, and Norman lay quietly on the floor; his eyes were open but not seeing and he was totally unresponsive. Cel ran to the main house to call the local doctor, who dispatched an ambulance to take the child to the nearest hospital. She did not even think to call Morris at that moment because she knew she just had to get back to the bungalow.

Norman continued to remain unresponsive until just before the ambulance arrived. At that point he seemed to come out of the trance and merely said, "I tired... go sleepy now."

"What's happening to him?" Joey questioned.

"Joe... I have never seen anything like this before. I just don't know. We'll have to wait until the doctor sees him. Stay with him, I have to go call your father."

With that Cel again ran to the main house and called Morris at the factory. She quickly told him what had transpired and suggested he meet them at the hospital as soon as he could get there. Then she went back to the bungalow and watched as the ambulance attendants put the now sleeping child on the stretcher and carried him into the vehicle. He looked so small and helpless, and even she could not help but feel genuine concern. She climbed into the ambulance, leaving Joey and Estelle in the care of the other residents of the Colony, all of whom were gathered around watching the macabre sight.

When they arrived at the hospital, Norman remained in a deep sleep and they were unable to awaken him. The doctor examined him and found all his vital signs were normal. The decision was a simple one; the child had to remain in the hospital for observation and testing. Cel decided to remain until Morris could get there, just in case Norman awoke and was frightened. She just sat by the side of his bed and stared ahead. She tried to sort out her feelings but decided that at that moment she just felt nothing at all.

Several hours passed before Norman woke up and said he wanted to go home. Cel tried to explain that he was sick and had to stay for the doctors to help him. Of course, he did not understand, and merely cried and kept repeating "Home...go home." This was the pathetic sight Morris saw when he first entered the room. He took the child into his strong arms and just held him. Cel quickly filled him in on what had happened and what the doctors had said up to that point.

"I'll stay here with him. Why don't you go home to the other children? It is really ridiculous for us both to stay and do nothing," Morris said, and Cel quickly agreed.

When Cel reached the bungalow, she found a very frightened Joey. He feared he would be blamed for what had happened and there was no consoling him, especially since there was nothing concrete to tell.

"Is Daddy mad at me?"

"Right now your father cannot think about anything else except your brother. He did not say anything about you, so I cannot tell you what he is thinking. I can tell you this. You have done so much for your brother this summer. You've helped him to develop so many skills he didn't have before. No matter what anyone says you've helped more than you hurt him. I'll do everything I can to make your father understand that. I'm sure what happened today would have happened anyway. You can't blame yourself."

Joey looked at her as though he was seeing her for the first time. He felt a closeness for this woman he had never felt before. It was as though she cared about him. All he could say was, "Thank you. That means a whole lot to me."

"Go to bed now and get some rest; we will need to be fresh in the morning," Cel responded as she gave him a pat on his backside and sent him off to his room. For herself, she needed silence; she needed time to put her own feelings into some perspective. Who knew what the future would hold for her now that it was obvious she not only had a retarded child on her hands but possibly a very sick one as well.

Morris came to the bungalow very late that night. He had stayed at the hospital watching Norman sleep, a sleep of the dead. When he came in, he found the entire place draped in darkness and he was surprised to find Cel sitting on the couch.

"Why are you sitting in the dark?"

"I was thinking. This day seems like a nightmare and I am having trouble sorting out my feelings. The children are both asleep."

"What happened here today?"

"I must say that I do not think what happened is the cause of all of this. The boys were playing. As you know, I insist that Joey play with his brother for a couple of hours each day, and he has been wonderful for Norman."

"Okay, I can accept that. But what happened just before Norman went into convulsions?"

"Norman was walking with his feet on Joey's feet and lost his grip on Joey's hands. He fell backwards and hit his head on that metal cabinet in the kitchen. Then all hell broke loose."

"Did you tell this to the doctor?"

"Of course. I have to tell you that Joey is very upset. He feels responsible."

"He should."

"Morris, please don't blame him. A normal child might have been knocked out for a few minutes. This is something else, of that I'm sure."

"It's late; let's get some sleep. Tomorrow maybe we will know more."

They went to their bedroom and undressed in silence. That night Cel needed to stay close to Morris, as if by doing that she would get extra strength. He, for his part, seemed lost in his own thoughts and fears.

Morning came all too quickly and the tension in the bungalow was so thick, it was intolerable. Morris did not speak to Joey and the boy could hardly eat his breakfast. He feared his father's wrath and Cel could not say anything to break the tension. Only Estelle seemed unconcerned as she got ready to spend the day with her friends. Joey refused to remain at the colony and insisted on going to the hospital with them.

When they arrived at the hospital, they quickly went to Norman's room, only to find him gone. It turned out that the nurses had taken him downstairs for some testing and they assured Morris that the child was alert and had even eaten very well. The night had been a quiet one and there was no further episode. That was a relief for everyone concerned. Together the family sat in the room and waited for the child to return. No conversation took place as each seemed lost in his own thoughts. Finally, Norman was wheeled into the room and seemed excited to see his brother. He put his little arms up and hugged Joey around the neck.

"I scared."

"It's all right, little guy. Everything is going to be all right. Before you know it we will take you back home."

"You stay here."

"Yes, I'll stay. Would you like me to read a book to you?"

"Okay."

Cel and Morris walked out of the room as the two boys sat together on the bed looking at the pictures in the book. They wanted to find the doctor and to try to find out what was going on. At the nurses' station, they found him writing up charts.

"Well, can you tell us anything at all?" Morris asked.

"It looks like he is epileptic. Let me try to explain it to you as simply as possible. Epilepsy is a disorder in the brain affecting the nerve cells. Normally, the brain cells produce some electrical energy, which then flows through the nervous system and activates the muscles. In the epileptic patient, the brain fails to limit or control this release of energy and then a seizure such as the one that occurred yesterday happens. There are three types of epileptic seizures. One is the grand mal, which is what we think Norman experienced. The others are called petit mal and psychomotor seizures. In a grand mal attack, the person loses consciousness and the muscles jerk uncontrollably. Most gran mal seizures last a few minutes and then the person goes into a deep sleep. That is exactly what Norman did. A petit mal attack is different in that the person loses awareness of his surroundings for a few seconds. These seizures are not always noticeable, and we think Norman probably had been experiencing them for some time and no one knew it. In a psychomotor attack, the patient is withdrawn and behaves strangely for a few minutes and then it is over.

"We did take x-rays and they seem to indicate an area of the brain is pinched. Given the history of his birth and development, it is probable that the injury to his brain occurred during the birth process. The fall yesterday just jarred his brain into releasing the uncontrolled energy. I want a neurologist to see him, but I do not think there is anything to do surgically because it is my initial opinion that any surgery will leave him a total vegetable. I think this is a case to watch and wait. Maybe he will not have further episodes if we can prevent jarring of his brain. If the seizures continue, then we will have to see if medication or diet or a combination of the two will help alleviate them. This is not an unusual situation and the fact that this was his first episode is in our favor."

"Can't he hurt himself during one of these so-called seizures?" Cel asked.

"Yes. If he hits his head or bites off his tongue, he will be permanently affected. He might have to wear a helmet to protect his head and we will show you how to use a wooden spoon to protect his tongue. Otherwise, they usually do not inflict injury upon themselves during a seizure. Time will dictate how we manage him. I am sure, in time, if there are repeats of this episode, you will learn to read the signs indicating when they will occur and you will learn how best to prepare for it."

"But, doctor, he is supposed to start school in the fall. What will happen if it happens there?"

"School? Surely not a public school? He does not belong in a regular classroom and if he goes to a special school, you will have to tell them about his condition. I'm sure they have faced this before and are trained to deal with it."

"Is he retarded because of the epilepsy or did being retarded cause the other?"

"Neither. It is entirely possible that both are caused by the same injury to the brain. Epileptics do not have to be retarded and, in fact, most live fairly normal lives. In this case, I think both conditions were caused by some trauma and some pinching of the brain during delivery."

"Now what?" asked Morris.

"Now, you will take him home and watch him closely. I want to know if there is another episode. I know you folks live in the city and I think it would be best to see a neurologist there so he can monitor the case. I will give you a list of some men I can recommend in Manhattan."

"What should I do if this happens again?"

"Protect his head as best you can and try to put a wooden spoon in his mouth to keep the teeth from biting down on his tongue. Do not try to control his arms and legs because if you restrain them, you could cause injury. To help prevent a seizure, I would suggest the child be kept relatively quiet. Don't over-stimulate him or allow him to become overtired. We often see more seizures when the person is fatigued."

"Will he become more retarded?"

"No one can say to what degree he will develop. He is about four years behind in mental development now. This may be all that he is capable of or he may continue to develop at a slower pace than a normal child. Time will tell."

"Should we keep him out of school?"

"That is not an option. The law requires he go to school; whether that be a residential facility or a day one, he must attend a school. I think it is best he remain with his family and attend a day facility because that would be less traumatic for him. He is very attached to the family, that is obvious. Now you will have to find a school that is prepared to address both of his problems. That is not to say that I am sure there will be repeat seizures. I do not know that for a fact. My guess is there will be."

Cel felt as though someone had hit her with a two-by-four. Now, for sure, Morris would not entertain any idea of a residential school. She was doomed. She just could not imagine how she was going to handle Norman. My God, she thought, this is bad enough if it is your own child, but to have to deal with all of this and have it be someone else's child was too much. She was jarred out of her thoughts by hearing Morris saying, "Well, thank you, doctor. Please prepare the list of the doctors in the city. We will take your advice and get him to one of them as soon as we can get back there. Is it all right for us to take him home now?"

"Yes, by all means take him home. Please don't leave for the city for a few days at least. I would like to keep an eye on him, and please call me if there is another seizure."

"Of course. Thank you again. Come, Cel, let's take the boys home."

As they walked away from the nurses' station, Cel touched Morris' arm.

"We have to talk for a few minutes before we go back to the boys."

"Let's talk."

"Look, Morris, this is too much for me to handle alone. I just cannot stay here with him and be by myself. You cannot appreciate how horrible the whole thing was for me to watch and if it happens again, I don't know if I can manage."

"I understand. I will make arrangements to remain up here with you until we can take him back to the city. Believe me, I don't want to just leave him."

"There is another thing. I want you to promise not to blame Joey. The boy has been wonderful all summer and he has really helped Norman to be able to do more things by himself. The child is really upset and blames himself more than anyone can blame him. You heard the doctor say the fall did not cause the condition. Will you promise not to punish Joe?"

"If that is your wish. I will try. I do appreciate you taking his side like this. I have to admit I am a little surprised. You are always so hard on him."

"Hard, yes. But I do try to be fair. I know he is not my child but he is a good boy, most of the time. I saw his face when this all happened and let me tell you, he touched my heart. He did not mean to hurt his brother in any way, form or manner."

"But we must be assured something like this will not happen again."

"I doubt if you need worry about that. I am sure Joey will not attempt to do anything like that again. My guess is that he will always try to take care of the child, especially after this."

"Thank you, Cel. Your concern means ,more than anything. I know this is not easy for you and I truly appreciate your attitude. I know my sons are a burden to you."

"One thing has nothing to do with the other. Yes, Norman is a burden, has always been a burden and probably always will be a burden. But we must accept what we cannot change. Let's go back to the boys and let's go home."

Morris walked down the corridor with a heavy heart but a much lighter step. Maybe, just maybe, this woman had softened in her attitude towards the boys. Maybe, just maybe, they could be a real family, not just people living together because of their individual needs.

The rest of the day passed quietly. Joey was ever so attentive to Norman and played with him all afternoon. Only Estelle seemed untouched by the events that had transpired. She completely ignored Norman and was only concerned with the fact that she could not meet her friends and go to the movies with them. Even Cel seemed annoyed with her selfishness, though she said nothing about it. She simply felt drained and was looking forward to finishing the dinner dishes and climbing in between the cool sheets to rest. Morris also was tired and wore his concern on his face. He knew in his heart that what laid ahead was going to be difficult and just hoped he had the wisdom to see his family through the hard times.

That night when the children were in their beds, Cel lay close to Morris as though she was getting strength from his firm body. The silence of the bungalow was shattered by the sound of Norman thrashing in his bed. Before they got to his room, they knew he was having another seizure. Cel and Morris stood helplessly in the doorway as they watched his contorted body shake. Finally, Cel ran and grabbed the pillows from their bed and placed them around his head to prevent him from injuring himself. Morris tried to hold his arms and legs but it was useless and he let them go before the child could be hurt. The force of Norman's movements astonished the grown man. How was it possible that someone so small could have such power and strength? Just as quickly as it all started, it ended and Norman was in a deep sleep, his body wet with perspiration. Cel wiped him off with a dry towel before returning to her bed, knowing she would be able to sleep as the nightmare was over for this night at least. No words were spoken between them as Cel and Morris clung to each other; each knowing their lives were forever changed and each wondering what was ahead for them and the other children.

The next morning they decided it was pointless to remain in the country and they started packing to return to the city where they would seek out whatever help was available for Norman. It was too bad that Estelle and Joey also had to return to the hot city and give up their summer and their friends. Estelle complained bitterly but Joey wanted to help prepare for their return. Cel tried to explain to Estelle that she was being selfish and that there would be other summers to spend in the mountains. Finally, she gave up trying to persuade Estelle and just told her she had no choice but to comply with their wishes. Cel swore she could see Sophie's face in her daughter and felt ashamed that the child could be so self-centered and so uncaring. She even questioned herself briefly that maybe she was being too lenient with the child and was giving her too much. However, she decided that was a problem to be dealt with at a later time; there were just too many problems right now.

The doctors in the city were not any more helpful than those in the mountains. It was agreed that Norman had epilepsy and that it was probably a product of his birth. They felt that surgical intervention was too dangerous. The doctors explained that they could possibly go in and relieve the pressure on Norman's brain which they believed was causing his seizures, but that the area was a difficult one to get to and if the surgery was not perfect, they would leave him a virtual vegetable, unable to function in any manner. Morris would not entertain the thought of doing any such surgery. Now, at least, the child could function on some level and his seizures were only at night. He felt, and even Cel had to agree, they could manage this way and who knew what developments might come in the future. Hopefully, some medication would be developed that could control his seizures or maybe an operation would become available that would not have such inherent risks. For now, everyone decided to leave Norman as he was and to try and live with the situation as best they could.

Cel did pressure Morris to allow her to enroll Norman in a school for children like himself. She found one in Manhattan where they had other children with epilepsy and where they knew how to handle the children should they have a seizure while in school.

"Morris, you just cannot send this child to regular school where they will just let him vegetate. He needs special stimulation and attention which he can never get in the class for retarded children at the local school."

"I know you are right and this time I really believe you are doing this to help him and not just because you are ashamed of him."

"This has nothing to do with my feelings, which were selfish before now. This child needs special attention and we would be doing him an injustice if we do anything less for him. No one can say how much he is capable of learning or if he is capable of learning anything. But he does deserve a chance. He might even need to live at a facility in the future, but for now, he must go to a place where there are trained people who know how to handle him and his condition. If we are forced to send him to the regular school, I feel he will be victimized by the other children. You know how cruel children can be to someone who is different and we can no longer deny he is different."

"How would it work with this school you found?"

"Very simple. Every morning they will pick him up by bus and transport him to the facility, and they will bring him home each afternoon between four and five o'clock. He will be here for dinner and we will be told what they worked on each day so we can reinforce what he has learned to do. If they teach him how to tie his shoes, let's say, they will expect us to let him practice that skill. Their goal is to help him learn to be independent and they will try to teach him how to read and write as he is ready to learn."

"Do they have any idea if he will ever be ready to learn to read or write?"

"I took him there and they observed him with me in the room. They were very kind and gentle with him. It is their opinion that he is currently at the level of a two-or three-year-old. No one can tell me if he will ever get past this level but they have many others and say that it is likely, with the proper stimulation, that he will develop. It is doubtful if he will ever catch up to his chronological age, but only time will be able to answer that."

"Cel, I cannot believe you did all of this."

"I did what had to be done and now I am asking for your approval. I want you to come and see the school for yourself. This child needs this type of help and we must give it to him. He needs it and so do the other children."

"When can I go?"

"Tomorrow would be fine. I asked them and took it upon myself to make an appointment for nine in the morning. We can go and you can see for yourself how they handle Norman and then you will still be able to go to the factory."

"Thank you."

"No thanks are necessary."

Morris took her in his arms and kissed her, all the time holding her tightly to him. He could not believe how caring she had become, when before she seemed to resent the child so much. He decided not to bring up the past but knew he would be forever grateful for the change in her attitude. At that moment he loved her as he never thought he would love anyone again and holding her made him realize it had been entirely too long since they had been intimate.

Cel could feel his hardness against her body and she too wanted him and so wanted to enjoy his body. She hoped this night would be a quiet one; one of lovemaking rather than the terror of watching Norman convulse. Arm in arm, they walked to each child's room and checked to make sure the children were asleep. Then they went into their bedroom, closing the door to keep out the problems and fell onto the bed still holding each other. The hunger they felt exploded as each tried to hurriedly enjoy the moment, knowing they could be interrupted at any second. Afterwards, they fell asleep still holding each other.

The next morning the anxiety could be felt in the house as everyone prepared to leave. Estelle and Joey were walked to school by both parents and from there they took Norman with them for the meeting at his special school. Cel feared that Morris would find fault with the place and then she did not know what she would do with the child. Morris feared that this would not be a place that would help his son and he really wanted to make the right decision, placing Norman's needs before those of Cel or anyone else. He was keenly aware that Cel could have ulterior motives in placing Norman in a school where he would be out of sight of the other parents and children. However, he kept reminding himself to keep an open mind as they boarded the subway to go downtown to the school.

The building was anything but impressive as they approached. It was just another brick building in a row of buildings and had no distinctive markings to indicate that it was a school. There was not even a playground that could be seen from the street. However, once inside the atmosphere changed. Everything was at a child's view and colorful posters decorated the walls as the family walked to the administration office. As they opened the door, Mrs. Silver came right out to greet them and proceeded to pay special attention to Norman, who was hiding behind his father. She suggested they walk with her to a classroom where Norman could be with the other children while they toured the school. The classroom was a cheerful place and Morris was relieved to see that just five children were in the room with two adults.

"Is this the way you keep the children all the time?"

"We try not to have more than six children with every two teachers or at least one teacher and one aide. That way we can ensure each child will receive individual attention. All the children in this class are developmentally delayed but not all have epilepsy."

"How will you manage to make Norman comfortable so that we can leave him?" Morris asked.

"Please just watch and follow my lead. Now, Norman, I want you to come with me and meet the other children," Mrs. Silver replied.

Norman just stood and held on to his father as though he was afraid. He hid his face in his father's trousers and started to cry.

"There is no need for tears," Mrs. Silver said, as she gently took Norman's hand and led him over to the group of children who were listening to a story. "Mommy and Daddy will stand right over there and watch you. I think you will like the story Miss Greenberg is reading. Let's just listen for a few minutes."

Morris and Cel watched and saw Norman relax as the teacher encouraged him to become a part of the group. He kept looking over to where they were standing and each time he glanced their way, they waved at him. Norman was about the same size as the other children and he did become involved in the group. He did seem to relax and his eyes began to close. Cel was sure he would be asleep in just a few minutes and she was correct.

"Okay, we can go and tour the building now. If he wakes up, Miss Greenberg will come to get us," Mrs. Silver said, as she gently led the parents out of the room.

Morris was impressed with the cleanliness of the building as they went from room to room. Each area had small groups of children engaged in many different activities, each of which was patiently described by Mrs. Silver. Few of the children were just sleeping and Morris did observe that often the teacher would go over to a sleeping child and awaken him or her.

"We get to know each child and know when we should let him sleep and when he is just trying to escape by sleeping. We do not allow the children to just sleep away their time here. However, if we feel the child really needs to rest, we do allow it so that we do not overtax the attention span. Each of these children have special needs and we really work within those needs," Mrs. Silver explained.

"How would you stimulate Norman to do things? We find it very hard to get his attention at home," Morris asked.

"Time and repetition usually works. We keep repeating a task until he can master it and we make a game of each task. We use this technique to teach the alphabet as well as such tasks as tying a shoelace or buttoning a shirt. Often when they see another child doing something, it encourages them to try to do it. Everything with these children takes time and patience."

"Do you think Norman can learn?"

"Norman can learn as long as our expectations are within his limits. Right now we do not know his limits and we will only know them after he has been here for a time. We will have a psychologist work with him as well and she will advise us as to how we can proceed. I can promise you this, we will help him to develop to his capacity, whatever that might be. At least in this environment he will get the attention he needs. In a regular school there is just not enough staff to give him what he requires."

"I think it will be hard for him to be away all day and to have to travel on a bus."

"Every parent thinks that way at first. The bus is supervised by either a teacher or an aide. We watch each child for signs of fatigue and we will allow him adequate rest time. In the beginning we might require that your wife remain in the building to give him a feeling of security. Usually that only lasts for a short period and then he will be ready to travel by himself and to remain here alone. We communicate regularly with our parents so you will know what is happening each day. Of course, you are welcome to come and observe whenever you wish, as long as it does not disrupt the other children."

"Well, I think we have no other choice but to try this. It certainly is a better solution than placing him in a special class in the regular school," Morris stated, to Cel's relief.

"Norman can stay today but I would want Mrs. Beckman to remain as well. That way we can alleviate his fears."

"Of course I will stay. Just tell me what I should do and I'll do it."

"Basically I want you to be within his sight but to try and let him develop a relationship with Miss. Greenberg. Let her indicate to you if she wants you to be involved or not. Today, she will do little more than to try and make him feel comfortable and to try and get him involved with the group. This group is composed of children who are all new to the program and she is wonderful with them. Our goal is to get them to socialize and to try and have them relate to each other. These children often are not able to socialize at all, though I doubt that will be Norman's problem since he does play with his siblings."

"Norman is able to play with his brother better than with Estelle because Joey is more patient with him."

"That's fine. It is still a start in the right direction. Now let's make our way back to his group and you can try to awaken him."

When they returned to the room where Norman was, he was still asleep on the floor. The other children were no longer listening to the story and were having a snack. Morris went over to the sleeping child and gently awakened him by saying his name over and over again.

"Why don't we go over and see what the other children are eating? I think they are having cookies and maybe you would like one too."

Norman's face lit up. He loved cookies and quickly went over to the group for one.

"Now would be a good time for Daddy to leave if you wish and then we'll see how he reacts."

"He is used to Morris leaving. After all, he goes to work everyday," Cel injected. "Where may I sit so that I am out of the way?"

"We keep that chair for the mothers. You will find some magazines on the table. Please feel free to read them. Just sit there where he can see you until Miss. Greenberg indicates that you may leave. Then I will see you in my office to go over the necessary paperwork."

An hour later, Cel was in Mrs. Silver's office.

"Miss. Greenberg said to leave. Norman seems to be playing very well with the teachers, though he doesn't seem to want to talk to the other children except to demand whatever someone else is playing with."

"That's normal. Remember he functions much like a two-year-old and it is not unusual for that age group to want whatever the other has. He will learn to share in time. We are used to that type of behavior and everyone in that group behaves the same way," Mrs. Silver replied. "You will be taking him home early today so that he will not be too over stimulated. Tomorrow you will come down on the bus with him. I have arranged to have you both picked up as one of the last stops in the morning. That way he can get used to traveling on the bus and hopefully he will be able to spend more time without you being in the room. Usually the mothers can stop coming within a week."

"Whatever you want me to do, I'll do."

"Your cooperation is essential and we really appreciate your attitude, especially since we know he is not your child."

"I still want whatever is best for him. He needs help."

"Hopefully, he will develop to whatever level he can and that is all we can desire. No one can promise he will ever catch up with his chronological age but he does give every indication of being able to learn."

CHAPTER 10

Everyone can get used to things no matter how challenging the situation. Cel had that thought as she stood over the sink washing the breakfast dishes. The house was quiet; all the children were in school and Morris was at the factory. Cel was thinking about her day. Today would be her day! Today was the day she planned to meet Sam and to enjoy the afternoon with him. They both knew they were playing with fire but they decided to meet anyway. Sam was restless and claimed that Sadie no longer was interested in any type of physical relationship. He had often let Cel know he was interested in more than just a friendship between the two couples. As for Cel, well, she was just bored. Morris and she were not really able to have any fun any more with the children being around and with Norman always threatening a seizure. Their sex life had diminished to almost a non-existent level. A smile crossed Cel's face as she chuckled to herself.

"All of this is just rationalization. I just want to have some fun. Sam is pretty handsome and it would be fun to see how he performs. After all, Sadie always brags about what a great sex life they have and I believe her. I know Sam was just saying that he and Sadie no longer have a sex life to get me interested in him and to alleviate any guilt I might have about betraying my friendship with Sadie. Now I can see for myself and no one ever needs to be hurt. Sadie and Morris will never find out and I do not intend any emotional involvement."

Cel took extra time showering and fixing her hair. She was glad that she had allowed the beautician to put some color in it. Now there was no gray and her hair seemed to shine as she brushed it. She was amazed at how excited she felt and how young she felt. For a few hours she would not have to think about providing for Estelle, or mediating a dispute between Joey and Estelle or Estelle and Norman. For a few hours she would not have to think about Norman having a seizure or have to deal with Morris. For a few hours she was going to be a desirable woman, not a wife or a mother or a woman approaching middle age.

It was amazing that she did not even think about violating Sadie's friendship. Sadie was such a know-it-all. She always seemed to have all the answers, all the angles, and was always flaunting her jewelry as if to brag about how much her husband loved her. If she only knew the truth! Cel knew for a fact that she was not to be Sam's only afternoon encounter but she did not care. For her this day was an experiment to see if she still was a woman, a desirable woman. She was glad that she had convinced Sam to get a room in one of the downtown hotels. That way she did not have to deal with any of the neighbors seeing him coming to the apartment in the middle of the afternoon. These buildings have a thousand eyes attached to a thousand mouths that have nothing to do but gossip. She had convinced Sam that a hotel was the only way they could be guaranteed some privacy and that way also no phone calls would interrupt them. She had assured him that she would be worth the expense. Now she laughed out loud as she thought, "Now I had better perform!"

A final glance at her image in the mirror was satisfying and Cel grabbed her handbag and walked out of the apartment with a clicking of her heels on the tiled lobby floor. She was glad that she did not meet any neighbors in the hall and proceeded down Bennett Avenue to the 184th Street subway station without seeing anyone she knew or having to make any excuses. As she boarded the train the cadence of the wheels seemed to say, "You wicked bitch..." over and over again. Cel smiled to herself, knowing she was letting her imagination take over and enjoying it. She was wicked and she was liking it. At 42nd Street she left the subway and took a bus across town to First Avenue; it was only a short walk to the Beekman Towers Hotel on 39th Street, and the air felt fresh and clean as Cel walked the city blocks. Sam was waiting on the north corner as she approached. She was glad that he had gotten there first as they planned to enter the hotel together and register as man and wife. Sam was even carrying a small overnight bag for the sake of appearances.

Registration went smoothly and they walked to the elevator. Cel's heart was beating so fast that she was sure everyone in the lobby could hear it. Never would she have imagined that she would be so nervous and she wondered if Sam was experiencing the same emotions. Probably not, she concluded, because this was not new to him.

Sam opened the door to their room. It was a lovely room, furnished in Victorian style with wooden furniture and heavy drapes to close out the city and shield the room from some of the traffic noises from below. As Cel walked over to the window, she was amazed at the view of the East River and, looking uptown, the Triborough Bridge could be seen in the distance. As she stood there, Sam came over and put his hands on her shoulders.

"I thought you would like the river view...it is very pretty. May I hang up your coat? I hope you are not nervous... you know we don't have to do this if you have cold feet or something."

"Don't be silly. I am not nervous, just excited and anxious," Cel replied, taking off her coat and laying it on the chair in front of the window. She then decided she would take the initiative, and put her arms around Sam's neck and kissed him passionately on the lips.

—

"Does that feel like someone with second thoughts?"

"Whoa – what's next?"

"Your turn," Cel said, taking her shoes off and unbuttoning her blouse so that her ample breasts showed. Sam came over and put his hands into the blouse and caressed her breasts, then slowly moved his hands around to the bra hooks, which he opened, and then helped her out of her blouse and bra. Kissing her, he slowly moved his lips down her neck and over the top of her breast before putting her nipple in his mouth. Cel could feel herself getting wet as he sucked her breast until the nipple hardened. He then opened her shirt, and she willingly took off the shirt and her underpants, leaving only her garter belt and stockings on. She watched as he undressed and they both lay down on the bed. She sucked his member as he continued to touch her and excite her until she could no longer wait for him to penetrate her body. She came with a force that she had forgotten was possible and she felt him go limp too.

"Satisfied, or do you want more?"

"Oh, Cel, I want more. I just don't think I can do it again. That was great!"

"I can make you hard again, just say the word."

"You amaze me. I never thought you would suck me like that. That is something I would never expect from you."

"The name of this game is sex. I wanted to make you feel good and to feel good too. I guess if I were hung up about it, I would not be here," Cel said, as she took his penis into her hand and started massaging it until the hardness returned. Then she got on top of him and hung her breast over his mouth so that he could suck it, while she reached back and continued to massage him. His groan signaled his readiness and she lowered herself down onto his erect penis and moved with long deliberate strokes until she felt him come again. Then she pulled him over on top of her and again pushed his mouth onto her breast. While he sucked her breast, he touched her and she felt herself let go and it was wonderful.

They both lay there, allowing the satisfaction to bridge the gap between them. Then Cel got up and went to the shower, where she scrubbed her body as if to wash away her guilt. The sex was great and its illicitness added to the excitement, but it would not happen again, Cel told herself as she stepped out of the shower and re-entered the bedroom. Sam was asleep as she dressed and she considered leaving without waking him, but decided against that, as then she would really feel like a whore.

"Sam, I have to get started for home."

"What time is it?"

"It is almost two and the children will be home by three thirty, so I have to go."

"We must do this again; it was great!"

"We'll see. I just hope I can face you when I see you with Sadie without thinking about this afternoon."

"I'll never face you without thinking about it and enjoying the thoughts."

"Seriously, Sadie and Morris must never find out about today; so think what you wish but keep your mouth shut."

"Don't worry; there is no reason for them to ever know. I have no need to hurt Sadie or Morris. Though I am jealous that he can have you whenever he wants. You are great!"

"Thanks – I enjoyed it too. I needed to know I am still a desirable woman and you showed me I am. Now I must really get going."

On the subway ride home Cel kept thinking that everyone around her could smell that she had just had sex. The cadence was now saying, "Whore – you are a whore – whore..." and the guilt was making her nauseous. There was no excuse for what she had just done. It was wrong, just plain wrong, and no justification would make her feel any better about herself. Morris was a fair man who was a good provider and a decent husband. He did not deserve to be betrayed, and to be betrayed by a supposed friend. She and Sam were both at the bottom of the friendship barrel. "How am I going to face Sadie and listen to her brag about how great her sex life is?" Cel thought, shaking her head. "It's going to be harder lying to her than it will be keeping the secret from Morris. Women know."

That afternoon and early evening Cel felt as if she was watching herself from outside of her body. She went through all the motions of greeting the children when they came home from school and making dinner without any thought; she refused to allow herself to think about anything except the correct number of hours necessary for the diaphragm to remain in place. She was literally counting the minutes for its removal as if it was the last sign of her guilt.

Morris came home and seemed very preoccupied. He sat in the living room reading the *New York Times* and the Jewish newspaper, *Forbes*. Even the children sensed his mood and stayed in their rooms. When dinner was ready, Cel called everyone to the table and started the conversation by asking the children about their day at school. Even Norman contributed to the conversation, relating his attempted tasks.

"All of this is good, but has little meaning considering what is happening in the world," Morris stated. "I was talking with Morris Ruben, the buyer from Kleins, today. He has family in Germany and is really worried about them. It is clear to him that Hitler hates the Jews and there is going to be trouble in Germany for the Jewish people. Morris wants his family to leave and come here, but they keep saying it is ridiculous and everything will work out; after all, they are German citizens. That in itself is frightening because I can remember my family saying the same thing about Russia before the Cossacks came to wipe out the Jewish communities."

"Times are different now."

"Different? No different. Look, in the past three months Hitler has managed to take over Poland, Denmark, Luxembourg, the Netherlands, Belgium and France. War in Europe is sure to erupt on a large scale and I can't help but believe that the United States will become involved. The German economy is already taxed by the reparations they have had to pay because of the last war; now money will be even tighter there with all of it going to finance Hitler's aggressions. If money is tight, the Jews will be affected; I feel certain of that. Hitler makes no secret of his hatred of the Jews and his desire to have a perfect Aryan race."

"That's impossible. There is no way that anything horrible can happen. After all, this is 1939 and we live in a civilized world. Hitler will be satisfied now that he has control of France and everything will quiet down over there without our country becoming involved. You'll see."

"I doubt that you are right. I see big troubles in Europe and we will become involved. I see it so clearly that I am preparing the factory to produce clothing for the military."

"You're spending money for something that may never happen?"

"Cel, I feel I am right and it is necessary to prepare."

"We'll be bankrupt."

"Don't be ridiculous."

"I know the factory and its operation is your business, but I cannot help feel that it is wrong to spend for something that we all hope will not happen. No one wants us to become involved in Europe's problems; they are not our concern."

"That is wrong. Our economy is not based only on our own country; it depends on the other countries that buy our products. If Europe is unable to buy American products, we will all be affected."

"Oh, so we go to war to protect our money...That is wrong."

"Right or wrong... that is a possibility. However, we are not about to decide that now. I think I will go to the Temple. I want to discuss what Morris told me with the Rabbi; he said he would be there tonight."

Cel was relieved that he was going to go out and did not say anything; all she could think was that it worked to her advantage that he was so preoccupied with worldly affairs that he never even asked about her day – nothing said, no lies necessary. By the time he came home from the Temple, the children and she would be asleep. This was too perfect to believe.

The next morning at breakfast, Morris was really agitated. He reported that the Rabbi was also very concerned about the Jews in Germany and, in fact, arrangements were being made to find housing in Washington Heights for German families who were currently trying to leave Germany. He wanted Cel to help find things these families could use and for her to contact all her friends and have them donate things.

"The Rabbi is saying that the Jews are leaving with nothing. They are not being allowed to remove any of their possessions or money. The ones that are coming will have to make totally new lives for themselves and their families, but they feel they are doing the right thing. They all fear what will happen if they stay in Germany. Did you know that in his book *Mein Kampf*, Hitler outlined his plan to create a perfect German race? The Rabbi says that his perfect race does not include Jews."

"When will these families arrive?"

"We do not know, but the Temple is making space for the items we collect and when they get here, a committee at the Temple will dispense everything. Talk to the women in the community and let's get going on this. You all have things that you haven't used in years and will never miss. These people can use everything."

The entire Sisterhood of the Temple was mobilized. Before long, each woman was going door-to-door in her building requesting items the displaced families could use. The items were taken to the Temple, where they were inventoried and placed in boxes awaiting dispersal. Cel actually enjoyed her involvement, but found it hard to believe the accounts being circulated about how the Jews were actually being treated in Germany. There were tales of the Germans making the Jews wear Stars of David on their clothes so that they could be easily identified on the street. Other tales were that the Jews were being rounded up and put on boxcars that took them to concentration camps, where they were being forced to do hard labor. Cel even heard that some of the Jews were being killed in the camps. The more outrageous the tales, the harder it was to believe, especially with the reports from the American Red Cross that denied any mistreatment of the Jews in Germany. It was as if the whole thing was a mystery that would be solved in time.

The first German family arrived and was placed in an apartment on Bennett Avenue. They gladly took whatever the Temple offered and explained that they had left without anything because the German government would not allow them to remove their possessions from Germany. The family did not personally experience any other hardship, but feared that soon the government would not permit them to leave. The rumors were that the Jews would not be allowed to leave or to travel outside Germany's borders and the family did not like what they had seen or knew about Hitler. They decided not to take any chances. Several other families also came, and as time passed each family told of greater hardships and perils endured during their departure. Some left in the dead of night and traveled on foot through the mountains until they crossed the border to France. That border was now closed since Hitler took control of France so that he could have a port on the Atlantic Ocean. Some reported that friends and family had just disappeared in Germany and were never heard of again. They were sure that concentration camps were a reality. They all feared Hitler and worried about Germany's future. They even worried about the future of Europe; many saw the signs that war was about to erupt.

Cel was enjoying her role at the Temple. It was rewarding to help the new families establish themselves in Washington Heights. They all made her feel important as she distributed the items to each family and helped organize the attempts to replenish the shelves at the Temple. She felt that even Morris looked at her with new respect. Every evening they discussed her day, and she had new things to say and new reports to offer about the situation in Europe. Joey was particularly interested, and kept asking his father about the chances of a war and whether or not America would become involved. It was sobering to think that Joey was old enough to think about war and the draft; after all, he was only fourteen years old!

Two months had passed since the rendezvous with Sam, and Cel was pleased that their secret had remained at the Beekman Towers. Then one morning she awoke with the most terrible nausea. She tried to raise her head off of the bed but was too dizzy to even sit up. When Morris came over to her, she told him she had a stomach virus and asked him to help the children get ready for school. But in her heart she knew this was no stomach virus and she made plans to call the doctor that very day. The timing was too close for comfort and she knew she was pregnant with Sam's child; a child she was determined would never see the light of day. She felt as though her whole life was about to unravel and everyone would know her shame if this child were to be born. No way was she going to have this child, or any other child for that matter. Life was finally becoming tolerable now that the children were older and in school all day; no way was she going to start over with diapers and all of that mess.

Cel had heard about a "doctor" who helped women who were in trouble. Ironically, it was Sadie who had told her about a friend of hers who used this so-called doctor when she discovered she was pregnant at a time when she should have been going through her menopause. It was expensive, but worth every penny, and Cel decided she would use part of her saved nest egg to pay for the abortion. The only problem was how to get through it all without Morris knowing anything about it. No way would he permit it if he knew in advance and if he ever found out about it after the fact, he would be furious. Cel decided the only thing to do was to call Sadie and ask her for help. What an emotional payback!

She called Sadie just as soon as everyone had left the apartment and asked her to come right over.

"I am pregnant and you have to help me get rid of this baby."

"Cel, this is ridiculous. You and Morris have no children together. He would love to have another child."

"No way. I will not be tied down with a baby again. I have waited all these years for Estelle to grow up and now I want to enjoy my life. Besides, Morris and I have an agreement that there will be no more children. He has a terrible fear of pregnancy. This baby will not be born and I need you to help me get to the doctor your friend used."

"How do you know that you are pregnant? Have you seen Dr. Hillman?"

"No, I haven't seen Dr. Hillman, but trust me, I am pregnant. I woke up this morning and promptly proceeded to throw up my brains. I had not thought about it, but I now realize it has been two months since my last period. You do not have to be a genius to know what all this adds up to."

"God, Cel, why weren't you more careful, especially considering your feelings?"

"Oh, Sadie, I was careful. I always use my diaphragm. But who knows how these things happen? Maybe I took it out too soon – maybe the jelly was not fresh enough – maybe it slipped during the night. Who knows? Who cares? All I know is that I am pregnant with a child I do not want and will not have and I need your help. You are my best friend."

"You are putting me in an awful position. What if something happens to you? How would I explain things to Morris?"

"Nothing is going to happen to me. You told me about your friend. She did well. I am a strong person. I'll do well. Just get me in touch with that doctor so we can get this over with quickly. I cannot be throwing up every morning without raising Morris' suspicions."

"I'll call and get you the number, but I want you to know I do not agree with you. I feel this is the wrong thing to do and that you and Morris should discuss it before you go and do this crazy thing."

"No way. There will be no discussions with Morris, ever. He must never know about this."

"Cel, is this Morris' child?"

"Of course it is! What type of woman do you think I am?"

"Don't get excited. I only asked."

"Will you help me or not?"

"I said I would get you the number. As soon as I get it, I'll call you."

When Sadie left, Cel felt totally drained. She could not help but wonder how Sadie would react if she knew this was Sam's child. What a mess she had gotten herself into. But it had to be resolved and that's that.

A few hours later, Sadie called with the doctor's number and even offered to go with Cel if she decided to use it. Cel called immediately and was told the doctor would see her the next morning. She was instructed to come to his apartment at 125th Street and Amsterdam Avenue, and that she could bring one person with her, preferably another woman. Cel told him she would be there promptly at nine-thirty and then called Sadie to ask her to come. They were both nervous about going to an apartment in Harlem, but there was no choice in the matter as far as Cel was concerned.

Morris came home for dinner and was happy to see that Cel was feeling better.

"What did the doctor say?" he asked.

"I called him, and he told me a stomach virus has been going around and that it usually passes in a few days. He told me to eat lightly and take it easy for a few days, and that if I am still sick, to come in to see him after the weekend."

"It is not like you to be sick. I was really concerned this morning."

"It's nothing and I am feeling better now. Let's see what tomorrow brings."

Cel was shaking inside when she awoke the next morning. She ran to the bathroom, where she promptly threw up, and was grateful that the bathroom was up the hall and away from the bedroom so Morris would not hear her. She decided she would make herself appear to be feeling better so that he would not worry about her, and would not be suspicious if he called and did not find her home. It literally took all her will for her to make the coffee that morning, but she did it because she had to; everything had to appear normal.

Once everyone was safely gone, she dressed and met Sadie in front of the building. They took the A train to 125th Street and walked to Amsterdam Avenue. The building was old, as were all the buildings on the dilapidated block. Once this area was the home for the wealthy; now it was rare that a white face was seen in the neighborhood, and all the people stared at Cel and Sadie as they walked into the building. It was no secret what the "doctor" did and the neighborhood people knew why the women were there. The apartment appeared clean as the two women entered the hallway and were greeted by an elderly man, whose white hair was neatly combed but whose clothing looked as though it needed a good washing.

"Do you have the money?"

"Yes. I guess you want it now."

"You bet!"

Cel's hands shook as she handed over the three hundred dollars she was requested to bring.

"Go in there and get undressed from the waist down," the man told her, pointing to a room that doubled as a bedroom. "Your friend can wait here. When you are finished undressing, come into the kitchen and we'll get this over with."

Cel was relieved to see that the kitchen was relatively clean. On the table there was a pillow for her head and on either side of the table were tall back chairs. Above the table was a lighting fixture, which Cel stared at as she lied down.

"Put your legs up on the back of each of the chairs. We do not have stirrups here, so you have to keep your legs up there or I cannot see what I am doing."

Cel obeyed and looked for a sheet to cover her exposed body but there was none. Modesty was not an issue here.

Then she felt something really cold going into her vagina and she knew he was spreading her open. Next she felt a sharp object piercing her; the pain was intense and she bit her lip to prevent herself from crying out because, as part of his instructions the previous day, she was warned not to make any noise for fear that the police would be called by a neighbor. It felt as if he was scraping her insides, and Cel began to wonder how much more she could take when she heard him say, "Okay, you can get up now. When you get home you will have cramping and bleeding. That's normal. If the bleeding becomes extremely heavy, go to the hospital, but normally it stops in a few days and that's that."

"What about infection?"

"Infections happen, go to the hospital and they will help you. There is nothing more I can do. I have done my part. You paid for an abortion and you are having an abortion. Now get going; I have other women coming and I need the space."

As Cel stood up she felt weak and as soon as she took her first step, she felt the blood coming down her legs. It was warm and sticky, but she actually felt grateful because it was done.

"I need a sanitary napkin."

"There are some in the bathroom. Help yourself, but please hurry, the others are coming soon."

"I am doing my best."

When Cel came out into the so-called living room, Sadie was frightened by how white she looked and how shaky she seemed.

"That was not fun. Let's get out of here."

"Are you all right to go home?"

"Just let's get a cab and get home. I'll be fine once I lie down. This creep has it scheduled so that there is not time in between women and he wants us out of here now."

Once in the cab, Sadie looked at Cel, who appeared ready to pass out, and wondered how her friend was going to be able to keep this from Morris. On thing was for sure, that man was no fool and he would know something terrible was going on as soon as he saw Cel.

"How will you ever get this past Morris?"

"That's easy. I am going to tell him I am having woman's problems and that I am having a really bad period. He'll believe that and when this is over, things will go back to normal."

"Cel, I have known you for years. You never complain about your periods."

"One can always start."

"When we get home, you go right to bed. I'll fix something for dinner for Morris and the kids."

"Thanks. That would help. I really feel rotten."

When Morris came home for dinner, he was surprised to find Cel in bed. She really looked pale, but he accepted her explanation without question and just urged her to stay in bed and get some rest. Morris and the children warmed the food Sadie had left and then together they cleaned the kitchen. Cel even smiled when Norman brought her a dish of food.

Cel barely touched the plate of food prepared for her and was asleep when Morris looked in on her. He was aware that she was restless throughout the night and heard her whimper in her sleep throughout the night. But when Morris awoke in the morning he nearly panicked. Cel was as white as her pillowcase and there was blood on the sheets. There was no question that she needed medical attention.

"I am going to call Dr. Hillman right now and I'll take you there."

"Don't be silly. You have to get to the factory. Call Sadie. She'll go with me to the doctor."

"No way. I'm taking you myself. Do you need help getting dressed?"

"I'll be fine; don't worry so much."

Morris never responded to her assurances. He went directly to the phone and called the doctor, who promptly told him to bring Cel directly to Lenox Hill Hospital where he would see her immediately. Cel was very quiet in the taxi and just kept thinking of what she could possibly tell the doctor about her predicament. As soon as he examined her, she was sure he would know what she had done, but she knew she needed help or she would just bleed to death. What a mess.

Luckily, it was just Cel and Dr. Hillman in the examination room. As soon as he started the exam, his alarm was evident.

"What have you done?"

"I had no choice, but Morris must not know the truth. You must tell him that I've had a miscarriage or something. He definitely does not want any more children and I promised him I would never become pregnant."

"Cel, that is ridiculous. Had you discussed it with him he would have preferred your having a child to this mess. Your insides look like someone mutilated you. If you are lucky, I'll be able to stop some of the bleeding. If not, we'll have to do a hysterectomy. I don't know how to explain that to your husband."

"He'll believe whatever you say. Just tell him I have had a miscarriage. Nothing else!"

Dr. Hillman just shook his head and feared that if he pursued this conversation, Cel would become hysterical and that would only make matters worse. He wanted to get her to the operating room before she bled out and hopefully he would save her life. Then she would have to deal with

Morris. If she died, then he would tell Morris the truth; of that he was sure.

Dr. Hillman was able to tie off the bleeding vessels and he did not have to perform a hysterectomy, which he felt would have been too traumatic considering her weakened condition. He was appalled by the horror the abortionist had effected, and was sickened that women had to seek out such animals and expose themselves to infections and other complications. Someday, maybe things would be different but, until then, he knew he would have other cases like Cel. Whatever makes these women so desperate will never change. He was sure that the child was not her husband's; why else would she refuse to tell him? It was obvious that she was lying about her motives, but it was not his business and right now she needed all the support she could get to regain her strength. There was nothing to gain by becoming involved in their marriage, so Dr. Hillman decided to honor Cel's wishes and lie to Morris; at least for now.

He met Morris in the waiting room outside the surgical suite. The man was obviously concerned and seemed beside himself.

"I think she will be all right. We were able to stop the bleeding and she is coming out from under the anesthesia as we speak. I think you will able to see her shortly."

"What happened?"

"Your wife has had a miscarriage. I am sorry but there was nothing I could do to save the child."

"I don't care about the child. Will she be all right?"

"I think so. She is young and strong and I think she will come out of this Okay. I doubt she will ever be able to have any more children because there was some damage to her insides but I don't think we will have to perform a hysterectomy at this time. That is all I can tell you for now.

We will watch her carefully and hopefully, in a few days, she will be able to go home."

"Thank you, thank you."

Dr. Hillman felt sorry for the man standing in front of him. He seemed so concerned, so distraught. It was obvious that he really cared for Cel. He wondered if she appreciated her husband. His thoughts would never be answered because he would never believe Cel's answers if he ever broached the subject with her.

Cel recovered and was able to leave the hospital within a week. Morris accepted her being extremely quiet because he was sure she was upset about having lost the baby and he decided that the less said the better. Hopefully she would return to her own self and their lives could continue the way things were before. They certainly did not need another child. In his heart, he was glad that this could not happen again. Dr. Hillman had repeatedly told them that he felt she would not be able to have any more children. The doctor thought this was a sacrifice but Morris was relieved. At least he would not have to see anything like this again. It was hard for him to accept that he could have lost another wife because of his selfishness. If there was any chance that Cel could become pregnant again, he would never have any relations with her. That was that. Obviously whatever she was using to prevent pregnancy was not effective.

Cel could not help but think of the child that would never be. Was it a boy or a girl? Would it have looked like Sam? She remembered how thrilled she and Henry were when she was pregnant with Estelle. But that was another lifetime. This could never have been. Had she permitted this child to be born, it would have forever been a reminder of her infidelity and would have been the object of her hatred. Her entire life would have been ruined and she would be trapped by the child. She was convinced that she had done the right thing but...but nothing! She had to get her life together and put this horror behind and forgotten. She had to stop thinking about holding a newborn and cuddling it and loving it. She had to stop thinking about that horrible man in that horrible apartment in Harlem. Yes, she had to stop thinking about the pain and fear and the lies. She had to stop remembering her words to Henry spoken so long ago stating that she would never have an abortion. That was another lifetime! She had made her choices and now she had to go on with her life.

CHAPTER 11

Time and life pass like the blink of an eye. Before Cel knew it Joey and Estelle were graduating from George Washington High School. Joey was to go on to the Fashion Institute to study design and hopefully be able to go into the business with Morris. The boy definitely had talent and an eye for clothing but he was so wild and headstrong. He traveled with a tough crowd of boys, and he and Morris were having communication problems, to put it mildly. Joey thought that whatever Morris said was ridiculous and was totally convinced that he knew more about everything than his father. As for Estelle, Cel insisted that she would go on to secretarial school so that she would have some skills that she could use to earn a living, at least until she married and had children. Norman was still a problem. His mental age was now about six, while his chronological age was twelve. He could do simple things for himself but there was no judgment of right and wrong and he had to be watched all the time. He would undress and fondle himself without thinking about who else was present. Cel feared that before long he would make advances to some girl or even force himself on Estelle. The teachers and doctors at his school really did not expect him to mature past this level and it seemed hopeless to Cel. After all, he was almost as big as Morris and as strong. He could definitely inflict physical harm if he became really angry and the neighbors were afraid of him. Even Cel harbored some fear, though she could still control him.

The other problem in Cel's world was the war in Europe. Hitler had conquered France and there were confirmed reports that Jews were being taken off the streets and never seen again. The refugees arriving in New York were more desperate with each new group that arrived and they feared for the relatives left behind. A new German community had formed on Bennett Avenue and there was talk of starting a new Temple that would be Orthodox. These people were more dedicated to Judaism than ever before, and even those who previously were not religious and who had declared themselves Germans first and Jews second now felt a renewed need to practice their religion. Even Morris was following a more Orthodox version of religion. In the past several years, he had increasingly demanded more attention to Orthodox beliefs. He no longer worked on Saturday and walked to Temple every Friday and Saturday. The dishes in the house had to be separate for meat and dairy and only kosher foods were permitted. Cel could not believe it when he requested that they prepare the toilet paper on Friday afternoon so that they would not have to tear the paper from the roll during the Sabbath. They also had to leave the burner on the stove on so that food could be cooked. That way they did not have to turn it on during the Sabbath. Cel could not believe that she had to do these things but would not argue with Morris once he had made up his mind, so she went along with his demands and made the children adhere to them, except for Estelle, who was allowed to see her friends as long as she did so quietly and did not let Morris know. Estelle kept telling Cel how ridiculous she thought Morris was to make them do all that mumbo-jumbo religious nonsense. Cel agreed but reminded Estelle that while they were living in his house, they had to do things his way, regardless of what they thought, but if they were discreet, they could work around it.

Joey was not willing to be discreet. He wanted to challenge his father and repeatedly refused to honor the Sabbath. Morris was constantly upset with the boy and Cel decided that the best thing for her to do was to stay out of it. If they had differences of opinion, they had to work it out without her help because there was nothing for her to gain by being in the middle. Everyone was telling her that boys go through rebellious stages before they realize that their fathers are not complete fools. One thing that Cel knew was that time would tell how their relationship would be once the boy became a man. She felt that he would quiet down once he became involved at the Fashion Institute and learned what it was like to have to make a living.

Joey also amused Cel with his attempts to date girls. He was totally unaware of how to please a girl. He did not even know how to kiss a girl and she took it upon herself to teach him. It was exciting to her to feel his lips on hers and to smell his young body when he was close to her. She sensed that she was arousing him and that pleased her; after all, she was old enough to be his mother. She refused to allow herself to go beyond the kissing because she had vowed to herself to never, ever permit herself that pleasure again, but it would have been really easy to let herself go. It was obvious that Joey was about to experiment with sex and she decided that she had better watch that Estelle and he did not try anything. What a mess that could be. Luckily, Estelle kept telling her what a jerk Joe was and Cel was determined to keep it that way, though it was obvious to her that in reality he was an extremely sexy male who was on the cusp of maturity.

Estelle had become a very beautiful girl. When she entered a room, people would stare at her. She had a way of carrying herself that made everyone notice her and it was obvious that the boys at school were all eager to date her. Even Sadie's sons were hanging around looking like hungry puppies. Cel decided it was definitely time for a strong mother-daughter talk about protection and morals. She approached Estelle early on Sunday morning.

"We have to talk."

"Talk about what?"

"About how you should conduct yourself. After all, you are no longer a child and it is quite obvious that the boys want to get into your pants."

"You sure know about that. I know how you have been teaching Joey to kiss. What else do you want to teach him?"

"Stop being so mean. I was just trying to help him; he did not even know how to kiss a girl. That is not the issue now. The issue is that I care about you and I want to be sure that you do not do anything to mess up your life. I know how hard it is to be a woman alone with a child. Believe me, it is not easy and I was forced into situations that I do not want you to experience."

"Yeah, I know it is all my fault that you had to marry Morris and raise his horrible children..."

"Look, Estelle, I am not saying it was your fault and I definitely have tried to do everything possible for you so that you would be happy. It was not your fault that your wonderful father died and left us penniless. I just want you to be able to have different options; options you will not be able to have if you screw things up. And I mean that literally."

"Don't worry, I will not get pregnant. I have no intentions of allowing that to happen. You do not have to give me the birds and bees talk, I know about protection, etc, etc."

"Are you sexually active?"

"That is none of your business."

"Oh, there you are wrong. It is my business. You are my daughter, living in my house and being supported by me. That makes it my business."

"I will be graduating this June. Once I get out of secretarial school, you can be sure I will get my own place and support myself."

173

"We'll see about that. You are crazy if you think you will be earning enough money to live on your own."

"Everyone tells me that if the war does happen, jobs will be plentiful and women especially will be able to earn really good money."

"Estelle, I want you to continue to live right here until you are married. That is what a decent girl does. Only tramps live otherwise. Do you understand me?"

"I understand you. But I can tell you that you cannot control my life, who I date or what I do. I promise that I will not embarrass you. What more do you want?"

"I want you to be a good girl so that eventually you will have a good marriage and a wonderful life. I don't want you to have to get married to someone you do not love. That's what I want. And if you get a reputation of fooling around, you will ruin your chances. I want your life to be better than mine. I can remember how wonderful it was to be in love with a special man and to enjoy getting up each day knowing he loved me as much as I loved him. Your father would want that for you as much as I do."

"I get the message. Just remember that this is my life. I plan to live it my way and I will not tolerate your attempts to control me. You should be able to remember how you hated your mother for constantly interfering with your life. Don't be like her."

"I am not trying to interfere. I just –"

"Enough!"

Cel got up and left Estelle's room, shaking her head. Her precious little girl had grown into a rather headstrong young lady. Hopefully, she would be all right and not mess up her life. There was nothing more she personally could do without running the risk of losing Estelle forever, so what was to be, was to be. Estelle would have things her way just as everything else was always done to keep her happy. Maybe that was where the mistake was from the beginning. Sophie always said that she was ruining the girl and overindulging her. But all Cel ever wanted to do was to make up for the fact that her father was dead and to try and make the child happy. Things would have been different if Henry had lived. Now all she felt she could do was to leave Estelle alone and let things happen as they would. Maybe, someday Estelle would realize that she knew what was best for her and that she really cared. Until then, she would only stand by and help if she was needed. No way would she be her mother.

Thinking about Sophie really hit a nerve in Cel's being. It had been several years since she last saw her mother. Sophie had moved to Florida with Mr. Richman, whom she eventually married. They had a small bungalow colony where they rented space to New Yorkers who wanted to spend the winter in Florida and they were supporting themselves that way. Mr. Richman seemed like a good man who really cared about Sophie, and Sophie had softened and was not as domineering with him. Both Morris and Cel were happy to have Sophie out of their daily lives and Morris kept insisting that Cel visit her mother whenever she wanted to. He would not make the trip and Cel could not arrange to have anyone take care of Norman, so she did not go either. In her heart, Cel only hoped that Mr. Richman would live a long life. She really liked having Sophie too busy to bother with her and the fact that it was long-distance, made phone calls few and far between. At least that was one wish that had come true; she finally could live her life without Sophie. Now if only she could get rid of Norman, life would be more bearable. No matter how she tried to convince Morris to put him into a boarding school type of place, Morris continued to refuse to give it a thought. Cel even tried to make him realize that it was dangerous to have a man-child in a building with so many young girls. Norman, after all, had no concept of right or wrong and could easily force himself on a young girl. Physically, he was ready. But Morris still refused and seemed to make light of Cel's fears, saying that Norman was still a child and that if no one put the thoughts into his head, they would not get there.

Cel did not know if she was looking forward to Estelle and Joey graduating or dreading its arrival. One thing was certain, life would again change once they left high school and she was unsure what road she wanted to take. Once Estelle was able to earn a living, Cel wondered if she could leave Morris and strike out by herself. That had been her original goal, but she could not really say that she did not care about this man with whom she had lived for twelve years. When she really thought about him, all she could think was that he really was a good person who certainly had treated her well. She would never forget his kindness after her supposed miscarriage; he could not do enough for her during her recuperation. Morris never seemed to refuse her anything. If he had the money, she could have anything she wanted, whenever she wanted it. She had to question her motives. Looking for a storybook love at her age was ridiculous. What man would want an overweight woman who was thirty-five years old and not wealthy?

Sex – was that what she really wanted? Better, more exciting sex? Cel knew that was the root of the problem. Sex with Morris had become routine. They both seemed to know the other's moves before they occurred. The thrill was gone and she did not know how to rekindle it but in her heart, she wanted more excitement; she wanted to feel orgasmic release and to know that her partner was equally excited by her. After all, there was no reason for her and Morris not to engage in relations as often as they wanted to; she could not become pregnant again and that should have put his fears to rest. Right after the "miscarriage" he seemed afraid of sex and Cel knew he was remembering Lilly's death. Often she had tried to talk to him, but he seemed embarrassed whenever she broached the subject. There was no talking. That was the other factor that was missing. They rarely spoke about their feelings and she really wanted to be able to do so. That was one of the things that was so special about her relationship with Henry; they could explore each other's feelings without judgment being passed.

But do you leave a good man because he doesn't express his feelings and you are not getting the amount or type of sex you want? The question seemed ridiculous even as Cel posed it in her mind. Where would she leave to? She had to admit to herself that she was infinitely better off here with Morris than she would be if she were forced to move in with Sophie, God forbid! Estelle would make a life for herself, a life that would not include Cel any more than she would want to be included. She could not see herself living with Estelle once she married. In reality, there was no place for her except right where she was and she knew she had better make the best of it.

Graduation day approached and with it came new concerns for the family. War was a reality in Europe. All the peace concessions did not appease Hitler and he kept advancing. France was now under German control, but England would not capitulate. Hitler and Mussolini had formed an alliance and there were fears that America would somehow become involved in the conflict. If this were to happen, many of the boys graduating would be going off to war before their dreams could be realized. It was hard to look at the young faces and to wonder who among them would not return if they went off to war. Every parent had the same thought and every parent hoped they would be spared the ultimate grief.

The boys did not share their parents' concern. They seemed excited at the prospect of going off to war. Many seemed to consider it a chance for thrills and glory, and some expressed their plans to immediately join the English army to help them in their effort to ward off the Germans. That seemed like the most ridiculous action. Cel could not understand why anyone would want to go to war to defend a far-off country. Luckily, Joey did not have any such ideas; the only place he was going was to the Fashion Institute. Hopefully, the war would end and Americans would not have to die.

Morris and Cel were alone after graduation. Estelle and Joey went off to parties with their friends and Norman was exhausted from all of the excitement of the day.

"The house seems exceptionally quiet, doesn't it?" Cel asked.

"I would guess we will have to get used to not having the children here. They have grown up."

"What about us?"

"What... what about us? Cel, what do you want?"

"I want us to try to rekindle some excitement in our relationship. The kids have grown up but I am not an old woman. I am only thirty-five years old, and I am not ready to sit and knit."

"How and what do you want to rekindle? I thought things were going well."

"Morris, we could almost be sister and brother. You rarely show any interest in me and when we do anything, there are no sparks. I want you to excite me, to make my body want yours, and to make me feel like a desirable woman."

"Cel, you know you are a desirable woman. I am seven years older than you and I am tired when I get home from the factory. Sparks are the last thing I can think about."

"There you go, making light of what I am trying to say."

"No, I am not trying to minimize what you are saying. I am just trying to make you realize that I am tired when I come home and I am very content to just sit and read the newspaper."

"Morris, I need you to do more than read the newspaper. I understand that you are tired but I have needs that have to be satisfied. I need to feel loved and I crave the excitement we had early in our relationship."

"It's hard for me to let go."

"But you have nothing to worry about. Remember Dr. Hillman said I cannot become pregnant again. Is that what you worry about?"

"What if he's wrong?"

"He's the doctor. He would not say things like that if he had any doubt. Anyway, I have not used any precautions since the miscarriage and nothing has happened."

"Cel, it is because I care about you that I am fearful. It hurt me deeply to see you suffer and I would not want that to happen again."

"Is it better to make me suffer all the time? I am not happy this way. Think about it."

Cel walked out of the room, amazed that she had actually spoken that way. Sometimes she wondered what would come out of her mouth next. She wondered how her veiled threat would be taken.

Norman was fast asleep when Cel checked him. It was going to be a quiet night, she could just tell. Cel then went into the bathroom, showered and powdered herself so that she knew that her smell would remain in the room after she left. She then went to the living room and told Morris she was going to bed early. She hoped he would take the suggestion and join her. It worked. He too came to bed freshly showered and lay down next to her, pulling her to his body. Cel felt excited feeling his chest hair on her breast and she responded to him by running her hands down his body slowly coming to his erect penis. Slowly, she came down and placed it in her mouth, making long and slow movements until she could hear him groan with pleasure. She too felt the excitement rise and she knew she was becoming nice and wet. Then she stopped and waited for him to make the next move. She wanted to be brought to the edge before he penetrated her body. Morris took the initiative and started to message her clitoris as he sucked her ample breast. Excitement raged within her until she could no longer stand it; she pulled him on top of her and felt her entire body let go as he entered. All the tensions seemed to leave and for that moment she felt at peace with herself. It was not long before Morris just collapsed next to her. He fell into a deep sleep and she just lay there enjoying the moment.

Cel felt beautiful the next morning. She resolved that she would attempt to lose weight and keep herself more appealing so that she would not have to feel that she had to beg for sex in the future. She would make Morris want her. She would make the best of the situation she was in and she would make sure that he never wanted to deny her anything she wanted. Eventually, she was sure that she would manage to get rid of Norman too. Then her life would be even better.

CHAPTER 12

That summer the family took a bungalow in the mountains. Cel and the children went shortly after graduation and both Joey and Estelle seemed to want to enjoy every minute of what could be their last summer of innocence. There was a nice group of youngsters their ages in the colony and they all seemed excited with the prospects ahead. Some would start college in the fall; others would be going off to special schools, like Joey and Estelle, where they would learn a trade. All of them seemed to want to put any talk of a possible war out of their heads. They just wanted to enjoy swimming in the lake and hanging out together. Estelle seemed to particularly enjoy the company of a nice boy, Larry, whose family was new to the colony. He was going off to college to become an accountant and it was obvious to everyone that he was totally infatuated by Estelle. Joey, on the other hand, did not seem to want to stay with any one girl. He would even go to the other colonies when there were socials. Cel only hoped that both of the children would stay out of trouble and she kept reinforcing the importance of using protection.

Norman did not fit in anywhere. He was too big to play with the children at his intellectual level and too immature to associate with the others. He spent most of his time playing alone or just hanging onto Cel. Next summer, she decided, she would just stay in the city and let him continue going to his school, where a summer program was offered. At least that way she would have some peace during the day.

Morris came up on Friday nights and stayed until Sunday evening. He always looked completely exhausted when he arrived but seemed to rejuvenate during the weekend. On Saturday, he would walk to services and he no longer insisted that Joey join him. It was easier to leave the boy alone than to continually fight. Morris hoped that someday he would feel a need to practice his religion, but he now realized that need had to come from within Joey and he could not demand it. Norman, on the other hand, loved to go with his father but would not sit still during the services. It was hard to accept that the child would be thirteen soon and would not be able to be Bar Mitzvahed. There was just no way he could learn any of the prayers and it was impossible for him to even read them in English.

Cel and Morris were inhibited in the small bungalow. The walls were thin and if they engaged in any relations, the children were sure to hear no matter how careful they were. Sometimes Cel paid Joey to take Norman with him to a movie so that she and Morris could be alone. Of course, Joey and Estelle snickered when she made the request. Jokingly, Joey would remind Cel to make sure she used protection.

All in all it was wonderful to be away from the city in the heat of the summer. The long walks on the mountain paths, the lake, the beauty of the Catskills all reminded Cel of the wonderful years with Henry and her youth. She kept putting out of her mind the thoughts that her life might again be changed and that she and the children would never be able to enjoy the magic of the Catskills again.

War in Europe was a reality. The flow of refugees had all but stopped when Cel returned from the country. There was basically no reason to continue the activities at the Temple because those who had come were now pretty much settled and no one could predict if future refugees would be coming. Rumor had it that Hitler wanted to solve the Jewish problem and he was rounding up the Jews and taking them to camps. Some of the later arrivals said that they were sure the

Jews were being killed at the so-called camps. Those who were not killed were being forced to work to support the German troops. It seemed that there would be no way to stop the German takeover of Europe. France was completely under German control and it appeared that England would never last long with both Germany and Italy attacking. Even the newspaper spoke of the nightly bombings and how the people would try to survive in the underground shelters. It was truly scary, especially to Cel and Morris, who worried about America becoming involved and the possibility of Joey being drafted. However, the war still was far away in September 1941. The entire family was excited about the new schools that both Joey and Estelle were attending and everyone was surprised at the talent Joey seemed to have. His designs kept winning all the competitions at the Fashion Institute and Morris began to get excited that maybe, someday, they could work together. Joey could design the line and the factory could produce it. No matter what happens, people need clothes and now that the Depression was a distant memory, they were willing to spend money for quality clothing. Then, of course, there was Kleins and Alexanders where a less expensive market existed. These discount stores were becoming more popular in the city and Morris was doing very well selling copies of the more expensive garments. He would walk past the windows where the finer dresses were sold and sketch them so that he could make the patterns and produce them cheaply for the Kleins' market. But with Joey's talent, they could manufacture dresses for the likes of Saks Fifth Avenue or Lord and Taylor or Altmans; no more cheap dresses.

Estelle and Larry were still seeing each other. He was going to City College to study accounting and both Cel and Morris were impressed with his intelligence. He was a quiet boy but an impressive young man who stood six feet tall.

When he and Estelle entered a room together, they were a couple to be noticed and admired; he was tall and handsome, and she was ever so beautiful. The only drawback was that his family seemed to be all messed up. His father had died and it was whispered that he had died of alcoholism. People also said that his mother liked to tip the bottle more than she should. He had an older sister, Barbara, and a younger brother, Martin, but he rarely spoke of his family and tried to avoid answering any questions about them. Estelle was totally unconcerned about his family and totally infatuated with him. No matter what he wanted, she did it without question. She was even reading books that he liked so that they could discuss them. She even spoke of possibly going to college herself so that she could become a teacher. That was the most amazing thing for Cel to hear because Estelle never liked school and really did not like children. She was never one to babysit or to enjoy spending time with the children in the neighborhood or at the bungalow colony. But Cel knew better than to voice her opinion because she was sure that if she said green, Estelle would say blue and accuse her of trying to ruin things for her and Larry.

For Cel, things were going exceptionally well. She and Morris had definitely rekindled their physical relationship and he would do just about anything for her; anything except put Norman in a school. Norman remained a problem that she could not solve. He was physically as big as Morris but his intellectual development was only at age seven or eight. The seizures were occurring less often now that he regularly took Dilantin but they did still happen, especially at night. Cel had taken to putting him in a helmet so that he would not experience any head injury if he had a seizure but there was little else that could be done. To date he had learned to feed himself and cut his own food. He could get dressed by himself as long as someone put out his clothing and he could zipper his pants and tie his own shoes. But reading and writing were not something he seemed capable of learning, so it was apparent he would never be able to live independently. He would never be able to earn a living for himself and Cel kept reminding Morris that the likelihood was that they would be outlived by this man-child and then what? It would be totally unreasonable to expect Joey to take care of his brother; after all, Joey would probably marry and most likely his wife would want nothing to do with Norman. But Morris was not going to give in. He would just tell Cel that they would deal with it when the time came closer, not now.

December 7, 1941 was sure to be a date that would go down in infamy. When the news reached the streets of the city that the Japanese had bombed Pearl Harbor, everyone knew the War was no longer other people's concern; it was America's concern too. The young men flocked to the recruiting offices throughout the city in response to Japan's declaration of war against the United States. Everyone knew that it would not be long before we were also involved at the European front. Neither Cel nor Morris were shocked when Joey came home that night and told them that he had enlisted in the Air Force. Larry had enlisted in the Army and Estelle had signed up to work as secretary in the New York Headquarters for the war effort.

"When will you have to report for training?" Morris asked Joey.

"They will call me. Needless to say, things are a little confusing but they do expect to get us together really quickly. I will probably report to Fort Dix in New Jersey for basic training and then be assigned to an Air Force base. I am really excited that I was accepted into the Air Force. That will be where the action is."

"But you have never been in a plane. How do you know anything about it?"

"I've never been in a war either. I'll learn and I just think that the Air Force is the most exciting branch of the services. You have to have perfect eyesight to be even considered and I am excited that they accepted me. But, who knows, maybe I won't be able to complete my training. Then I will have to serve in the regular army. You know that is where Larry is going. He wanted the Air Force too but he needs glasses so they wouldn't take him."

"This whole thing is too scary for me. I have been afraid of this war for some time and now..."

"Spoken like a mother. But this war is a reality and it probably will become even bigger in the next few days. It is our duty to defend our country. We can't let the bums just bomb our ships and kill our people and not do anything about it. Those Japs are real bastards. Here they were talking peace with Roosevelt while they were planning to destroy the entire Pacific fleet. It's unbelievable."

"I only wish that you could do something to keep yourself here in America and not have to actually fight."

"That is not an issue. I want to do my part. I have to do my part. And I will go wherever they send me."

"Does Larry feel the same way?"

"You bet he does. I think the Army guys are going to ship out first. They will probably report within a day or two for their basic training. A lot of planes were destroyed in today's attack so the Air Force guys may be delayed until they figure out what to do."

"Have you seen Estelle?"

"She's with Larry – probably shacked up. Can you blame them?"

"Stop being so crude."

"Maybe they should get married. That way she could at least say she was married if she has a kid."

"She is too smart to let that happen."

"Like mother, like daughter."

"What do you mean by that remark?"

"Nothing – I guess I am just being a little testy. Let's drop it. What's for dinner?"

The next four days passed as if a whirlwind had come into their lives. By the time that Germany and Italy had declared war on the United States on December 11, 1941 it seemed as if the entire nation had been mobilized. Morris' plant was already producing clothing for the war effort because he had made all the necessary preparations long in advance. Larry had his orders to report to Fort Dix in New Jersey; Joey was to report there too. Estelle had taken a job in a defense plant in Manhattan and Cel was busy getting the necessary rations so that she could put food on their table. Roosevelt quickly ordered the rationing of the food in the United States so that the rapidly growing armed forces could be adequately fed and no one on the home front was arguing with his judgment. Even Norman's life was changed because many of his teachers were leaving the school to become involved in the war effort. Cel was fearful that he would not be able to continue at his school and she knew it would not be possible for him to survive in the regular school's special class, but now was not the time to try to persuade Morris about putting him into a boarding-type school, so she kept quiet.

The men who had been receiving basic training when the war started were being dispatched to both the European and the Pacific theaters. Every newsreel showed the tearful goodbyes as the soldiers left their loved ones and everyone wondered just who would be coming home and in what condition. Cel and the other mothers all remembered the First World War and for them there was no glamour in war; they felt their generation was being doubly punished to have to face two such horrible wars. They all knew it would not be long before the body bags started arriving.

The news out of Germany was even more desperate. The Jewish community was hearing of mass murders in the concentration camps and of inhumane conditions. The only hope for the Jews of Germany was a quick American victory so the Americans could free the captives. The Red Cross was no help because their reports were rosy renditions of life in the camps. American Jews wondered how the Red Cross officials could be so easily fooled by Hitler and his goons. How Hitler could have become so powerful was a question on every thinking person's mind. How could the Jews have permitted themselves to be rounded up and forced into concentration camps? This was inconceivable to the American Jewish population. Everyone kept talking of the signs that the refugees had seen early on during Hitler's rise to power, but too many did too little to stop the mad man and now the entire world was going to suffer.

CHAPTER 13

Both Joey and Larry were good about writing home while they were in basic training. Fort Dix was closed to visitors for security reasons and the line waiting to call home was too long to deal with, so the boys wrote letters, and Estelle was particularly good at answering them, especially Larry's. The training was rigorous and accelerated, and before anyone could realize it, Larry was being shipped off to the European theater, where he would be a part of the Signal Corp. Joey, on the other hand, was being shipped to Wichita Falls, Texas, where he was scheduled to study weather forecasting.

Cel knew he was miserable being sent to some God-forsaken place in Texas instead of being sent to Europe, but she was relieved that at least he would be safe for a while. She felt that if they kept him out of planes, they had a chance to keep him alive. She could not picture Joey in a fighter plane. He was such an undisciplined boy; it was hard to imagine him taking orders and responding without question. However, it was also hard to picture him being involved with weather forecasting. He had never expressed any interest in the weather and both Cel and Morris wondered how he ever got that assignment, unless it was a random one.

Cel did question Joey in her letters about how he became involved with weather forecasting but she never received any sensible answers. Joey's letters seldom dealt with any real issues. Instead, he wrote about the other boys and how he was having fun making fun of them. Typical Joey, Cel kept thinking. He always wanted to make himself appear better than others and always enjoyed making fun of other people. Joey was one who had to always have the upper hand in his dealings with others and Cel always thought that was because his early life had such horrible upheaval. Now that he was not living at home, it was easier to see him as he really was and to appraise her relationship with him. When she was honest with herself, she realized that she really loved the boy and would be really upset if anything happened to him. He had been difficult to raise; always wanting his own way and always knowing just how to provoke her. And Cel knew she had been hard on him and often unfair to him because she always wanted Estelle to have the best and the most. Somehow Joey had come to accept the idea that Estelle came first. He was a survivor and Cel kept hoping that, being a survivor, he would live through the war. Someday, she would let him know that she really loved and cared about him, but that day would only come when he was back home. She knew she could never express her true feelings in a letter and he would never allow her to do so over the telephone.

Morris refused to talk about the war and Joey being in the Air Force. It was as if he felt that if he did not deal with the situation, it would just go away. He was working very hard at the factory, where they had to put extra shifts on just to fill the orders for the clothing. Morris often spent the night sleeping on the cutting table so that he could cut more fabric if it was needed. He was still making some dresses because, after all, the women needed clothing too so that they could go to work, but the majority of the work was being done producing clothing for the military. The military was also paying extremely well for the clothes and money was no problem for Cel and Morris. They were actually putting a great deal of money into savings and, as always, Cel was able to put a part of it into her own separate account. She figured that by the time the War ended, she could be financially independent and, though she was not planning on leaving Morris, it would be a good feeling for her to know she could do so. Where would she go? She was now almost middle-aged and definitely too heavy. No new man would be interested in her and the fact was simply that Morris was good to her. He gave her anything and everything she wanted and he even seemed to enjoy her more than ample body.

Estelle was rarely home. During the day she worked as a secretary at one of the war offices and in the evenings she donated time preparing boxes for the troops overseas. When she was home, she spent most of her time in her room either writing to Larry or rereading his letters, which she kept hidden. Cel figured that when the war was over, they would marry. It was obvious to her that Estelle had really fallen in love and she was happy that her daughter could know such love. The memories that were rekindled still brought bittersweet happiness. Cel only hoped that nothing would happen that would shatter Estelle's happiness and life. After all, the girl had experienced such a horrible loss when her father died. Cel felt just as helpless as she did when she was watching Henry die; there was nothing she could do.

Joey graduated from weather forecasting school and the next thing the family knew, he was being sent to Fort Worth, Texas. Once there, he wrote home that he had a new interest, hydraulics. When Cel questioned him as to what hydraulics meant, he explained that he wanted to learn how to fix the brakes, bomb bay doors and all the other parts on the plane that worked by hydraulics.

"Look, if I can get good at this, I'll get to see more of this war than I ever will forecasting the weather," Joey explained during one of his calls home.

"What exactly will you have to do?" Cel asked.

"Planes need constant repair and I would be doing that repair. I am told that most of the work is done at bases but at least I would be doing something real."

"How long is the training? After all, you don't know anything about mechanics."

"I am told that it is a five-month training course back at Chanut Field in Wichita Falls. With my luck the war will be over before I am finished."

"From your mouth to God's ears."

"Anyway, I have put in for the transfer and if I get it, I think I will like it. Have you guys heard anything about Larry?"

"Estelle and he write nightly, but he is not allowed to give us any information about his whereabouts or any details about his activities. Estelle keeps telling us that she doesn't know anything."

"I bet it's exciting. He is in the real war."

"I wouldn't call it exciting. I'd call it awful. Boys are dying in this real war."

"I know, I know. What else is new at home?"

"Your father is working too hard. The plant is operating around the clock just to get the orders out. He's exhausted. Otherwise, things are about the same here. We are lucky that the butcher knows us for so long. He always makes sure there is meat for us and he even gets us fresh eggs from time to time. Of course, he needs a wheelbarrow to carry off all of his money. But it's real simple; if you want it, you pay for it."

"The food here is just okay. No one here knows how to really cook like you guys in New York."

"But you are getting enough to eat?"

"Yeah, don't worry about me; I'm fine. Listen, I have to go. Love to Dad and tell him to hang in there."

"Please write."

At least he will be safe for now, Cel thought, as she looked at the telephone in its cradle. Things always have a way of working out if you let them and, besides, there was nothing she could do about any of this mess. With that thought the telephone again jarred the silence of the apartment.

"Hello."

"Cel, it's Sadie. Are we going for lunch or not?"

"I'm so sorry. Joey just called and I was speaking to him and did not notice the time."

"How is he?"

"Good – I'll tell you all about it when I see you. I'll be there in ten minutes, if you still want to get together."

"I will meet you downstairs and we can go to Bickfords; they advertised that they would be serving sandwiches for lunch today."

"Great. I really like their coffee. I hope they have some. Meet you in ten."

When Cel took off her coat in Bickfords, Sadie was amazed at how heavy her friend looked. Never had Cel had a stomach like she now had.

"My – you are gaining too much weight."

"I know. I just cannot help it. No matter how little I eat, my stomach keeps getting bigger. I really have to call Dr. Hillman. I think I might have a tumor, because now I am not even getting my periods."

"A tumor? Are you sure you are not pregnant again?"

"Don't be ridiculous. You know very well that Dr. Hillman told me there was too much damage done to my insides and that I could never become pregnant again. That was years ago and Morris and I have not used anything since then. If I could have become pregnant, it would have happened before this. I am sure I have a tumor."

"Well, if I were you I would make an appointment soon before that tumor gets too much larger."

"You are right, of course. It's just that with Morris working so hard, I do not have anyone to watch Norman if I should have to go into a hospital."

"Cel, they would work it out. Morris can always take him to the factory if he has to. You cannot let this thing keep getting bigger. Who knows what type of damage it could do? Haven't you learned your lesson?"

"Okay, okay. I will call his office as soon as I get home and I will make an appointment. Now let's get that sandwich and a cup of coffee."

The two women enjoyed their lunch and used the time to gossip and catch up on all the boys. Sadie's sons were also in the military. Milton was lucky because he was a musician and was assigned to a band that was entertaining the troops. He was traveling from base to base and they were putting on shows for the men to help keep morale up. Andrew was in the army and stationed somewhere in Europe. Like Larry, he could not reveal his whereabouts for security reasons. Sadie was really worried about him.

They also gossiped about the new refugees. The Germans were really an odd bunch of people. They kept to themselves and really did not want anything to do with anyone else. True, they took the things donated to them, but that was the end of their involvement in the local temples and schools. They quickly established their own synagogue and used the place to set up their own school for their children. The school was more like a yeshiva and the children were expected to study the Torah. Both Sadie and Cel were amazed that the women shaved their hair and reverted to following all the strict Orthodox practices. It seemed crazy that anyone would want to live that way in this day and age. It was rumored that the Germans felt that had they practiced their religion more strictly, Hitler would never have gotten to power and they felt they would never again be anything before being a Jew. In Germany, they had been Germans first.

"Well, I am glad that we helped them get established here, despite their ingratitude," Cel said.

"I don't know that it is ingratitude. I just think they have been through too much and now they feel that if they isolate themselves, they can survive."

"Well, I think that had they had the courage or the intelligence to fight Hitler, the whole world would not be in such an uproar."

"Cel, there really was no fighting that madman. Germany was left in an awful position after World War I. It was ripe for someone like Hitler to come along and offer the people a solution to their problems."

"Some solution. Kill the Jews."

"It is always easy to blame the Jews. Somehow they always manage to make money when others don't."

"Oh, now it is wrong to make money!"

"I never said anything about it being right or wrong. All I am saying is that is the basis for the problems over there. Had the Germans not been saddled with such horrible war debts, their economy would have been better and probably none of this would have happened. I think that we are not really fighting a new war, just a continuation of the old one."

"I never thought of it that way."

"Really the only new player is Japan and they are in it for more power. Those Japs really think they can conquer the world. Do you know what I heard? I heard that the United States government is actually putting Japanese American citizens into some type of camp to prevent them from giving information to the Japs."

"Is that legal?"

"Legal – all is legal. We're at war."

"I know. It just doesn't seem right to me. How can we put people away before they do anything wrong? It's like putting Jews into concentration camps; there really is no difference."

"The difference is that the Japs are not being killed."

"It's still wrong."

The conversation turned to other matters, including what their husbands were doing and how they would get more than their rationed amounts of meat, eggs and milk. It definitely was a challenge to the women to make sure they were getting more than their neighbors.

When Cel got home, she kept thinking about what Sadie had said about going to see Dr. Hillman. She even went into the bathroom and took off her clothes and looked at her body in the mirror. There was no question that her body had changed. Beside the roundness in her stomach, her breasts had also gotten larger and the nipples were darker than she remembered. Shaking, she went to the telephone and called Dr. Hillman's office. No way could she be pregnant; he would tell her she had a tumor and that would be that. After all, he had said it would be unlikely that she could ever become pregnant again. She called his office and demanded an appointment for the next day. The receptionist detected the urgency in Cel's voice and gave her a morning appointment.

That night Cel barely slept. All she could think about was that she did not want another child. What would she do? How would Morris react? After all, he really did not want any more children from the start. Now she was finally getting to the stage in her life where she could be free; no way could she picture herself tied down with an infant. Abortion was not an option this time. She was certain that it would be disastrous, even if she could find the courage to place herself in the hands of another horrible person. She could never again walk into another dirty apartment and place herself on a table and let someone rip her insides out. No way! But how could this have happened? After all, she and Morris had practiced unprotected sex for several years now. Surely she would have become pregnant before this, when she was younger. "My God, I am thirty-six years old," she thought. "I could be starting menopause."

The next morning Morris noticed how tired Cel looked and asked if she was feeling okay.

"I just did not sleep well. It's nothing important. I will get some rest later after Norman goes to school."

"Just call me at the factory if you need anything. I can go shopping on my way home."

"Thanks, but that's not necessary. I actually have everything I need for dinner tonight. The butcher has been really good to me and he makes sure we have enough meat and eggs."

"I guess it was good that you shopped there all these years. I always felt you were overpaying but now it is paying off."

"I was overpaying, but his quality was always good. When it comes to food, we never scrimp."

"Try to get some rest."

After Norman left for school, Cel showered and dressed. The trip to Dr. Hillman's office was not a long one but Cel kept imagining that the train's wheels were saying, "You're in trouble...you're in trouble."

Dr. Hillman's office had not changed much through the years. The receptionist was the same woman who had worked there since Cel first started going to him. She was a pleasant person who knew not to discuss any personal matters with the patients. When Cel was called into the examination room, she promptly removed her clothes and wrapped the sheet around her. She could not help but shiver, despite the fact that it was really not cold in the room.

"Well, Cel, what brings you here today?" Dr. Hillman asked as he came into the room.

"I think I have a tumor and it is getting bigger."

"Let's take a look."

Dr. Hillman said very little as he did the internal examination. He was a gentle man and Cel had always felt comfortable with him.

"Well, I don't find any tumor. Cel, I think it is wonderful that you are getting a second chance. I seriously never thought you would be able to conceive but you have. I would say you are about four months pregnant."

Cel jumped up into a sitting position as though she had been shot.

"You don't understand. I don't want to have another child. I am too old to have a baby."

"Sometimes we don't always get what we want. Cel, you are definitely pregnant and you will have another child. Hopefully, it will be a healthy baby."

"This is impossible. Morris and I have not used any birth control in years. How is it possible that now I am pregnant?"

"Cel, I really never thought it would be possible, but it has happened and there is nothing we can or will do about it. I promise you that if you even think of doing anything foolish, I will personally call your husband and tell him everything. Am I making myself perfectly clear?"

"I understand. I just don't know how I will be able to tell Morris about this. He really never wanted to have any more children. You know he is eighteen years older than me. No way does he want to start with a baby at this stage of his life."

"Don't underestimate him. Last time he was really upset that you lost the baby."

"Isn't there something we can do?"

"Nothing! Nothing at all except make sure that you and I do everything possible to make sure that this child is born healthy. You have to start taking vitamins and make sure you eat well and get enough rest. This baby will be born in about five months. I really don't want you to gain too much weight but I do want you to eat nutritious food. I think that it is important for you to keep your weight down just in case we have to perform a section. The possibility exists considering what happened in the past."

Cel felt that she was not really listening at all. It was as if a voice was coming from another planet. All she could think about was getting out of the office. She knew only one thing for certain; she would never love this child.

The trip home passed as if Cel was in a fog. No thoughts came into her mind and she noticed no one who passed her on the streets. Then suddenly she was in her own apartment and the silence was deafening. She could not stand being alone, yet she really did not want any company. She tried the radio but the noise annoyed her. The thought of having to go through raising a child was appalling. It seemed impossible that this could be happening to her at a time in her life when she could conceivably become a grandmother. She really could not think of any plan of action. She definitely did not have the courage to place herself in the hands of another abortionist. It would be easier to just kill herself than to lie down on another table in another dirty kitchen; yet she could not imagine taking her own life.

That night Morris noticed that Cel was particularly quiet and she did not eat much of her supper at all. He thought of asking what was on her mind, but decided to give her some time to work things out by herself. "Hopefully," he thought, "she will come to me and share her problems." Theirs was certainly a strange marriage. At times he really thought she cared about him, while at other times he could not help but think she wanted to be free of him and everything about him. He never for a moment fooled himself to think that Cel loved him; at times she needed him, at other times she desired sex with him, but at no time did she love him. A part of him longed for the type of love he had known, just as he was sure Cel longed for the type of love she knew with Henry. But there was no point to these thoughts. Fourteen years together was a long time and what is, is.

Cel decided that she needed some time before sharing the news with anyone. She knew that once the words were spoken, her choices would be limited to one. She planned to sleep on the whole situation and hopefully she could better face it the next day. She was actually amazed the next morning that she had indeed slept and somehow in the morning light the whole situation did not seem as desperate. She could have this child. Morris would probably adjust to the idea. Estelle could be a real help with the baby, especially since she was not dating since Larry left for the army. The reality of it all was that she was not going to leave Morris, child or no child. He was a good provider and she was practical enough to know that men did not want overweight middle-aged women.

That night she fixed an extra-special dinner for Morris, who was rather surprised when a different Cel greeted him. She actually had makeup on and was wearing a flattering dress. Dinner conversation passed uneventfully. Morris kept waiting because he just knew something was coming, so he was not at all amazed when Cel told him she had to speak to him about a really important matter.

"Tell me what it is; I am sure we can work things out together."

"I just hope you will understand that I have no control over what has happened."

"Are you leaving?"

"No, don't be ridiculous. Where would I go? No, I am not leaving, nor do I want to leave you."

"Good."

"Morris, I am pregnant. Dr. Hillman feels that I am about four months gone and the baby will be born either at the end of June or the beginning of July. He has no idea as to how this could have happened. He really thought I could not become pregnant again after the miscarriage."

"Pregnant? At our ages? That's incredible."

"Incredible or not, we are going to have a baby and there is nothing I can do about it."

"What would you do? Of course there is nothing to do. This will be wonderful. I was really disappointed when you had the miscarriage. I thought then that it would have been wonderful to have a child together and I think that same way now. The only thing you can do is to take good care of yourself so that the baby has every chance to be born normal and healthy."

"You had always said that you did not want any more children. I do not understand."

"I know that I said it, but that was out of fear. Now I can admit that I do and probably always did want to have another child. I know I will love this child."

Great, at least one of us will love it, Cel thought as relief overtook her. She did not know what she expected Morris to say, but she was grateful that he seemed excited about the pregnancy. His reaction would make things easier. Now all that remained was to tell Estelle and to write to Joey about the baby. Who could imagine how the children would take the news? But it really did not matter what they thought because they would be going their own way and would really not have much to do with this child. Norman on the other hand, could and probably will be a problem. Who knows what he might do with a little baby? But now was not the time to bring up that topic. Cel knew that this baby just might be her release from taking care of Norman, but she also knew that she had to play it out so that Morris would be ready to accept the idea that the boy belonged in a boarding type school.

When Estelle came home from work that evening, Cel sat down with her and told her the news. At first Estelle seemed amazed.

"This should be interesting, explaining to my friends that my mother got herself knocked up."

"Don't be so crude. I am a married woman and it is normal to have sex."

"At your age?"

"Estelle, as hard as it is for you to accept, I am not an old woman. I am only thirty-six. I know that is older than most women who are pregnant but it certainly is not any world record."

"I guess you're right. It is just that pregnancy is such a topic for all of my friends. We all worry about becoming pregnant, especially if our boyfriends are shipping out...and now you are pregnant. It's ironic."

"And I am married too."

"Okay, Okay. But are you really going to have this kid?"

"Yes...I have seen Dr. Hillman and there is no choice, especially considering my history. I cannot risk a backroom abortion, nor do I think any woman should ever subject herself to such a risk."

"Does he think it is safe for you to have this child?"

"He considers this a high risk situation and only time will tell. If I have another miscarriage, I will also have a hysterectomy so that this will not happen again. If this child is born, there is also a strong possibility that a hysterectomy will be necessary. I very much doubt that my life will be in jeopardy, if that is what you are asking."

"Are you sure that he is the right doctor?"

"Absolutely. He saw me through the last miscarriage and he is a very respected man at Lenox Hill Hospital. I would not consider having anyone else."

"Okay then, let's just assume this kid is born. Are you going to insist that I babysit?"

"When you have a child, are you going to insist that I babysit?"

"You bet!"

"Then I guess you have your answer. You can babysit when it is convenient and I will do the same when you have your children. Look at it as if it were a savings account. Whatever you put in, you'll get out in the future."

"My pregnant Mom and Confucius at the same time!"

"At least you have something to write to Larry about. I know that Joey is going to have some fun when he gets the news."

"I doubt that Larry will care either way. This just has no effect on his life. As for Joey, who cares what he thinks? He probably will not come back here to live after the war."

"This child will be his sister or brother just as it is yours. Family can be very important and this child could be his only blood relative."

"Why? He has Norman."

"Norman...who can know what will be with Norman?"

"Who can know what will be with this child? This child could also be born with some defect."

"No, that will not happen."

"Now you're not only a prophet, but you have the powers of God."

"No, I just have a strong feeling that this child will be perfect."

"I hope so for your sake. I would hate to see you having to take care of two children who are mentally handicapped."

"Enough with all the negative thoughts," Cel replied, as she walked out of the kitchen to end the conversation. It was just like Estelle to voice all of the same fears that Cel had.

Cel decided not to write to Joey but instead to wait until he called to tell him the news. She figured it was more personal to tell him about the new addition than to put it on paper and then not share his initial reaction. Somehow, it was important to her to have Joey be excited, or at least happy, about the news. She could not figure out why this was important, but it was. Norman did not appear to care one way or the other about it. Neither Cel nor Morris got any reaction from him when they told him and Cel could not care less.

Joey called the next week all excited about the hydraulics training. He explained that it would be a five-month course and then maybe he would be shipped to the war front, either in Europe or the Pacific. When he finished speaking, Cel said, "Well, five months can bring many changes. Maybe the war will be over by then."

"It would be my luck to miss all the action."

"I would consider it more than good luck!"

"Spoken like a mother..."

"Talking about being a mother, I have some news for you. We're going to have a baby in about five months."

"Going to have what?"

"You heard correctly. I am pregnant."

"Whoa – blow me away. I didn't think the old man still had it! It is his kid?"

"Joey! Of course it is! Don't get insulting."

"Okay, Okay – don't get excited. I was just asking. After all, you are much younger than my father."

"And I am married to him."

"Let's not start a lecture on marriage and faithfulness. I got it. Whoa, I can hardly believe this. I would love to be able to see you pregnant."

"Why?"

"I bet you are one sexy pregnant woman!"

"I take that as a compliment, though I frankly do not think any pregnant woman is particularly sexy."

"I always thought of you as a really sexy woman. Remember when you were teaching me how to kiss a girl...I have yet to meet a girl who can stir me the same way."

"Stop thinking about that. Looking back on it, I am not sure that was the right way to teach you."

"It was a hell of an experience."

"Joey, can we redirect this conversation?"

"Yeah, sure. It is just that when I think about it, I realize you are sexy enough to make the old man's juices stir."

"His juices are just fine! And now we are going to have a child that will be your sister or brother. You will forever have a responsibility to this child. It will be your family."

"Blow me away. Hell, I am old enough to have my own kid."

"Don't get any ideas."

"Yeah, yeah."

"What was my father's reaction?"

"I was really surprised. I had always thought that he did not want any more children, but he is excited. He told me he was very disappointed when I had the miscarriage and he cannot wait for this baby to be born."

"I guess it would be nice for him to be able to enjoy a baby. Lord knows he could not enjoy us. I just hope that it is a normal child."

"Dr. Hillman assures me that there is no reason to think it will be anything but normal. After all, Norman is not the result of any genetic problem."

"Talking about Norman, how did he react to this news?"

"There was no reaction. We could have told him we are taking out the garbage for all he cared."

"Hopefully he will like playing with the baby."

"Time will tell," Cel replied, but thought that was never going to be the case.

"Well, take care of both of you and tell my father that I said good going. I am sure he is proud of himself."

"Maybe give him a call at the factory. I'm sure he would love to hear from you. You know it is not the same when I tell him I've spoken with you. Good luck with your new assignment and do let us know how to reach you as soon as you have the information."

"All I can say is that you definitely one-upped me with your news."

"I don't know why, but it was important to me that you be somewhat excited about this baby."

"Well, I guess I am excited. I'll know for sure once the shock wears off. I don't know of another guy here whose mother told him she was pregnant. Most of the guys hear about pregnancies from their girls."

"I can appreciate the shock factor. I, too, was completely shocked by the news. But it is real and I am getting used to the idea."

"Well, I will try Dad at the factory and congratulate him. Take care and we'll speak as soon as I get settled in Texas."

"Stay safe and take care of yourself. Remember to think before putting your hands into those engines or whatever they are. It would be horrible if you cut off a finger or something."

"Stop worrying. I am going to be going to school first and I am sure they will teach me how to do everything I need to know."

"But now they are teaching everything too fast and taking too many shortcuts, so keep your head about you and stay out of trouble."

"Yeah, you sound just like a mother!"

"Well, I qualify."

When she hung up the phone, she kept looking at it. She had to admit she did love Joey. There was something about him that definitely triggered deep feelings within her. Hopefully, she would have the time to show him just how much she cared. With that thought, she put her hands on her stomach and said out loud, "Maybe you will be close with your brother and sister; that could prove to be special."

CHAPTER 14

Amazingly, time seemed to pass quickly. Cel could not believe how big she was as the pregnancy advanced. When she was carrying Estelle, she seemed to remember that only her stomach seemed to expand. This time she felt as if she was carrying extra weight all over her body; even her arms and legs seemed heavier. This only added to her resentment, as she was now sure she was doomed to having to wear tent-like dresses forever. Everyone would certainly take her to be the grandmother and not the mother, just as most people just assumed that she was just getting fat and not that she was indeed pregnant. This really upset her. After all, no one wants to feel old. The other thought that surprised her was that even when she felt the baby move, she felt really detached from it. In reality, it was as if she was observing this pregnancy and not participating in it. In no way was she bonding with the child and she seriously wondered if she would ever be able to bond with, let alone love, it.

Conversely, Morris was so excited that it was if he was a young boy again. All he could talk about was the baby and all the things he would do with it if it were a boy. He was really planning on making up for all he missed when Joey and Norman were children. Cel only hoped he would not be too terribly disappointed if the child turned out to be a girl. She kept reminding him that it was a possibility. Morris seemed not to understand that concept, so Cel could only hope. It really did not matter to her at all. All that mattered was getting it over with. She could not wait to have the pregnancy over and to reclaim her body as her own.

The other reason Cel wanted the pregnancy to be over was that she had made up her mind that once the baby was here, Norman was to go. She had even made inquiries about different boarding schools that could accommodate his needs. One was up in Rochester and that would be perfect. It was too far away for weekends at home and yet they could manage to go up and visit him. The best thing was that it specialized in epileptics and had special training facilities for the retarded boys. Cel was sure that Morris would acquiesce, especially if he thought that the baby could be endangered if Norman remained at home. It would be almost too easy for her to make Morris accept the concept and that seemed to make everything better. At least something good would come of all of this.

It was the beginning of July 1943. Cel's feet and ankles were so swollen that she could not wear her shoes. It was an effort for her to do even the simplest household chore and she sensed that it would not be long. There had been no news about the war ending and everyone seemed to just be accepting the war, the rations, and worst of all, the heat. There was no air to be had in the apartment and some nights, Cel just sat on the fire escape hoping to get whatever breeze there was. How she longed for the fresh mountain breezes!

July 9th came with the start of yet another heat wave. The radio kept warning people not to engage in any outdoor activities because of the oppressive heat and humidity. That morning Cel could barely get out of bed. With great effort, she dragged herself into the kitchen to prepare breakfast for Morris and Norman. While standing at the stove, the pain gripped her entire body. There was no doubt that this was the day.

"Morris, please call Dr. Hillman. We have to get to the hospital."

"Get to the hospital? What do you mean?"

"What do you think I mean? Call the doctor and then call Sadie to come and watch Norman."

"Yes, yes, of course. I am just too excited..."

Cel could hear Morris speaking on the telephone in the hall when she was gripped by a pain so severe it took away her breath. Grabbing her stomach and trying not to fall to the floor, she was vaguely aware of the sound emanating from her. Morris' white face appeared in the doorway. No one had to tell him how urgent the situation was. Cel was surrounded by a pool of blood. He gently helped her down onto the floor and ran to call for an ambulance. He knew there was no time to waste if Cel and the baby were to live. His next call was to Dr. Hillman to explain what had just happened. Dr. Hillman tried to calm the man but reaffirmed what Morris already knew; get Cel to the hospital as fast as possible. He told Morris that the operating room would be ready.

As Morris replaced the receiver, he could hear the police sirens approaching the building. He looked in at Cel, who was unconscious, and ran to the apartment's door to let the police officers in. They entered, followed by a breathless Sadie. One look and the officers decided that there was no time to wait for the ambulance; the dispatcher had told them the ambulance was a minimum of ten minutes away.

"Let's just carry her to the patrol car and get her to Lenox Hill. If we wait, she will surely bleed out," the older officer said as they lifted Cel, ignoring the blood that was running down their uniforms. Morris ran ahead to make sure the elevator was there for them and once outside they got the bleeding woman into the car. Morris jumped in beside her, trying to hold her on the seat as they sped off with their siren blaring.

The trip to the hospital was a blur for the man who had already lost one woman and now feared he was about to lose another at what should have been an exciting and wonderful time. As the car pulled up to the Emergency Entrance, Dr. Hillman was standing beside the gurney. Intra-venous medications were quickly placed into Cel's arm and a transfusion started before they even entered the building. Dr. Hillman was sure that the uterus has ruptured and he only hoped he could save Cel, let alone the baby. As they raced to the operating room, Morris was left with the police officers, and someone from the admitting office who wanted information. Bewildered, the man seemed to find some extra strength and responded to the questions asked by the hospital clerk and the police, who also had to complete their reports.

When the questions ended, Morris looked at the two officers as though seeing them for the first time. Before him stood two strangers, their uniforms stained with his wife's blood; their faces showed their concern and their silence showed their respect for him. Morris knew that they could leave, but also knew that they would stay to learn the result of their efforts. Morris turned to them as if to speak, but instead, the men just put their hands on his shoulders and steered him to a chair in the waiting area. The gesture declared that there was no need for words; they would simply wait and hope.

For Morris, the wait was increasingly becoming more hellish with every passing minute. Memories flashed back to when he waited for Lilly to give birth; memories of the difficulty of having a baby who did not have a mother; memories of knowing the child would forever be handicapped. Was it all happening again? It was too unbelievable to have to face the same tragedy twice in a lifetime. In his heart, he hoped that if the doctors had to choose between saving Cel or the child, they would save Cel. He had to acknowledge that his feeling had changed about the child. The excitement and wonder he felt while anticipating the birth had now turned to fear, a bone chilling type of fear.

Morris' thoughts must have made him shudder, as he was suddenly aware of a hand on his shoulder.

"Thanks, I really appreciate you being here. She was a really good person," Morris said.

"Let's not count her out yet. The docs here are really good. My religion teaches that where there is life, there is hope," replied the older officer.

"My religion also teaches that and maybe things will turn out right. It's just hard to sit here and not know what is going on. I wish someone would let me know if she is still alive."

"My guess is that she is still alive. I would imagine if she were dead, someone would tell us. I am looking at it that the longer this goes, the greater the chance that your wife will survive."

"God, I hope you are right, but my experience does not support your optimism. My first wife died in childbirth."

The three men lapsed back into silence. The officers felt a compassion for the man who at that moment seemed so small and helpless. Each of the officers felt that there were times on the job when things just seem so pitiful that there were no words to help; this was one. They had no doubt that the woman would have bled out if they had waited for the ambulance to come. At least they did everything they could but that did not make them feel any better. All they could think was, "God, why do bad things always happen to good people? Here were people who wanted to have this child and everyday they would hear about babies being abandoned. Life is not fair."

The sound of heels clicking on the tiled floor jarred the men from their thoughts. Before them stood Estelle, whose beauty astonished the officers.

"Where is she, where is my mother?"

"In surgery. She was hemorrhaging badly when we arrived and Dr. Hillman rushed her right to the OR."

"Is she going to make it?"

"We don't know any more."

"Whoa, what a bummer."

"Estelle, these are the officers who brought your mother here. We could not wait for the ambulance. I am sorry but I don't even know your names," Morris said, embarrassed that he had never even asked them for their names.

"I am Daniel Casey and this Tim O'Brien."

"Thank you ever so much for all of your help. I am sorry if I came in screaming but I am just worried about my mother. This is all so unbelievable."

"We understand; we are all concerned."

"My God, look at your uniforms. They are ruined."

"That's the least of it; it's part of the job."

"I've heard that you guys have to buy your own uniforms."

"If your Mom makes it, your Dad can buy us new uniforms," replied Dan with a little smile, as if the words would break the tension.

"That would be the least I could do. You guys were wonderful."

"Did anyone call Joey?"

"I have made no calls to anyone. How did you know where we were?"

"I called home to check on Cel and Sadie told me. Can I get anyone a coffee or something to eat?"

"No," replied all three men at once. And with that the conversation ended and each returned to his own thoughts as the wait continued. Dan and Tim were surprised at the obvious age difference between this beautiful young woman and the unborn child. They both knew that this was a family that had experienced tragedy and hoped that another one was not about to unfold.

It was another hour before Dr. Hillman appeared. The concern on his face told them that the news was not good.

"They are both alive. The baby swallowed a good deal of blood and we had to aspirate her lungs. As for Cel, we had to remove the uterus and give her several transfusions to stabilize her. Right now she is in recovery and, though I have reservations, I think she will make it."

A cheer went up from the three men.

"When can I see her?"

"Cel will be in intensive care for a while. I will be able to let you see her later but I seriously doubt she will be conscious. She is in shock, induced by the loss of so much blood. Her body had shut down and we have to watch her very carefully for the next few days."

"And the baby – what about it?"

"It is a girl and my guess is she is going to be fine. The pediatrician has ordered that she be placed in the intensive care unit for pediatrics and the staff there will keep a close watch on her. If you want to see your daughter, we can arrange for you to do so. The neonatal intensive care unit is opened to parents all day and night."

"We would all like to see the baby. These men deserve to at least see her."

"We will arrange it. Just give me a few minutes to clear the officers into the unit."

"Dr. Hillman, do you have any idea as to why this happened? Everything seemed to be going just fine until this morning."

"Morris, there is no doubt that the uterus was severely damaged by the last miscarriage. It could not withstand the stress of delivery. We wanted to do a caesarean section but unfortunately, the baby decided to come before the anticipated date. When I saw Cel the other day, there were no indications that the baby was near birth. She was not dilated and was still carrying very high. Believe me, I too wish we could have avoided this horrible experience."

"Dr. Hillman," asked Estelle, "how did the uterus become damaged by a miscarriage? I don't understand."

"This is not a time to discuss the past. Your mother will have to answer your questions when she can. I can only report the facts."

"That was no miscarriage – am I right?"

"Estelle – that's your name, right? I think this is inappropriate to discuss at this moment. Please –"

"No, Dr. Hillman, I have to know," replied Morris. "I have my doubts about the last time too. I could never understand what happened."

"Morris, I promised Cel to never discuss the case with anyone. Please respect that promise. I can only tell you there was damage to the uterus and it could not withstand the delivery. Beyond that there is not any relevance to the current situation and in my opinion I would concentrate on what is now and let the past remain in the past. Cel is going to need your support, not your questions. I must go and check on her, and I will send one of the nurses down for you as soon as you can see the baby."

"Thank you, doctor. We all really appreciate all of your efforts," answered Morris.

As Dr. Hillman retreated, Estelle seemed very angry. The two officers also removed themselves to give the man some privacy with the young woman, who obviously had something to say.

"Estelle, there is no need to confront your mother. Believe me, I am not the fool she sometimes thinks I am and I am very aware that there are suspicions about the last miscarriage."

"Stop calling it a miscarriage. It had to be an abortion!"

"I do not know why she would want to have an abortion or where it could have been done, but I feel for the sake of the family, I must respect her privacy and accept her explanation, and I think you should do the same."

"Morris, you never fail to amaze me. Do you love her so much?"

"My love for your mother has grown over the years and I truly appreciate all that she did for my sons. I know we were both looking forward and were very excited about this new child, and if I thought it would help anyone to know the truth, I would ask. It is no longer relevant and I agree with Dr. Hillman; let the past remain in the past. Your mother has to live with her conscience and if she had an abortion, she has to be able to come to terms with it. Hopefully she will survive and be able to be a good mother to this baby. That is all we should be concerned about now."

"God, I hope Larry will prove to be half the man you are. If I ever did not show you the respect you were due, please accept my apology. You are a man who deserves respect and love."

"Thank you, Estelle, I value your feelings. Come, let's find out if we can see your sister."

The neonatal intensive care unit had the shades drawn over the windows but the hum of activity could be heard in the hallway. Morris tentatively knocked at the door to the unit and waited for a nurse to appear. Despite the sign that parents were allowed to enter anytime, he felt it was best to just wait. Fear gripped him as he pondered what this child would be like and what type of future she would have. Everyday when he looked at Norman, he wished his life could be better and wondered at the "gifts" of modern medicine. Hopefully, they were not saving another only to sentence her to a lifetime of frustration and pain.

The door opened and Morris was jarred back from his thoughts.

"You can come in. Please wash your hands and put on the hospital gown in the locker before you come over to the baby," instructed the nurse as she hurried back to her duties.

As Morris approached the incubator he was amazed at the sight before him. There was this tiny naked person with blonde hair and strangely-colored skin attached to what appeared to be a million tubes with monitors going off constantly. All he could think was, "What a welcome into this world!"

"Don't worry about her coloring; it's just because of the blood she swallowed. All her vital signs are good," said a voice from behind. It was as though the nurse was reading his mind.

"Can they determine if there was any brain damage?"

"It's too soon to tell, but she is breathing on her own and that is a good sign."

"Then why are there so many tubes attached to her?"

"We cannot take any chances. Most of this is precautionary and allows us to monitor her constantly. If she does develop any problems breathing we will know instantly."

"Is she warm enough?"

"The temperature in the incubator is especially controlled. We will be putting diapers and a receiving blanket on her later on, if we can remove some of the tubes. But, believe me, right now she is quite comfortable and is actually sleeping. She has had a really hard day."

"Well, we will leave you; we just wanted to see her."

"You can come in anytime; please feel free to do so. We encourage the family to make contact with the baby."

"Thank you so much for your kindness."

Morris and Estelle left the unit in silence. Each wondered if that tiny person would indeed survive and develop into a normal human being. Estelle feared that if something happened to Cel, and if the baby survived, her life would certainly be changed forever. She shuddered as she pictured herself taking care of a baby. "What a bummer that would be!" she thought to herself as she put her arm through Morris' and they walked back to the waiting-room and asked the two officers to come in to see the baby.

Neither Morris nor Estelle were aware of how long they had been sitting in the cold waiting-room. Each was totally absorbed in private thoughts and each was respecting the other's need for silence. Time has no relevance in a place that knows neither day nor night; a place where there is hope as long as one is there; a place where strangers witness some of one's most private emotions.

Suddenly Dr. Hillman appeared in front of Morris. Morris never saw him coming and actually jumped to attentiveness.

"You can see Cel now. She is awake but very weak, so please do not make her talk, but I do think it would be good for all of you to see each other. Then I think you should go home and get some rest. There is really nothing you can do sitting here."

"How is she? I mean, is she going to be all right?"

"Cel surprises me every time there is a crisis. I really would be shocked if she does not come through this one. She has lost a good deal of blood and we had to transfuse her twice. But there is no active bleeding now and her vital signs are stabilizing."

"That all sounds pretty good. Does she know she has a baby girl?"

"She asked about the baby and seemed relieved to know she too seems to be doing well. I think she was really surprised to learn the baby had survived at all."

"Does she know we are here?"

"Actually, she has asked several times about you and expressed her concern that you would be worried."

"Let's go and see my wife," Morris said, as he took Estelle's arm and started walking toward the door. His words and voice seemed to reaffirm to Estelle his desire to focus on the present and let the past remain in the past. Again Estelle was amazed at the man's loyalty and love.

No matter how much Morris had thought about the moment he would see Cel, he was still unprepared for the white face that seemed almost lost on the pillow. Her eyes seemed too large for her face and her cheeks looked as though they had sunk into the back of her head. He could not help but shudder as he took her free hand into his and quietly stroked her arm.

"Are you okay?"

"Don't you worry about me, I am fine. You just think about getting your strength back. I saw our daughter and even though her color is a little funny, she is going to be one beautiful child who definitely needs her momma."

"I am amazed that she survived all of this."

"There were two policemen who were wonderful in helping to get you to the hospital. They even stayed with me until we knew you were going to be all right."

"That was nice..." she replied with a voice that was fading and Morris released her hand and turned to Estelle.

"It's time we leave, she needs to just rest."

Cel remained in the hospital for two weeks and wanted nothing to do with the baby. The doctor assured Morris it was just from the trauma and he seemed certain her rejection would vanish. When the time came to bring them home, Cel still seemed totally uninterested in the child and Dr. Hillman recommended that a nurse be hired to care for both of them. He also recommended that she be watched carefully because women who seemed as depressed as she could inflict harm on themselves and the child.

Morris could not understand such a concept. To him it was totally inconceivable that any woman could hurt her own child. But he listened carefully to the doctor and took heed of his words. A nurse was hired to take care of Ann (Morris had chosen the name in honor of his mother), and a housekeeper-companion was hired to watch Cel while he was at the factory. At night, the nurse stayed in the same room as Ann. Cel was shown the baby several times a day and even encouraged to hold her, though she did not seem to care. Once again, Morris was patient with his wife and let her come to terms with the child in her own way and in her own time-frame. He felt that Cel would change and that it was important not to force her too quickly.

The baby was a whole different matter. Morris was truly in love with her. He could not hold the child long enough or stop marveling at the tiny hands, fingernails, toes, eyes that seemed to shine up at him and a mouth that was like a rosebud. Everyday he promised to make sure the world was a perfect place for his princess.

The other problem that Morris had to address was Norman. Unfortunately, the boy was very jealous of the baby and resented that everyone was paying attention to her and not paying any attention to him. There was no way to reason with him and though Morris repeatedly told him that he was still loved, no one could change his attitude. Even Cel remarked that she was concerned about how Norman was reacting to the baby being there. Morris knew in his heart that his man-child was heading on a collision course with a destiny that would forever alter his life and Norman's. The one thing he knew for sure was that in no way would Norman be allowed to harm the baby and that he would do whatever was necessary to protect her, even if that meant placing Norman in a boarding school facility. The baby was too fragile, too helpless and too vulnerable, and it was as if only Morris could save her from the harm that seemed to be all around her. He cautioned the nurse never to allow Norman to be in the room alone with Ann, even if it meant taking the baby with her to wherever she had to go.

Estelle was a totally different story. She not only accepted Ann but she demonstrated such love for the child that to strangers it appeared as if she were the mother, not the sister. Morris loved to watch her coo back at the baby and talk the nonsense that all mothers talk to their infants. The baby seemed to know the love she was receiving and followed Estelle with her eyes whenever she was there. Morris could not keep from wondering how long Estelle would be willing to keep her life on hold and keep giving so much time to the baby. He was smart enough to realize that once Larry returned from the war in Europe, Estelle would be starting the next phase of her own life, marrying Larry and having a family of her own. He prayed that by the time Larry returned, Cel would have snapped out of her depression and be able to assume her rightful role as the mother of the precious child. Larry was another worry. His last letter said he was going on the offensive somewhere in Europe and probably would not be able to send any letters home for quite some time. It was hard to imagine someone as gentle as Larry being involved in active combat.

The days continued to pass. The hardships of a nation at war continued. Meat was almost impossible to buy and Morris had to pay black-market prices in order to get the meat that the doctor said was so important to help build Cel up physically. The factory was still producing garments for the war effort and luckily Morris was able to keep all of his employees working so that when the war was finally over, he would be ready to resume making dresses that women could afford. He had big plans for the factory once the war was over. Now women were working outside the home and it was unlikely that they would ever return to their pre-war lives. Working women need dresses and changes that the homemakers never envisioned. His factory would produce those dresses at a cost the average working woman could handle. Morris knew he could copy the most expensive dresses and make them for a fraction of the original cost. All that would be needed would be a store where the women would go that would carry the copies and keep the costs down. If necessary, Morris planned to open such a store and let Joey manage it, assuming he came home after the war. Unfortunately, Joey had not been keeping in touch with Morris so there was no way of knowing what he was doing, except that he was in the hydraulics division, stationed in Texas.

CHAPTER 15

The routines of life had encompassed the family and everyone just seemed to know their individual responsibilities. Even Cel began to demonstrate some interest in the baby, and seemed to enjoy taking her out in the carriage and hearing the neighbors remark on the child's beauty, which was enhanced by the beautiful clothes Morris made for her. Morris, more than anyone else, worshipped his daughter. Ann could do no wrong around her father and he was sure that would be the way it would always be for him and his miracle child. She was his princess and he would laugh when visitors would refer to her as "The Princess". Being with the baby made him feel young again and encouraged him to look forward to the end of the war and the implementation of all of his dreams.

The reality of the war struck the little family on a June night in 1944. Morris came home to find the apartment strangely silent. He walked up the long hall toward the kitchen to find Cel holding a sobbing Estelle. Cel attempted to wave him away, but there was no moving Morris and Cel told him that Larry had been badly wounded during a battle that had happened in a place called Normandy, somewhere in France.

"A telegram arrived today at Larry's house. He is supposed to be evacuated to a hospital in England but we do not know anything more. His mother said something about there being a big battle at Normandy which was supposed to lead to the liberation of France. She heard about the battle over the radio or something but no one had any idea that Larry was there," Cel explained.

"I heard about the Battle of Normandy. Commentators are very excited about it and they do keep referring to it as the liberation of France and the start of the end of the war. I heard that it was a big battle with many injuries and a great deal of damage to the town itself. I just cannot image Larry being a part of such a horrible thing."

"I know... he is such a gentle person. I cannot picture him killing anyone. Now I only hope we see him walk through that door and return to his life. Hopefully his injuries will not make him a cripple."

"When can we expect word about his condition?"

"Your guess is as good as mine. Hopefully he will be able to write but we know nothing at this point."

"Security has to be decreased since word of the battle has come over the radio. I would imagine that prior to the news release, the government had to keep the whole encounter a secret for security reasons. That would explain why Estelle has not heard from him for so many weeks. He probably was not permitted to even write home, but now he will be able to so, let's not assume the worst and let's be hopeful that his wounds will be able to heal quickly."

"Morris, the optimist! Go and pick up the baby and let's get her fed before it gets too late. I'll sit with Estelle until she gets herself under some control. Oh, by the way, Norman walked out during all the excitement. I really do not know where he went."

"What do you mean, he walked out? Where could he go?"

"He has been just walking out of the apartment and he usually refuses to tell me where he is going or what he is doing."

"Cel, why haven't you told me this before?"

"I didn't think it was important and besides, what could you do about it anyway? You cannot be here during the day and no one here can control him. He's stubborn and very difficult to handle."

"I still feel you should have told me the first time he walked out without your permission."

"Morris, this is not the time for us to have a discussion about Norman. Estelle needs me now and that is where I am going and Ann needs you. Norman will come back and you can discuss this whole thing with him later."

Morris turned his back on Cel and felt a sickness in the pit of his stomach. First the news about Larry and now the worry that Norman was walking the streets getting into who knows what type of trouble. She never really cared for the boy and now it appeared as if she had simply washed her hands of any real responsibility toward him. Life just seemed to get harder all the time. It was clear that a decision about Norman's future was at hand and Morris silently prayed he would be able to make the correct choice, but who really knew what that choice should be or even if he would be given the opportunity to make a choice. Norman, after all, was physically large and he could do something that could get him arrested or into some other serious trouble; then there would be no choices.

Morris contemplated going out to look for Norman. But where could he start, and what if the boy came home while Morris was out? It seemed futile to run around the neighborhood so Morris simply took Ann into his arms and held her close to his chest. Her smell eased the moment and he could not help but smile as she started playing with his face and hair.

It seemed like hours had passed before Morris heard the door to the apartment open. He walked to the hallway and watched Norman come in as if nothing had happened.

"Where have you been?"

"I went to my friend's house and we did things together."

225

"Who is this friend and what type of things did you do?"

"She lives in Sadie's building and we like touching each other and kissing."

"Where are her parents?"

"She doesn't have parents. She just lives in the apartment by herself."

"How old is she?"

"I don't know but she is very nice to me and we like kissing and stuff."

"Norman, you just cannot walk out of here and go to someone's apartment and kiss and stuff."

"Oh yes I can. Joanie said I could come to her house anytime I want to and that I can stay there as long as I want to. She said it's okay."

"Norman, I'll tell you what. I would like to meet this girl. Will you take me to her apartment?"

"Sure, but I am hungry now. Can we go later?"

"I'll tell you what... I will make you a sandwich and then when you are finished eating it, we'll take a walk together to see Joanie."

He put Ann to sleep before he and Norman left the apartment together. When the door was opened, Morris almost fainted. Before him stood a woman old enough to be Norman's mother. She was dirty, ill-kept, horribly obese, and obviously mentally handicapped. She and Norman embraced and started walking into the apartment as if Morris was not standing there in the doorway. When he managed to find his voice, he attempted to find out about this person and how she managed to live in the apartment by herself. But the information was not forthcoming and he quickly realized there was little to gain from the visit except that he had to do something to stop things before Joanie got pregnant. At that moment he knew he would have to find suitable living arrangements for Norman where he would be taken care of properly and given every opportunity to develop. His man-child was a time bomb waiting to explode and it was obvious that he had to diffuse that bomb before any serious damage could be done.

On the walk back home, Morris formulated his thoughts. He knew he would have an ally in Cel when it came to placing Norman in a boarding school. However, he really wanted to broker the deal and try to guarantee that Cel would become a better mother to Ann; after all, Estelle would be moving on with her own life and that baby deserved to be loved. So he decided to make it a deal that if Cel became a more active, loving mother, then he would see to it that Norman was placed in an alternative living arrangement. However, if Cel continued to refuse to be a part of the baby's life, then he would bring Norman back home. Something good had to come out of this whole situation.

Cel readily agreed to Morris' conditions and even actively started to look for a suitable school for Norman. Through his school in New York, she learned of an institution upstate that specialized in housing retarded epileptic students. Norman would live there and attend school on the same premises. Since the males and females were completely segregated, there was little chance that he could have a relationship similar to the one he had with Joanie. Best of all, the school had a reputation of helping its students develop to the best possible level and the older residents were even able to work and earn spending money. Visitation would be a problem since the institution was six hours away but it was still doable, especially when the war ended and gasoline was no longer rationed.

The day came to tell Norman of their plans. No one was prepared for the reaction that ensued. Norman became uncontrollably furious and blamed Ann for his father wanting him to go away. Norman promised that no matter how long it would take, he would kill Ann to punish her for what was happening to him. Morris tried to reason with his son and to explain that the baby had nothing to do with their plans, but there was no talking to Norman. It was obvious that the baby had to be watched constantly until Norman was expeditiously enrolled in his new institution. Morris decided that he alone would accompany Norman upstate and that they would leave the following weekend. Morris viewed the whole situation as another failure but he knew he had to do everything to protect his daughter, even if the end result was the sacrifice of his man-child.

Cel felt as though life was in fast-forward. She had to prepare Norman's clothing, keep a constant vigil over Ann and continue to support Estelle, who still had not heard from Larry. It was a great relief when a letter finally came from England. His wounds were serious, but not life threatening, and he felt that it would not be long before he would be shipped home, though he could not give them any idea of when that might happen. The letter contained no information about how he was wounded or exactly where his wounds were, but Estelle was still greatly relieved and even started talking about planning their wedding so that everything could be in place for when he came home.

Norman and Morris left early that Saturday morning. They were to take the train to Buffalo and then they were to be picked up and driven to the school. There were no goodbyes that morning and Cel was shocked by the sudden quiet that descended upon the apartment after their departure. This was what she had always wanted, but now it felt really strange. The key to everything was going to be how Morris would act when he came home. If he could keep this whole thing isolated in his mind and if they could be a real family, then it would all work out. Cel remained prepared to keep her end of the arrangement and to start taking care of the baby, the house and to try once again to be a decent wife. Lord knew, Morris deserved that much from her.

The train ride to Buffalo seemed to last forever. Conversation was, at best, always difficult when he and Norman were alone, but today it was impossible to maintain. Morris felt haunted by Lilly's memory and the undeniable feeling that he had failed both her and his son. He had always imagined that Norman would just remain a part of his household and that someday Joey would assume the responsibility for him. Never did he think there was any reality in the thought that he would be putting the boy into an institution; call it what you may, it was an institution for people who could not function in the real world. Right now he truly felt it would have been better had the boy died; then he would have grieved for his son and would have been spared this day and all the upcoming days of guilt. FAILED...FAILED...FAILED, the cadence of the train seemed to be yelling at him as he stared into the window and watched the countryside whiz by.

He finally looked over at the boy, who was slumped into his seat, sleeping. Norman had spent much of the night crying in his room and asking over and over again why he had to go to a new school and why would he not be able to come home at night. Cel had assumed the responsibility explaining to him that the decision had been made to help him learn how to live by himself, so that one day he would be able to have a family of his own. This Norman did not understand; he kept on telling her that he already had a family of his own and did not need more. Even Cel seemed to feel sorry for the boy when he told her that she just did not want him any more because she now had Ann to baby and take care of. Cel tried to make him understand that the decision for him to go to a new school had nothing to do with Ann; it was best for him and that was the only reason. The blank look in the boy's eyes told them he would never believe them again.

Finally the train pulled into the station at Buffalo and Morris quickly took the boy by the hand while the porter gathered his luggage. A car from the school met them at the station and the driver tried to make the trip interesting by explaining all the sights they were passing. The city seemed very small compared with New York and the tree-lined streets were certainly pretty, especially now that it was early fall and the leaves had started to turn. Morris could only imagine how beautiful it would be in a few weeks when nature had completed its mastery of colors. He wondered if Norman would even notice the beauty. Probably not... what a shame. Hopefully this place would be able to make him more aware of his surroundings and more responsive to them. That was part of their promise, but right now, Morris was only hoping there might be a kernel of truth in the promises.

Norman seemed to try and get closer to his father as the car slowed in front of the massive building.

"We're here. This here building is the administration building and there are some classes in it. The buildings used for the dorms are in the back so that we can keep them secured. Each building has its own courtyard and playground so the kids can be supervised, and the younger ones are kept separated from the older kids," explained the driver.

"Do they take the children to the city or to a movie?"

"We have movies right here on the complex, just as we have a regular hospital should someone get sick. There is little reason for anyone to leave and go anywhere. However, visitors can take the kids when they come and the city does have lots of interesting places. You will be coming up to visit and you'll see for yourself."

"Can I take him home for a visit?"

"I doubt you will want to. Usually once the kids are settled, it is best not to take them away for any prolonged time because then they have to go though the adjustment of getting used to the place all over again. The counselors will explain all of that to you during their meeting with you today."

"Okay... lead the way to these counselors so we can show this young man how special this school is and maybe then he will know how lucky he is to be here. Right now, I think he is a little frightened and overwhelmed by everything. Right, Norman?"

The boy did not respond, but his eyes told Morris that he was more than just frightened...he was petrified.

As they entered the administrative building, a woman greeted them with such enthusiasm that Morris could not help but smile as he responded to her greeting but she completely ignored him and turned all of her attention to Norman, with whom she starting talking about the Dodgers and his favorite radio shows. Before Morris could believe it was happening, the boy started responding to her and seemed eager to go with her to the playroom down the corridor. Morris' relief was practically audible.

Morris did not see the boy during the admitting process, which seemed to be extremely efficient and friendly. He was repeatedly assured that he could call anytime and he could come and see the boy anytime he wanted to. They kept assuring him that the security around the facility was not to imprison the children but to keep them secure and ensure their safety.

"Here the children will attend school just as they did at home. The only difference is that here the school day is somewhat longer and the children each receive individual attention from our trained staff. Each child is encouraged to expand his or her horizons and explore new things."

"Will he be allowed to call us?"

"Not at first. We want him to adjust to being away from home so we do not allow any calls to be made or received. Once he is comfortable here, we will relax that policy and he will be allowed to call you collect and receive calls from you, as long as he does not become agitated by the calls."

"Norman can function to a good degree. How will you place him? I really do not want him with severely retarded children."

"He will be placed with children of similar abilities. I guarantee he will neither be the most advanced nor the least able to function. There will be some that cannot function at his level and he will learn how to help them, just as a family helps each other."

"What if I change my mind and want to take him back home?"

"We are a private institution. He can remain as long as you wish and, at anytime, we will help facilitate a transfer if that is your desire or a return home. I do think you have given this considerable thought and now you should give us a chance before you start having negative ideas. Our children are happy and you will see this for yourself as I take you around to meet them."

"I only hope that Norman will be happy too. He has had a hard time accepting this, especially with the baby being at home. He feels like we want to get rid of him now that we have Ann and, unfortunately, that is partly true. I guess that is why I feel so guilty. Before Ann was born, Cel was able to give him the time he requires but now she can't, and we are always afraid he will hurt the baby. But please don't think he is in anyway violent because that is not the case; he just doesn't always think before he acts."

"Mr. Beckman, I understand your concerns and your feelings. Sometimes we have to take the actions necessary to protect all the involved people. Here he will be supervised and protected, and there will not be any female students in his residency hall, so we will not have to worry about him getting into that type of trouble. He will still see the girls in shared classrooms and at social activities but it will always be under supervision. Come with me and I'll show you his living quarters and give you a tour of the facility. Then you are going to say goodbye and we will show Norman around."

Morris was very impressed with the facility. It was clean and neat, and the children seemed happy and interrelated well with each other. Of course, there were some who just sat and stared ahead without seeing, but there were many children who appeared to be normal and functioning. Morris could not help but inquire as to why they were in the institution.

"These children are here to help them reach their maximum potential. We are actively training them to live independently and hopefully one day they will be able to retain a job and function in the world at large."

"How will you determine when they are ready?"

"Actually, we will help place them in a job and they will continue to live here while they are working. We will get feedback from the employers and use all the information to make a determination. It is a long process but I can tell you we have had great success in placing our children in the local community."

"It is hard for me to envision Norman being able to live independently. He cannot even read simple signs and could never be permitted to take a subway or bus without supervision because he would certainly get lost. We have tried to teach him his address and telephone number, but even that does not get repeated correctly."

"I doubt that he has ever had the type of qualified attention we offer. I think you will be surprised at his progress in the upcoming months. I have reviewed all his

233

school records and I am very aware of his limitations, but I do not think he has been properly challenged."

"Okay...now what?"

"You will say goodbye and let him know you will be calling him in one week. There will be tears and possibly an expression of anger, but you will not waver and we will talk to him as you take your leave. Remember, he wants you to feel very guilty right now and he will do everything to ensure that you leave here with a very heavy heart."

"That is already the case. Right now I am beside myself with feelings of guilt and failure."

"You are very normal and if you did not feel that way I would question all your previous motives. You wanted to do the best by your son, and I am sure you did, but there are limits to what any parent can do with a special child and that is where we come into the picture. We can and will help your son to become an independent functioning individual."

"Let's get this over with before I completely lose my nerve."

The goodbye was as hard, if not harder, than Morris expected. Norman became hysterical and Morris had everything he could do to keep from crying. When the door to the administration building closed behind him, the tears just flowed down his face, blurring his vision, and he was very aware that his entire body was trembling. Before he knew it, the nice man who had driven them to the school had his hand on Morris' elbow and was guiding him to the waiting car. No one spoke and the car was put into gear and the trip back to New York City was begun.

As the countryside again passed before him, Morris started to regain control of himself. The tears slowed and the trembling ceased. In his heart, he knew he was doing the only thing he could to protect the baby from Norman and to protect Norman from himself. What life would be like once he returned to New York was not something he could imagine right now.

"Thank you for being so understanding. I guess you have done this before."

"The parents always take it the same way. It is totally understandable. All I can tell you is that most of the kids are playing when I get back from the train station. Our staff is wonderful when it comes to helping them adjust. You can call the counselors to find out how he is doing anytime you want."

"I am sure that I'll be calling within the next few days."

"Have a safe trip back home."

"Thanks again for everything."

CHAPTER 16

There is truth in the cliché that one day goes into another. When Morris first left Norman at the institution, he was sure that his life would never be free of the guilt he felt. Well, as the days passed, his normal activities took over and before he could even realize it, he was enjoying his life. The baby gave him endless joy. He could not do enough for her. In fact, the entire neighborhood called her "the princess". Every garment she wore was handmade by her father and she was always dressed just so. Even Cel seemed more relaxed and more eager to please him, in and out of the bedroom.

The only event that caused some stress was when Larry came home from the war. He came unannounced and shocked the entire family with his appearance. He had been badly wounded during the battle of Normandy. While his physical wounds had mended, there was a look in his eyes that was like a knife stabbing Morris in the heart. There was no doubt that the young man had seen things that had horrified him and would always challenge his sanity. Morris tried to get him to talk about his experiences, but he would just clam up and let everyone around him know that the topic was off limits now and forever. Morris had grave doubts that Estelle would be strong enough to be able to live with the changed Larry but there was no talking to her either. All she could think about was planning the wedding and getting an apartment for them to live in. The plan was that they would marry at Thanksgiving and Larry would start school in January to get his degree in accounting. Estelle would continue working and, between her salary and the GI Bill, they would be able to manage financially. Morris let them know that, should they need anything, he would be there for them so that finances would not be an added pressure.

The only missing link for the family was Joey. No one had heard from him and no one knew when he would be returning to New York. It seemed very strange that he had failed to get in touch with either the family or his friends now that the war was over. Everyone was returning and resuming their interrupted lives but Joey remained a mystery. There was no doubt that he was alive because had anything horrible happened, they would have been notified. Morris was hesitant to contact the service because he feared that Joey would consider it meddling into his life, but as a father he could not help but be concerned. Interestingly, Joey could have a great future in the garment industry. Morris' factory had done very well during the war and now was extremely busy turning out dresses for the post-war economy. If Joey did not want to learn to be a pattern maker, he could have a good future as a salesman and there was no doubt that Morris could use the help of someone he could really trust.

The mystery was resolved in the summer of 1945. A salesman came into the factory and congratulated Morris on the birth of his granddaughter. Morris was dumbfounded and told the man he had to be mistaken, but the man provided Morris with Joey's address and phone number in Dallas and told him that Joe was working in the children's clothing industry as a designer. That was how they had come into contact, as this particular salesman was selling some of the line that Joey had designed in addition to ladies' wear.

As soon as the man had left his office, Morris was on the phone calling Dallas. He had to know the truth and he had to know it immediately. The phone was answered by a woman who spoke with a heavy Southern accent.

"May I please speak with Joe Beckman?"

"Who may I say is calling?"

"His father!"

"Please hold for Mr. Beckman."

"Hi, Dad – I was going to call you at home tonight but I guess you beat me to it."

"Marvin Glassman was just here, and he is telling me you are married and have a child. I told him it had to be a mistake."

"It's not a mistake, Dad. Mae and I have a daughter. She was born last month and I would love to have you see her. She is really beautiful and a very good baby."

"Don't you think it would have been proper to have let me know you were getting married before you called with the news that I have a granddaughter?"

"Well… things kinda went very quickly."

"Oh… so you had to get married. Is that what you are telling me?"

"Sort of."

"Now you're going to tell me that she is not Jewish."

"With a name like Mae… did you have any doubts?"

"So you just killed all Jewish children that could have been born for now and for all future generations. You could do this after what Hitler has done to our people. That is inconceivable to me. How could you allow yourself to get involved with a shiksa, and how could you allow her to get pregnant?"

"Dad, shit happens. Why don't you get control of yourself? It is not the end of the world. I really think you might like her once you get to know her and our baby could grow up with Ann; after all, they are only two years apart in age."

"No…never…I can never forgive you for what you have done. You are not my son…my son died. I will sit shiva for him and for all the Jews that died with him."

With that, Morris hung up the phone. There was silence in the factory, and everyone was concerned because Morris had become stone white in color and was shaking uncontrollably. His secretary came running into the office after seeing him through the glass partition.

"Mr. B. Let me help you get home. Whatever it is, I am sure it will work itself out."

"Just call me a cab and let me go."

"You are going nowhere alone. I am going with you. I promise, once you are in your apartment, I will leave and no questions will be asked. But I cannot let you leave here in this condition. Can I call your wife?"

"No! I just want to go home."

When Morris walked into the apartment, Cel was horrified by how he looked. She tried to get some information out of him but he simply refused to talk. The secretary told her about Marvin's appointment but could not clarify the situation past that.

"Look, I want you to go back to the factory and get me Marvin Glassman's phone number. I really appreciate you bringing Morris home. Now go and call me as soon as you have it."

With that, Roberta left and Cel proceeded to get Morris to lie down. He continued to refuse to talk to her and even ignored Ann when she came and tried to get his attention. The next forty-five minutes seemed like an eternity and when the phone finally rang, Cel almost jumped out of her skin. Roberta not only gave her Marvin's phone number but also a number scribbled on the pad on Morris' desk. Cel immediately recognized that number as a Dallas exchange and decided that was to be her first call. It took only a few minutes for her to determine what had caused Morris to be so upset and, when she finished speaking to Joey, she told him she would do whatever she could to help rectify the situation, but she doubted that even she could get things patched up between him and his father.

"You know how he feels about marrying within the religion, especially now that so many Jewish people have been murdered just because they were Jewish. But that is only a part of this. Your father is devastated because he found out about this from a salesman and not from you. How could you have allowed that to happen? You are supposed to be a man now and a man has to take responsibility for his actions."

"Don't you lecture me. You made him put my brother in an institution."

"Joey! One thing has nothing to do with the other. You were wrong and you hurt your father deeply. I personally think that had you handled this differently, he might have accepted your wife and child; but now I have grave doubts."

"Try to make peace."

"I'll try, but you have to promise me one thing. You have to keep in touch. No matter how this turns out with your father, I want to know how to reach you should I have to. Do you understand me?"

"I promise, and if it makes it any easier, I know that I was wrong. It all happened so fast and to tell you the truth, I was really ashamed."

"Were you sure the child was yours?"

"Not at first, but now that I see her, I am sure I am her father."

"I just hope this doesn't kill your father. I have never seen him like this."

"He's a tough geezer and so unreasonable with this religious mumbo-jumbo."

"His religion is important to him."

"Do what you can."

"I will, but remember, keep in touch."

With that, Cel hung up the phone and went into the bedroom where Morris was just staring at the ceiling.

"Okay. I know what happened and I understand how hurt you are. Now what?"

"He is dead and I am going to sit shiva for him."

"He is not dead! Don't you want to see your granddaughter?"

"Never! I never want to see him, nor his bastard child."

"He made a mistake and he knows he was wrong, but he is your son. How can you just write him off as though he doesn't exist?"

"Cel, I am a man of honor and have always prided myself on my honor. If my son doesn't have any honor, he is not my son. It is final. He no longer exists and his name is not to be spoken in this house. Do you understand me?"

"Will you reconsider?

"No! Leave me alone to my grief."

Morris sat shiva for seven days. He tore his clothing and wailed in sorrow. There was nothing Cel nor anyone could do but leave him alone and hope he would come to his senses. The rabbi came to the house and prayed with him but could do nothing to change his mind. Joey was dead to his father and anyone who wanted to keep in contact with him had to do it secretly.

After the seven days of shiva, Morris went back to work and life resumed for the family, but there was a void that would forever be with them and they each had to deal with it in their own way out of respect for Morris and his wishes. Only Ann, blessed with youth and a lack of understanding, was untouched by the events.

Estelle and Larry had married in a small, intimate service with just the immediate family and a few friends present. Larry could not handle the thought of a big gala affair, and Estelle decided to honor his wishes. She said that she understood his pain after the loss of so many of his comrades. He continued to refuse to discuss the war and his experiences, but she did manage to ascertain that he was wounded in the Battle of Normandy and she could only imagine the horrors he had to have seen. Estelle only hoped that once they were married and he became engulfed in school and then a career, his thoughts would leave the battlefield. Now she was keenly aware that he was preoccupied with his own thoughts and the nightmares were not allowing him a night's rest.

Larry and Estelle moved in with Morris and Cel immediately after the wedding so that they could save money while Larry was still in college studying accounting. They were no problem for anyone since they both were out all day and it was fun having the family together for dinner. Cel arranged the apartment so that she and Morris used the living room as their bedroom and she gave the young couple the master bedroom. She converted the big dining room into a living room since they were no longer having large dinner parties and really did not need the huge table. She felt that someday, in the not too distant future, she would again redecorate and maybe even purchase new and more modern dining room furniture. But for now she was grateful for the young couple's presence as they definitely helped fill the silence that had crept into her marriage ever since Norman was relocated and Joey had so disappointed his father. She and Morris had lost the spark and only Ann seemed to have the ability to make Morris smile. In many ways, Cel was beginning to be jealous of the child, because only she had Morris' attention and love.

At the age of three, Ann was a precocious child. Morris had taught her how to read Hebrew and they would sit for hours in the evening reading together and singing Hebrew songs. From the time Morris came home from work until Ann went to sleep, she had eyes for no one else, and she would often disobey Cel and wait until her father had issued instructions before she would do anything. Cel would verbalize her frustration, only to be told that Ann was a mere child and she would outgrow this phase.

Unfortunately, the situation became more acute as Ann approached age four. One day, she was preoccupied in the apartment and believed the child was playing by herself in her bedroom. When Cel went to look for her, the child was nowhere to be found. Cel ran to all the neighbors to see if Ann had gone to one of the other apartments on the floor. But no one had seen her. In an absolute panic, Cel called Morris at the factory.

"How could that child have left the apartment without you knowing she was gone?"

"I have no clue. I was busy cleaning and I thought she was in her room playing. I can only assume I failed to hear the door because the vacuum was on, but that is only a guess. All I do know is that she is not in the building and we have looked in the courtyard and all around the block. There is no sign of her."

"Have you called the police?"

"No...I called you first."

"Do you by any chance think she could be coming down here?"

"How would she know how to get there?"

"I don't know. I am going to call down to the candy man at the concession in the lobby. He knows Ann, and if he sees her, he'll call me right away. I really do not want that child wandering in this building by herself. You know the problems I am having with the unions."

"I'll call the police. What if someone from the union has her?"

"How would they have gotten into the apartment?"

"Morris, I really do not believe anyone came into the apartment. I do think she left here because the door was unlocked when I started to look for her."

"You did check with all of the neighbors?"

"Of course, that was first thing I did. I thought she might have wanted to go and play with Steven down the hall. She really likes the little boy and they do play well together. But Harriet has not seen her all day and she and Steven were alone in the apartment all day."

"What about the Radius boy? She always talks about Michael as though he is her brother. Did you call Bea?"

"They live in the next building. How would she...?"

"Call Bea before you call the police and let me know right away. It would be easy for the child to go next door to their building. Bea might have even thought you sent her over."

"I doubt that. But I will call."

Time seemed to just stand still and every minute was like an eternity. No one had seen the child and there were no hints as to where she could possibly be. The police were canvassing the neighborhood but were constantly coming up empty. They had even spoken with the men in the change booths at the 181st Street and the 184th Street stations, but neither had seen a small child traveling alone. Morris was instructed to remain at the factory on the outside chance that someone attempted to contact him there, while Cel was to remain at the apartment. Of course all the neighbors came to the apartment and sat with her as Cel sat crying and shaking her head in disbelief.

Two hours passed before the ringing telephone broke the tension in the apartment. Cel jumped to grab the receiver. When she heard Morris' voice, she could not believe what she was hearing.

"Ann is here. She took the subway down to 34th Street and walked down the block to the building. Al at the concession saw her standing and looking around down in the lobby and called me. When I went down, there she was eating a pecan bar and telling Al all about her ride on the subway like a big girl."

"Why would she do such a thing?"

"She says she wanted to come and work with me."

"How did she get into the subway train?"

"She walked through the turnstile with an adult so that she did not have to pay. She said that was the way you and she always got into the station. She actually said she made believe she was the lady's child so she would not have to give the man any money."

"This is unbelievable. How could a four-year-old child think of such things? How did she even know which was the correct building or which station to get off at?"

"That's what took so long for her to get here. She said she went into one building but did not see Al so she knew it was not the right place. So she kept looking into the buildings until she saw Al and then she knew where she was. As for the station, she said she always counts the stops the train makes when she comes down here with you and so she got off by counting the stops this time."

"I'll call the police and let them know we have her, but I have no idea what we are going to do in the future. We can't have the child going off by herself like that."

"We'll talk when I get home. Obviously, we have to think of something to prevent this from happening again. Right now all that I can think about is that my child is safe. Everything else will have to be worked out when I can think more clearly."

"Right now I could kill her for causing so much grief."

"That would be productive."

"Come on, Morris, you know what I mean. That child needs to be reprimanded properly for causing so much grief. She has to learn a lesson so that this type of thing never happens again. If we do nothing, she will think it is okay to walk out and just leave."

"She is only four!"

"She is only four, but obviously too smart for her own good. I am going to whip her butt when she gets home and you are not going to stop me."

"We'll talk later. Make the necessary calls now."

Morris hung up the phone and reached out and took his child into his arms. She smelled so good and seemed so soft and vulnerable. He could not stand the thought of her being whipped by anyone and he knew he would forever protect her.

"You know what you did was wrong. You cannot just leave Mommy and come down here by yourself. There are bad people in this world and little girls are not safe when they're out all by themselves. We were really worried about you."

"I wanted to come and be with you."

"I understand that, and believe me I love having you with me. But you cannot just leave and come here. Mommy was scared something had happened to you and now she is really upset. I was afraid that someone would hurt you and I was worried sick. You do not want to make me unhappy and worried, do you?"

"No, but I like to be with you and not with Mommy. She is mean to me. She makes me stay in my room."

"Sometimes Mommy has things to do and she cannot just play with you. When that happens, you can take one of our books and read it. That way it will be as though we are together. Big girls do things like read, but it's wrong to just take off and leave the apartment without telling anyone. You cannot do that again. Do you understand me?"

"Daddy mad?"

"Yes, Daddy is mad at you for doing what you did and for scaring me that way."

"Sorry Daddy."

"I love you, baby, and you must listen to me."

Morris decided to leave the factory early because he was exhausted from all the stress of the day. It was hard to imagine how horrible it would be to have had something happen to Ann. She was the light of his life and life without her would be too dismal to endure. He knew for sure that he would have to take whatever steps were necessary to ensure her safety and, in the depth of his heart, he knew there were problems between the child and Cel. In front of him, Cel always seemed like the perfect mother; but a child does not leave home alone when the perfect mother is there. Could she be resentful of the child and could that resentment be detected by Ann? Morris was sure that the possibility could exist. Cel could be extremely manipulative and cunning, and he did know for a fact that there was no way that she wanted to have another child. One thing he did know for sure...Ann had to be protected and he would think of a way to do so.

The trip home went by quickly with the two of them playing word games. Morris would say a word in Hebrew and Ann would say the English equivalent. If Morris said an English word, she would respond in Hebrew. He never failed to be amazed at how easily she went from one language to the other despite their tremendous differences. The only difficulty he was noticing was when she attempted to read. It was as if she could not decide whether to read the letters from left to right or from right to left. He guessed that he would have to decide which language he wanted her to read.

247

As the train pulled into the 181st Street Station he felt the little hand tighten on his. As they exited the train, she seemed to hide behind him. He could feel the child's fear. He bent down and picked her up, hugging her to him.

"You do not have to be afraid. I am here with you."

"I am not afraid of you. I know Mommy will hit me for going away. She always hits me when I am bad."

"What do you mean?"

"Mommy hits me with your belt when I am bad."

"Does this happen often?"

"She says I am very bad."

"Why haven't you told me about this before?"

"She said she would really hit me if I told you."

"Don't you worry about that! I will talk to Mommy."

"No, she will be angry. I'm scared."

"Ann, don't you trust me? I am telling you I will take care of it and Mommy will not hit you anymore."

"Oh, she will hit me when you are not home and there will be nothing you can do. That is what she says."

"Did you leave the apartment because you were afraid Mommy would hit you?"

"I was very bad today. She yelled at me."

"What did you do that was so bad?"

"I kept talking and talking without stopping. Mommy kept yelling at me to leave her alone and I kept on talking."

"I'll talk to Mommy and I promise I will make it all right with her. You do not have to worry about being hit."

"Promise?"

"Promise!"

As he walked the two blocks to their apartment with the little girl in his arms, he wondered what she meant by being hit. He decided not to pursue the conversation any further, but there was no doubt in his mind that he and Cel would have a serious discussion this evening. A child should not fear her mother and Ann's fear was too real to be ignored. He shuddered, because in his heart he knew that Cel was capable of hurting the child. As he walked up the stairs to their apartment, he could only wonder what he would do to protect this child, and still be able to go to the factory and deal with the unions that wanted to take control of his workers and all the other problems he was having there. Life can become unbearably complicated in a single day. It was in the midst of that thought that the door to the apartment opened and Cel stood before them, her face contorted in anger. She started yelling at the child before they could even enter the apartment. Morris was sure all the neighbors heard every word and his embarrassment was overwhelming.

"Cel, control yourself. There is nothing to be gained by yelling at the top of your lungs. Ann is safe and she understands that she was wrong. Please let's discuss this situation intelligently."

"There is nothing intelligent about a four-year-old leaving her home and going on the subway alone. I want her to go to her room and to go to bed without her supper."

"I think it is a good idea if she were to go to her room so that we can discuss this situation."

Once the child was safely out of hearing range, Morris turned to Cel and told her what Ann had said about being hit and being afraid. When Cel tried to deny that she hit the child, Morris cautioned her not to lie to him because that was something he could not tolerate.

"Okay, okay...so I have given her a little hit on the behind. She exaggerates so. Believe me, she deserves to be reprimanded; she is a very headstrong child and doesn't listen to the most simple things."

"You know how I feel about physical punishment. Why can't you let me know if she is disobedient and allow me to punish her?"

"You only see her as being good. You don't see her the other way. I must be able to control this child or she will grow up like a wild animal. She is entirely too smart for her own good."

"Cel, I will not tolerate you hitting her. She is a smart child and needs attention, not being sent to her room to play by herself. She is more like a delicate flower than a wild animal, and she must be nurtured and encouraged."

"Now you want me to do nothing but amuse this child all day. How do you expect me to do my household chores and cook your dinner?"

"I'll hire a maid," he replied, as the idea formed that the maid could be the person to protect Ann. He could handpick the person and make sure that she reported only to him. That could be the immediate solution. Maybe just having someone in the apartment would help to control Cel. There was no doubt in his mind that the child had been truthful and that Cel was capable of abusing Ann physically and mentally.

"Now I want you to go to Ann and tell her that you love her. Try to explain that you are angry because you were frightened that something could have happened to her. There is no point in making this situation any worse than it is. I have explained that she cannot do this again but if you continue to scare her, who knows what will happen next time. This is a child you can reason with."

"I guess you are right."

Together they walked to Ann's room, and Cel opened the door and entered the room while Morris stood back, watching. The child was hunched in the corner of the room looking like a caged animal. His heart broke as he saw the fear in his daughter's eyes as her mother approached. He wanted to run to her and grab her into his arms but stayed back, hoping that mother and daughter could come to some degree of peace, but there was no doubt that he had to protect this precious child.

Cel did try to impress upon Ann that she loved her and hated the idea that anything bad could happen to her. The child looked into her eyes and tried to find the message behind the words but all Ann saw was emptiness. As young as she was, she knew that her mother did not love her or really care about her.

"I want to go work with Daddy," was her reply to her mother's declaration of love.

"But that is not a place for a child. You have no one to pay attention to you or play with you," Cel responded.

"I talk to all the people and I can sit on the cutting table and talk to Daddy. It is really fun to be there."

"We'll have to see about that. I'll talk it over with Daddy. In the meantime, promise you will not go down there alone. If you have to go, I will take you. I promise."

"Okay – but remember you promised!"

When Cel and Morris walked out of the room, they both knew they had to solve the situation immediately.

"Now you see what I am up against. It is not normal for a child of that age to be so hateful towards her mother."

"It must be very painful to you to hear her true feelings. But now we have to put aside our feelings and decide how to handle the situation. Initially, I think I will take her to the factory with me, but I will try to make it boring for her so that she will not be as eager to come. Next I think we have to look into some type of pre-school for her to attend during the day so she can interact with children her own age. I want you to call the Temple in the morning and see if they have a program for her. Once we have that information, we will be able to make a better decision."

"I don't know about our Temple but I do believe the Yeshiva has a pre-school program for gifted children. I will call them and find out more about the program and requirements the child has to have for admission. I just think that anything too restrictive might be too much for a child this young."

"Find out and then we can discuss it more. Of course, I would have to see any program before making any decision. I also want you to call an agency and set up interviews for someone to help around the house. That would free you up to give the child more attention."

With that, Morris turned his back on Cel and walked into Ann's room. He took the child into his arms and hugged her tightly.

"I know you feel that Mommy does not care about you but that is not true. She loves you dearly and really wants what is best for you. You must learn to listen to her and to obey her. She is your mother and really knows best what is best for you. Do you understand me?"

"Yes. But she is so mean to me."

"She wants you to learn and to become a really good person."

"Am I a bad person?"

"No, of course not, but you have a whole lot of learning to do before you can really determine what is good and what is bad. Today you did something very bad and you must never do that again. The subway and the streets downtown are not a safe place for a little girl to be if she is alone. Tomorrow you can come to work with me in the morning if that is what you want. But you will not be able to do that every day. Do you want to come with me?"

"Yes. I love you, Daddy."

Father and daughter became a regular sight in the factory building. Ann would come to work with Morris and seemed happy as could be trying to read the books he brought with him. She would also help the seamstresses by getting fabric for them or bringing patterns to them. But the best was when she would sit on the cutting table and talk to Morris as he cut the patterns. They would speak in Hebrew and in English, and the child seemed to love learning new things from her father. However, he could not help but notice that she was having trouble reading the English books. She would get confused as to the proper direction of the print and would see the words backwards. He wondered if he had made a mistake teaching her Hebrew before English. Hopefully the teachers in school would be able to help straighten it out in her mind.

Cel made little progress in finding a pre-school program for Ann. The Yeshiva required excellent reading skills in both English and Hebrew and Ann did not qualify. There were some pre-school programs at local churches where working mothers could leave their children, but they were really just babysitting services and had few enrichment programs. She did attempt to meet other mothers of children Ann's age who lived in the neighborhood, and she did arrange play dates for Ann who seemed to like playing with the children, especially little Michael, who lived in the next building, and Steven, who lived down the hall. Together, the mothers would take the children to Fort Tryon Park and to the movies in addition to allowing them to play in each other's apartments. On the days when there was a play date, Ann seemed happy to stay home with Cel and would animatedly discuss the entire day with Morris when he came home in the evening.

The other change that occurred was Stephanie. Stephanie was a Polish lady who came to work in the apartment during the day. She would sit and play games with Ann and the child seemed to be really fond of her. Ann would help Stephanie with the chores around the apartment, and Cel was free to go shopping and to do her own thing. This arrangement seemed beneficial to everyone and Morris could not help but notice that the child was more willing to stay home on the days that Stephanie came to work. He began to relax about the entire situation and knew they would get through the year and a half until Ann started kindergarten. The only problem that remained was getting Ann to accept Cel's love. That was not happening and Morris feared it would never happen. The child did not trust her mother and really wanted to keep a safe distance from her. Morris would always wonder what happened when they were alone together. He could not pursue this with Ann for fear that he would make matters worse. Stephanie never reported any abuse when he would question her and, of course, he never saw any inappropriate behavior when he was with them. But he could not ignore the fear he saw in his daughter's eyes and he knew it had to have some basis.

CHAPTER 17

It was a monumental day when little Ann walked into PS 132 on Wadsworth Avenue for the first time. She looked so little going through the huge doors and it was as if she was being swallowed by the building. Morris had taken the morning off from the factory so that he could walk her to school and he felt the tears streaming down his cheeks. His baby was growing up and soon she would no longer look to him as her major source of information. It would be interesting if she proved to be as intelligent as he believed her to be...time would tell. It was also going to be interesting to see how interacting with the other children would change Ann, who really was like an only child who associated mainly with adults. Hopefully the sparks of youth could be kindled and Ann would be able to laugh easily and smile instead of always being so serious and cautious.

At the very least he hoped that he would no longer have to worry about her traveling downtown by herself, and she could be protected from the union goons who were now actively trying to get Morris' plant to unionize. Last week alone there were several work stoppages when the union representatives held meetings with the operators. They kept promising better conditions, more benefits and shorter hours if the operators joined the union and paid the union dues. Everyone in the factory was upset because they felt that the union really only wanted the dues and did not have their interests at heart. They were even more upset when Morris told them that the new line was going to be discarded because styles had drastically changed and the economy was, in general, depressed, with people buying fewer dresses. The only hope for the factory was to sell the garments to the discount stores such as Kleins and Alexanders. Revenue was going to be really tight until they could produce the new styles, and hopefully jobs could be retained. Bankruptcy was a real possibility; many of the other factories had already declared bankruptcy and everyone knew there were many operators out of work in the garment district. All it took was a walk down 34th Street and you could not help but notice that there were fewer clothing racks being transported on the street. Morris was also hoping to combine his factory with his friend's suit and coat factory. Sol and he felt they could produce dresses, suits and coats and keep the overhead down. But it all depended on the unions and their demands and if the operators elected or were forced to unionize. In many ways it seemed strange to know that your future could be so easily altered and you could have no control over it. But one thing Morris did know: he would survive and somehow he would find a way to make a decent living, even if it meant working for someone else and not having his own factory and all the worries attached to it. People would always need clothing and he was an excellent pattern-maker as well as a designer.

These were his thoughts as he walked into his building that day. It was not until he was in the elevator and the doors had closed that he became aware of the two strange men in there with him.

"Are you Morris Beckman?" one of them asked.

"Yes, who are you?"

"We have a message for you from the garment union."

With those words, Morris felt a blow to his head and slumped to the floor of the elevator. He must have lost consciousness because the next thing he knew there was a group of people standing over him telling him the ambulance was on its way.

"I don't need an ambulance. I need to get to my factory and make sure everyone there is all right."

"You are not going anywhere until the doctor says you can. You really had one hell of a beating. Who knows if you have broken bones or internal bleeding? It is obvious that whoever worked you over means business."

"He said he had a message from the garment union."

"Just stay quiet. We called your cousin and he is locking the doors to the factory and keeping everyone inside until the police get here."

"I guess they win now. No one can risk standing up to these goons." This was Morris' last comment as he again lapsed into unconsciousness, never hearing the wail of the ambulance or knowing that he was being moved to Lenox Hill Hospital.

It would be several days before Morris would be totally aware of his surroundings. The doctors told Cel that he had bleeding within the skull and that once the swelling diminished, he should be able to resume his life. The doctors recommended rest and no stress until his headaches went away and his bleary vision cleared.

"I doubt that we can eliminate all stress. He will be worried about the factory, especially after all of this."

"First he has to recover, then he can worry all he likes. Do what you can. This man had one really bad beating and he is no spring chicken so he will need time to recover."

"This is too crazy for words. I cannot understand why they would do this to him. His operators have always had a great relationship with him and he always tries to do the right thing for them."

"From what we have been reading, this has nothing to do with the operators themselves. This was a message from the union organizers. According to the newspaper, the reporter felt they picked on your husband because he is considered a good guy by the workers."

"I don't understand, but I guess it doesn't matter if I understand or not. I will do whatever I can to help Morris get better."

During the weeks following the beating, Morris' physical condition improved but his mental attitude was definitely changed. The factory operators joined the union because they felt it was the only way to guarantee everyone's safety. Because Morris was not there, production came to a total standstill and operators had to be told not to report to work. The merger with Sol's factory was also put on hold. No one knew how much the union would demand and Sol's factory had not yet become unionized. Morris' first day back to work was marked by the silence of the sewing machines and the lack of the noise from the cutting blades. No one was in the factory except him and his cousin Jack who usually did the cutting of the patterns.

"What now?"

"I have no idea. There are no new orders and we did sell most of the garments at discount but where do we go from here?" his cousin asked.

"My first guess is that we should declare bankruptcy. You and I can get jobs on the street but I will forever feel sorry for the operators. Many of them cannot get other employment. They are the true victims of this whole mess."

"Is there any way we can salvage the factory?"

"We might have been able to salvage the situation if I could have arranged the merger with Sol. I don't blame him being afraid to get involved here. The union is still not going after the suit and coat operators, so he has some time to get things ready and maybe even arrange to get a union into his factory with which he can actually work. If I were him, I would not want to work with these goons. Maybe I can arrange to produce a dress line under his label. We will have to talk to him. Of course, you will come with me wherever I go."

"You sound like we are not only going to declare bankruptcy but are going to close the doors right away."

"I see no reason to fool around. This factory is done. We do not have a viable line to produce and it will take too long to get one, especially since we lost three weeks with me being in the hospital. It will be too expensive to keep the operators on the payroll while we try to get things restarted and there are just too many unknowns. So, yes, I think it is time to sell whatever we can and close the doors."

"Well, let's get going on it. You and I have been through too much together since we came to America so many years ago. I know you are right that we will survive this; it is just so disappointing to have the factory fail."

"Failures are part of our industry. We have been lucky up to now. But you know when one door closes another opens."

Cousin Jack got up and walked out of the office to start gathering up his cutting tools. One thing he knew – he had to get everything out of the factory just in case the creditors locked the doors. Morris could manage anywhere since he only needed a drawing board and paper to make his patterns, but the saws were too expensive to risk. He would lug as much as possible home tonight and he knew he could get the rest of it out in about two days. It would definitely be strange going to work for a new boss. His cousin had always been fair to him and to the other workers at the factory. Hopefully, they would be able to get established together. They were a good team and their reputations should help.

As he was about to leave, Cousin Jack walked past the office to say good-bye, only to find Morris unconscious on the floor. Once again the wail of the ambulance resounded through the building. Morris was again taken to Lenox Hill Hospital and Cel was once again summoned to the emergency room. This time she learned that he had had a massive heart attack and his condition would be touch-and-go. She did not know what she would tell Ann this time; nor did she know how they would pay the hospital bills. Luckily, they had always managed to save money and had lived below their means, always aware that fortunes could easily change in the garment industry. But who could plan for two hospitalizations within a month and a bankruptcy at the same time?

"What will happen if he dies?" Cel wondered to herself. "I cannot believe that I could be left with a young child again and no substantial savings. Who would want to marry me now that I am over forty and a size twenty to boot? God…how I wish I had gotten rid of that child before she could be born! The only positive thing is that I continued putting money away every week. That money is mine and I intend to keep it that way. No one knows about it and no one will know. If Morris does die, at least I have a little nest egg to start my life again." With that thought Cel shook her head as if in agreement with someone who was speaking to her and decided that changes would be made immediately within the household. The first change would be to get rid of Stephanie; that money could be saved and the neighbors would be happy to watch Ann while she was at the hospital. Who knew maybe she and Ann could still develop a relationship without Stephanie there to always take over and give the child whatever she wanted. As she walked home from the subway, she felt she could hear the resolution in her step. Things were going to work out one way or the other and Ann would just have to adjust.

Morris remained in the hospital for several weeks, gradually increasing his ability to walk in the hall. He knew his strength could not return until he was home and able to go for walks in the street. But he was resolved that would come in time. During his hospitalization several friends from the garment industry came by and offered him jobs once he was able to return to work. It would be different working for someone else, but there was no doubt that the stress level would be less and he would be able to count on a steady salary. Morris agreed to take a position with his cousin in the suit and coat business. He would be the designer and pattern maker and Cousin Jack would once again be his cutter. He was actually looking forward to going back to work.

Morris' contentment was to be short lived once he did return home. He found that Stephanie was discharged and Ann was much more withdrawn. The child had lost her carefree attitude and spent much of her time alone in her room. He questioned her but all she would say was that she missed him and that everything else was all right. He was afraid to ask about how Cel was treating her and figured it would all come to light once he was up and about. As for Cel, she actually seemed happy to have him home and she was really very attentive to him. He was to have six weeks of recuperation before the doctors wanted him to go back to work; six weeks at home would reveal a great deal about the day to day operation of the household. His main priority was going to be to draw Ann out of her shell and to have his happy little girl return.

Ann did go to school the next day and when she came home she went directly into her room and shut the door. Morris gently opened the closed door and sat down on the child's bed.

"What's up – how was your day at school?"

"I don't want to talk about it. Mommy says I cannot upset you."

"It will upset me more if you continue to not speak to me. Come on, tell me what is bothering you."

"I'm stupid. The other children can read and I am now in the last seat in the last row because I am too stupid to read."

"You're not stupid. Maybe it is just that you need a little extra help learning to read English. It is very different from Hebrew and you can read that rather well. I remember when I first came to this country, I had a really hard time trying to learn to read English, with the letters going the wrong way and so many words that can go both ways, and I was much older than you are."

"I'm just stupid!"

"No more talk like that. Tomorrow I will go up and see your teacher, and maybe between all of us we can help you. Would that be good?"

"I don't know what you can do. Miss Drake has tried working with me but I still don't get it. I like doing numbers but hate the words."

"It is much harder to be good at numbers. That should show you that you are not stupid. Let me try to help and we can even have fun trying. You'll see, it will be fun, like a game that the two of us can play together. I promise."

"Promise?"

"Remember how much fun it was when you and I worked to learn Hebrew? We used to spend lots of evenings together exploring new words. We'll do that again. Just this time we will do it with English."

"I love you, Daddy. I really, really missed you when you were in the hospital. Promise me that you will never go away again."

"I can only promise that I will try my best not to ever leave you again. What I think we have to do is to try to have as much fun as we can now that I am better and home with you. Now, come, let's go into the living room. I have a big surprise for you."

"But I can't leave my room. Mommy always tells me to stay in my room and be a good girl."

"Ann, I am home now and if I want you to come with me, you can come with me. Mommy will not mind, not one little bit. In fact, from now on I only want you to feel you have to be in your room when you want to go to sleep. I will tell Mommy and she will agree. You'll see."

"But she will hit me if I do not do what she says."

"No one will hit you. I will make sure of that. Now come with me and see your surprise."

The little girl's eyes lit up when she saw the television in the living room. It was just like Steven's, and the little screen came alive with people dancing right there in their very own apartment. It was even better than going to the RKO on the corner and seeing a movie. Now they could see things whenever they wanted to, right at home.

"I cannot wait to see Uncle Milton and the Texaco Hour right here. Sometimes Steven's mom invites me to stay and see the show with him but now you can watch it with me."

"Isn't this a good surprise?"

"It's the bestest!"

"The only thing I want is for us to spend some time every night working on learning to read English and then we can watch television together after that. Deal?"

"Daddy, I will try to learn, but I'm stupid."

"Stupid is not a word that we recognize."

The next morning Morris called the school and asked that Miss Drake call him at home. When she returned his call, she voiced her concern about Ann's inability to read and her lack of attention. He tried to explain that the child could read Hebrew and that she was having problems understanding the concept of reading from left to right since she was taught to read the opposite way. He suggested that Miss Drake send home some of the words that were part of the program and that he would try to work with the child on learning to recognize the different words and eventually put them together.

"We'll make it a game and a special time together and she will have fun."

"It would be wonderful if you can teach the child, Mr. Beckman, because her frustration level has been reached and she is shutting her mind to learning here at school. Any help you can give would be appreciated. I will send home the lists of words that the children are expected to learn and if I can do anything else, please call me."

"Thank you, and we will keep in touch."

That evening Morris worked on making flash cards for the words and drawing pictures that illustrated each word. He made puzzles for the flash cards and drew pictures without words so that eventually Ann would be able to put the word with the picture. And so the games began, and father and daughter worked together each evening. Little by little the child started to be able to realize the direction of the letters and began to make sense of the words. With each word learned, her excitement grew and she seemed even more eager to learn more words. Cel would watch them and maintain her distance. In some ways she resented the closeness the two had developed and in some ways she was grateful that she did not have to be part of it. Their time together was her time for herself. Often she would leave the apartment and go shopping or see Sadie or Estelle while the two of them worked together.

Morris continued to improve physically and he finally got the okay to go back to work. This was something Cel was truly excited about as she wanted him to go to work; first, to have the income, and secondly, to have the apartment back to herself during the day. She was tired of the role of nurse and companion and was sincerely worried that their savings were being consumed. It had been six weeks since she was able to take any money and put it into her private account. Morris did have a job at his cousin's coat and suit factory which would allow him to work and do his thing without all the stress of managing a factory and worrying if the line did not sell well. He would not have to deal with the union, nor would he have to handle the operators or the cutters. It was even better that he was going back to work now that Estelle and Larry were expecting their first child. She would be free go to their apartment and be with the baby during the day. It was incredible that her baby was having a baby.

Summer came and school was over for Ann. The city seemed unbearably hot and everyone's patience was taxed to the limit. It was amusing to see all the people sitting on the fire escapes trying to cope with the heat; some people even slept out there because it was just too hot to go to bed. It was during one of these hot spells that Morris came home and took everyone for a ride. They drove over the George Washington Bridge and rode on Route 4 for what seemed like a long time before they came to a dirt road. There was a lake there and at the corner of the lake stood a stucco house with a porch. Morris pulled into the driveway and stopped the car.

"What are we doing here? Do you know the person who lives here? You never told me you knew anyone in New Jersey. Had I known we were going visiting, I would have brought a house gift."

"Just come with me."

It seemed really strange that Morris had the key to the front door. He just opened the door and allowed Cel and Ann to enter the hall. Cel could see a living room with a fireplace and opposite that was a kitchen. There was no furniture in the living room and Cel's confusion just increased.

"What is going on here? Who lives here in a house without furniture?"

"You will be living here during the summer months. I bought this house for us so that you and Ann can be out of the city during the hot months and can enjoy the country, the lake and all that this place has to offer. There are four bedrooms, two downstairs and two upstairs, so there is room for Larry, Estelle and the baby. I thought you would like to pick the furniture. And I think we have enough extra dishes at home to outfit the kitchen. After all, I know you are no longer buying kosher meat, so there is no reason to have two sets of dishes and two sets of pots."

"How do you know that? I thought I was being careful to make you think everything was kosher."

"Remember, I went shopping with you one day after the heart attack and we went to the butcher. The sign in the shop says "Jewish cuts of meat"; it does not state kosher meats. You have been buying meat at a non-kosher store for years, so what's the difference now?"

"Aren't you angry?"

"Anger would not do anything at this point. This is the least of our problems, so let's just move ahead. What do you think about the house?"

"Think? What can I think! I'm shocked. Whatever made you do this?

"The city is just too hot. This will allow Ann to have a place where she can play and swim and have fun."

"How will you manage? It is a long trip to go to work from here."

"I'll come out on the weekends and the rest of the week, I'll stay in the apartment. I just think this place is better than any bungalow colony and in the long run it will cost less than if we rented a bungalow every summer. There are several families here and they all have young children, so you will be able to make friends and have children for Ann to play with."

"What about shopping? Where will we shop for food?"

"On the weekend we can take the car and do your shopping. If you need something during the week there are grocery stores within walking distance. I checked it out before I bought the place and there is a butcher in town who says he will deliver. Now let's look around the house and see what you think of it."

There was no question that Cel really liked the house. The bedrooms downstairs were separated by a big bathroom and the upstairs had its own bathroom. Off the kitchen was a dining area which looked out onto the porch and there was even a basement which could serve as a playroom for Ann. The grounds bordered the lake and there were big trees to offer shade. This was a long way from the fire escape in the city and the air here smelled as fresh as it used to on the farm many years ago. There were few cars on the street, which was a dead end, and the absence of horns blaring was welcomed.

"Where did you get the money for this house?"

"Cel, the question is, do you like it or not? That is the only question that needs to be answered; everything else has been taken care of."

"Of course I like it, but can we afford it?"

"Yes! Now let's go to town and you can order the furniture you want. I checked and they have some very nice furniture in stock and it can be delivered as soon as Monday if you like it. Otherwise you can pick out things and they can be ordered. I really want you and Ann to start enjoying this place as soon as possible. We can even pack the kitchen stuff and bring it out tomorrow."

And so the summer house came to be. Each summer as soon as school let out, Ann and Cel would go to the house in

Bloomingdale New Jersey, and the summer fun would start. Friendships were forged and the children all ran around barefooted. Even Cel had Margie, the butcher's live-in friend, and together they would sit on the porch talking and drinking coffee. For Ann the summers were the most perfect time. With Alice, the girl down the road, and Jackie, Margie's daughter, she swam in the lake, learned how to row a boat, and enjoyed a closeness that did not exist with any of the city kids. But the best time of all was when Morris came out for the weekend. Besides playing and boating together, they continued reading together and exploring new books and magazines. By the time second grade ended, Ann had moved to the top of her class and no one doubted her intelligence, not even her. Probably the greatest manifestation of her intelligence was her ability to make herself invisible when she and Cel were alone at the house. Ann arranged to spend hours playing in the basement with her make-believe family. There was a mother who loved her babies and never hit them like her own mother did; there the children felt safe, while she always was afraid when she was upstairs; there the children did not have to finish all the food on their plates before they could leave the table. Ann never could forget the time she refused to eat her fish because it smelled so bad and Cel would not allow her to leave the dinner table. Luckily, it happened on a night that Morris came out from the city. When he arrived and saw the child crying at the table, he went over to her to try to find out why. When he smelled the fish, he gently picked the child up and took her out onto the porch before he carried the putrid fish to Cel and made her smell it. Ann knew she would pay for her father's kindness and after he left to return to work, Cel did find some offense that triggered her anger and punished Ann for it with the belt she was wearing. The bruises were gone before Morris returned the following weekend and Ann never said a word to her father. This would be the pattern of Ann's life and the child learned to avoid any conflict in hopes of avoiding the painful beatings. She even sought refuge at the houses of her friends, where she was welcomed and where there was never any discussion of Cel's meanness. It would not be until long after Ann grew up that she would learn that Alice's parents were aware of how Cel treated her and how helpless they had felt because they could not change things.

Cel was not different when they were back in the city. If anything, the city was worse for Ann because there was no place to go in the apartment except her own room, and it was harder to be invisible there. When she was in the city, school was her safety net during the day, and at night, her world centered around her father. Surprisingly, Cel did not seem to resent the time the two of them spent together and Ann felt that, if anything, Cel was happy not to have to be with them. Most evenings Cel would go off with Sadie and do her own thing, or sit in the kitchen drinking her brandy. Cel was careful not to hit Ann where the bruises would show and Ann continued to make sure her father would not find out about the beatings because it would only make matters worse. At times, when she was alone with Estelle, Ann would ask why their mother hated her so much.

"She doesn't hate you; it's just that she feels trapped by having a young child again. She is really a very unhappy lady and it is her unhappiness that triggers her anger. She was the same way when I was your age and she was even worse in her treatment of Joey and Norman."

"I don't know Joey or Norman. Daddy never talks about them and Cel just tells me not to ask any questions about it."

"When you're older I promise I will explain everything to you. Now you are too young to know these things and knowing them will not help you to understand your mother. All you have to understand is that she has had a very hard life and it has left her a bitter person who cannot control her own feelings. Sometimes she just cannot help but take her unhappiness out on someone and you are the logical target. Just try to make yourself blend. I know how hard it is because I have been there, done it. I never wanted to stand up to her or to Grandma when I was your age and I always tried to do whatever they wanted me to do."

"I try, but no matter what she is always mad at me. When I couldn't read, she was mad that I embarrassed her by being stupid. Now she tells me I am too smart for my own good and that I think I'm smarter than she is. One minute she is happy that I read in my room, then she is angry that I do not talk to her. I just don't understand."

"Just do whatever she wants whenever she wants you to do it. That is the only way to keep her happy and not angry. Trust me, that is how I survived."

CHAPTER 18

Life continued in its own pattern until Ann's tenth birthday, when she felt the world collapse around her. That summer Morris was diagnosed with cancer of the bones. His pain was torturous and the child spent the entire summer trying to just make her precious father comfortable. Even as a ten-year-old, she knew he would not be physically a part of her life for long as she watched him become thinner and thinner with each passing day. He no longer went to work and passed each day sitting by the side of the lake under the weeping willow tree with the child by his side, and next to her was Skippy, the English sheepdog he had purchased for her the previous summer. He hoped the dog would be her companion long after he knew he would not be there. Her safety and happiness were his only concern as his days ebbed away. He feared what was to become of the child once she was alone with Cel. Despite all their efforts to conceal the abuse the child had sustained, he was all too aware of it. He just hoped the child would be strong enough to be able to become the woman he knew she could be without his help. He used his remaining strength to encourage her to be strong and to use her God given intelligence to protect herself from her mother. Even her tears would not stop him from talking about the future without him. Ann was devastated by her father's illness. Every fiber in her body wanted to die with him. She just did not know how to do such a thing.

School started that fall and Morris was now spending each day in bed, too weak to even walk around the apartment. The summer home was closed and Ann did not know if she would ever see it again. Larry and Estelle had the big old

Buick that had always been Morris' pride and joy and Cel had the prospect of widowhood looming before her once again. Cel did try to do everything possible to keep Morris comfortable, and for that Ann was grateful, as his pain had intensified following the radiation therapy which the doctors tried to use to stop the growth of the tumors. His skin was burnt so much that his back was actually blackened and needed to be swabbed with ointment regularly just to try to control the pain of the burns. Ann would always wonder if it had really been necessary to burn her father so unmercifully, especially since it really did nothing to cure him. She could actually smell the burnt flesh when she would walk into the apartment after being at school all day. It was a smell she would never forget.

Fall passed and winter set in and the gloom of the weather was surpassed by the gloom in the apartment. In December, Morris was rushed to the hospital suffering from malnutrition and dehydration. Seeing her father in the hospital and learning that his weight had dropped to just one hundred pounds from the one hundred and eighty pounds he had always weighed made Ann realize their time together was to be really short.

"Daddy, I know how sick you are and I know you realize it too. Don't you think it is time that you see your sons before it is too late for you and them."

"I sat shivah for Joey and to me he has been dead all these years."

"I know that, but he is not dead and I do have a brother whom I've never met. In fact, I have two brothers whom I do not know. You have two sons and despite everything they and you should have some time together before it can never happen again."

"Go, have your mother call Joey and have him come. Have him get Norman and bring him here too. You are right and wiser than I. I do have to make my peace with them."

And so it happened that Ann met her brothers for the first time. Joey came first and went directly to the hospital. He and his father cried over the lost years and all the stubbornness that had kept them apart. Mistakes were made and regrets were expressed. Both knew there was nothing that could be done to rectify the losses each had suffered, but Joey did promise his father that he would look after Ann and protect her.

Then Joey arranged to have Norman released from the institution so that he could see his father. He went to Buffalo to get Norman and bring him to the hospital. No one was prepared for the anger that Norman had festering within him. He hated Ann because he blamed her for his being put away. He could not stand to look at Cel and resented that his father had chosen them over him. On his second night he left the hospital before Joey and went back to the apartment alone. When Ann answered the door, the little girl was facing a man pointing a knife right at her.

"It's your fault that I was put away! I hate you!" he yelled, so loudly that Sadie, who lived next door, heard the commotion and opened her door.

"Norman, put that knife down right now. Do you hear me?" she commanded.

"I hate her! It's all her fault and now she is killing my father."

"Put the knife down! Ann, go into my apartment right now and close the door."

"But he could hurt you."

"He will not hurt me. Just do as I say, NOW!"

With that the child ran past the brother she did not know and into the apartment next door. Once in there she called her mother at the hospital and hysterically explained what was happening. Needless to say, Joey and Cel rushed back to the apartment and Norman was returned to the institution. Ann would never see Norman again except in recurrent nightmares and though the family kept telling her he would never have hurt her, she would never believe them.

To everyone's surprise, Morris actually rallied and was able to come home from the hospital. He was bedridden, but totally aware mentally, especially when the pain medications were not numbing his senses. It was during those times that he and Ann would be together, with her sitting by his bed listening carefully to every word he spoke. It was during these times that Morris made the child promise to marry a Jewish man. Over and over he would tell her to always remember that if she were to marry out of the religion all future Jews who would be part of their lineage would, in essence, be killed. He would also tell her that the best way to make sure she would keep her promise was to never even date anyone who was not Jewish.

"Remember, my kinda, that promises made to a dying person must be kept," he would tell the child, and she would always reaffirm her promises. The other promise he wanted her to make was that she would get her college degree.

"Follow your heart as to what you study, but make sure you get that degree. No one can take it away from you once you have it and it will always provide you with a sense of independence. You are a smart girl and you can pursue anything that you want to study. I will make sure there is money put aside for your education and no one will be able to use it for anything else. Just remember this promise and do not allow your mother or anyone else to convince you to follow any other path. Even if you fall in love and want to marry, remember that your education must come first. Any man who loves you will want you to do what is best for you.

Education and independence are just as vital for a woman as for a man and that will prove to be even more accurate as time passes. Mark my words. I have seen the roles women have in our society change ever since they had to fill in for the men in the factories during the war."

"Mommy keeps telling me the place for a woman is in the house, taking care of the children and cooking, and that I don't need a fancy education for that."

"Your mother lives in a different time. When she was a girl that was the way society viewed women's roles. Today the picture is changing. I believe women will be lawyers, doctors and professionals by the time you graduate from college. Of course, no one can dispute the importance of teaching as a career. It is wonderful if you have a family because you can be off from work when the children are home from school. That is something that you cannot do if you are a doctor; sick people do not take school vacations."

"Right now there is no way I could say what I would like to be. I feel that I would like to help people who are as sick you are and maybe be able to cure them."

"You have to be really tough to work with cancer patients. Most of us do not survive. Think about it long and hard because to work with death and dying takes its toll on a person. I saw it while I was in the hospital. I really feel sorry for those doctors. They try so hard to help and there is so little they can do."

"Daddy, please do not give up. Keep fighting to get better. I love you so much."

"If you love me so much, you will know when the time comes to let go and let the suffering end. I will always be in your heart and if there is any way I can protect you, my spirit will be there to do so. Just never feel guilty about wishing for the end of the suffering because that is the ultimate expression of love."

"Will I ever be able to do that?"

"When my pain becomes too great for the medications to relieve it and my mind shuts out the present, you will wish for the end and you will know that would be my wish as well."

October became November and Thanksgiving came and went without the usual turkey dinner because there was no one who felt like eating in the household. With each passing day, Morris grew weaker and the periods when he was able to speak with Ann grew shorter. Also the intervals between pain medications became shorter and shorter. Cel refused to listen to the doctors and just gave Morris the medication whenever he requested it. Her argument was that it was more important to keep him comfortable than to worry that he might become addicted to the medication. In her mind, any addiction would be too short to matter. Of course, sometimes it was difficult to actually get the prescriptions but, to her credit, she did keep pressuring the doctors to make them see her position.

It was shortly after Thanksgiving that Cel told Ann they would have to have a nurse in the apartment to help care for Morris, who now required attention twenty-four hours a day. Cel hired a male nurse and instructed Ann to always lock her bedroom door at night. The child could not understand why she was to lock the door, but decided not to challenge her mother on the issue. She was just happy to have someone in the apartment to help her father. By the start of the New Year it was obvious even to the child that her father would not be physically part of her life for much longer. He was now too weak to hold any type of conversation and when he was awake his pain made him groan in despair. The pain medications no longer seemed to help him and his back turned even blacker where it had been burned by the radiation therapy. In her heart she knew the time had come to let him go and though she cried herself to sleep each night, she prayed to God to end his suffering. Now Cel would even forbid her from going into his room and she would be beaten if she disobeyed her mother. One afternoon when the nurse was off for a few hours, Cel had to leave the apartment to walk the dog and she ordered Ann not to go into her father's room while she was downstairs. Ann was in her bedroom at the time and could hear her father calling for a glass of water. His cries became louder and louder and the child just wanted to run to him, but was afraid Cel would return and find her in his room. It seemed like an eternity before Cel returned to find the child crying in one room and Morris crying in the other. It was at that point in her life that Ann made a promise to herself never to allow anyone to dictate to her what her actions should be, no matter what the consequences might be. She would forever never forgive herself for not going to her father with a glass of water and would be plagued by nightmares recalling her terror.

Morris died on January 15, 1954. The day before he lapsed into an extremely deep sleep that was punctuated by occasional groans. He did not even awaken for the normal doses of the pain medications, and even Ann knew the end was really near and that it would be wrong to try to awaken him and prolong his agony. The child sat at the bedside through the day, refusing to go to school or to even eat in the kitchen. She finally fell asleep herself around one in the morning and Cel asked the nurse to carry her into her own room. At three in the morning the death rattle started and within the hour Morris had taken his last breath. Cel waited until the body was cleaned and looked as good as possible before she went to wake up Ann so that the child could spend a few moments with Morris before the hearse came. Even Cel was moved by the child's devotion and understood the loss would be most intense for Ann.

"Remember, my child, that your father did not want tears at his funeral. You will not cry and carry on. That would be disrespectful of his memory," Cel told the child as she approached her father's bed. "We will hold the funeral until Joey gets here, so there will be visiting hours tonight and tomorrow. People will come to pay their respects and you have to always be respectful. Sometimes people talk about other things while they are there; remember they do not share your grief, and many of them expected this and most hoped for it long before now."

"Are you telling me to expect people to laugh and that you expect me to appear happy?"

"No one expects you to appear to be happy. Just understand that others do not feel just like you do."

"I know that you don't feel the same as I do. You probably could not wait for this to be over so that you could be free to go on with your own life."

"That is really mean. I did everything I could to keep him comfortable and to make sure things were done properly for him. No wife could have done more than I did and you know it. And just for your information, I will miss your father very much. We have been married for twenty years and I was accustomed to his ways. In many ways, I would say that I had grown to love and respect the man. Few people are as honorable as he was. Once he gave his word it was as good as gold."

"I am glad to hear that you actually had feelings for him. It always seemed to me that you two just lived together in some type of an arrangement and that you really did not like him, let alone love him."

"Henry, Estelle's father, was the love of my life. I cannot deny that, and your father knew that from the start and accepted it. And, yes, we did have times when things between us were not perfect, but ever since his heart attack, things have been really good between us and our feelings for each other have definitely deepened. You and I share a deep grief and we cannot judge each other's sorrow; it is not a competition."

"Well, I cannot promise I will not cry." And with those words the child turned her back on her mother and walked over to her father's bed, where she took his hand into hers and buried her face against his body. Her sobs could be heard throughout the apartment and Cel elected to leave her alone and hoped, she would get all the hysteria out of her system before the ambulance came.

That night Cel took Ann to the funeral home. Next to the casket sat the crier, who had been hired to cry and stay with the casket all night so that it would never be left alone. There were people there from the factory and many who had worked with Morris years ago. Everyone went to Cel to express their condolences and few even noticed the child who sat away from her mother as though she were observing the event rather than participating in it. At one point Ann had to go to the bathroom. She tried to get Cel's attention, but that proved to be impossible, so she left the room and went in search of the rest room. After asking directions to the nearest ladies' room, she went the way she thought it was only to find herself in a room filled with caskets. It was a large room and it was very dark. Within moments she became disoriented and could not even find her way out of the room. Perspiration rolled over her body as she sank to the floor and just cried and cried. How long she was in that room, she had no idea. All she knew was that suddenly the lights came on and there were people standing around her and trying to comfort her. Who they were and what they were saying did not make any sense to her, but she was aware that she was being led to the ladies' room where Estelle was trying to dry her body and wash her face. Eventually the shaking stopped and Estelle took her home. It was then that a new nightmare was born: a nightmare that would plague her well into adulthood.

The funeral, shiva and all the rituals of death took place and Ann went through it all like a zombie. Little did she realize that the adults were fearful that she would be permanently mentally affected by her experience in the casket room and that everyone was making every effort possible to protect her psyche. All she knew was that the world as she knew it had ended and she would never again be a little girl.

CHAPTER 19

Days became weeks, weeks months, and before Ann realized it was time to light the yartzeit candle marking the year's anniversary of Morris' death. She could not believe that she had actually survived a year without her father, but she had. Her grades were really good at school, and she even found herself laughing when she was with Joanie, Debbie and Helen and the other girls who lived across the street. The only disappointment that occurred in that year was her visit to Joey's. To say she felt uncomfortable with his wife was a marked understatement. They really had nothing in common. Mae was a real Southern person, who seemed preoccupied with her appearance but could not have a conversation with Ann about anything. Unfortunately, the polio epidemic of 1954 further hampered the visit because all the community pools were closed and there was little to do during the day while Joey was at work. Ann was really happy to return to New York at the end of August, but was again saddened when she learned that polio had struck 56 Bennett Avenue and many of her friends had contracted the disease. The only one who had lasting paralysis was Joanie and by August she too was home and doing rehabilitation. Ann spent many hours with her, helping her to strengthen her unaffected limbs and encouraging her. It was as if the two injured girls developed a bond that helped each through the healing period.

The other incident that completely stressed Ann during that year was that Cel put her beloved Skippy down. During the summer, while Ann was in Texas, Cel had gone to the mountains to stay with her cousin, Helen. Helen had a really big dog who had pushed Skippy into a stone wall, injuring his hind quarter. Cel claimed that the dog was in a great deal of pain and that the vet could do nothing to help him. That was her justification for putting the dog to sleep without giving Ann an opportunity to even come to grips with the situation. For Ann, the incident was just another example of her mother's insensitivity. Ann knew she would always wonder if Cel had told her the truth about the dog or if it had just been more convenient for her to dispose of yet another burden. Of course, there was no discussing her feelings with Cel and Ann knew there was nothing she could do about the situation, so she elected to ignore it and just file her feelings away with all the other nightmares she had survived.

It was during the fall of that first year that Ann started going to Estelle and Larry's house every weekend. It was fun to be with the little children and Ann would help with the laundry and the kitchen cleanups to justify her being there. Best of all, she was away from Cel on the days when there was no school and that seemed to be a relief for both of them. Little did she know that her being away was affording Cel the opportunity to date. Cel had actually met several widowers through Sadie, who was acting as the matchmaker. The men were a good deal older than Cel, but her main criteria was that the man be wealthy and that was the most important attribute to her. She had narrowed the dating field to two candidates by late fall. First there was Joe Ravitz and then there was Morris Atman. Joe was the younger of the two, but he did not have Morris' wealth. The big stumbling block was Ann. Morris did not want to get involved with a woman with a young child and he wanted Ann sent to boarding school if marriage became a possibility. Cel knew that Ann would never accept such a proposal and that there would be no way to force her to go to a sleep-away school. Even Estelle was vehemently against the idea. Cel knew she would have to use all her skills to get Morris to accept the child as part of the package. It was lucky that he still enjoyed sex and she still knew how to use it to her advantage. Cel knew she was prostituting herself for money but she also knew she needed to have the money. After all, right after Morris' death she even had to take in boarders to make ends meet. Morris' illness had consumed much of their funds and that, after the bankruptcy, had really depleted the cash supply. The estate had to go to probate because of money left for Norman's care, so things were a real mess for Cel. Having two boarders in the apartment had been a real nightmare. Cel and Ann were sleeping in the former living room and each of the women had a bedroom. The situation was next to impossible for Ann. She hated sharing the bathroom and constantly complained about the way the women smelled. There was no making the child understand the situation. Money was not something she cared about or understood. Ann only knew one thing and that was that she would never live with strangers in her home again, no matter what. Cel knew her feelings and knew that because of them, she would never be willing to go to boarding school.

All in all, the year following Morris' death had been a hard one for Ann and deep down she was proud she had survived it. No one in the family knew that she had often thought about killing herself to escape the problems. She had even gone so far as to research how many aspirins it would take to do the job. But she had not done it and in a way she was proud of herself for surviving it all. Her father would be proud of her and she knew that for a fact. He had often told her that life's experiences would make her stronger and she knew he was right. There were other factors in her strength. Among them was her relationship with two dedicated teachers, Mr. Shapiro and Mr. Shore. They had an open door for Ann to come and talk to them, and they encouraged her to face each problem as it presented itself. It was because of them that Ann was able to do so well at school and she knew she would be forever grateful to them for their encouragement. Even at eleven years of age, she knew she would never be able to thank them enough.

CHAPTER 20

Ann started to notice changes in the apartment. The changes started before the unveiling of her father's stone and escalated following the event. It was as if Cel wanted to erase all signs of his existence. Ann found this hurtful but decided not to make an issue of it because she viewed it as hopeless. Instead she started to take small mementos of her father and hide them in her dresser. First there was his sweater, then his prayer shawl bag. His metal social security card with his name engraved on it became part of her wallet. Her search for things that belonged to her father was made easier as Cel was out more and more in the evenings. Cel would tell Ann she was going to Sadie's house but Ann suspected that was not the case. Each night Cel would dress up and make sure her makeup was just so. Ann was happy to have the time to herself, so she did not challenge her mother, nor did she really care if Cel was seeing other men. For Ann, life was forever changed by her father's death and instead of growing closer to Cel, she felt that in reality she was an orphan without either a mother or a father and she would have to make a life for herself without any help. Even Estelle did not fully understand how she felt. Estelle had also lost her father but she remained close to Cel. Ann, on the other hand, never felt close to Cel, nor did she ever believe that Cel loved her as a mother should. So why should she pretend things were different than they were? As for her friends from school, they had no frame of reference to understand Ann's feelings. They all had both parents and lived in homes where they felt loved. There was no point in confiding in them because they could not understand. So Ann, at the age of eleven, learned to live within herself and to make things that were important to her happen without relying on anyone else.

It was just before her twelfth birthday that Cel made Ann sit down one evening and told her that she had decided to remarry.

"I am going to marry a really nice man whom I want you to meet. His name is Morris, but he is not like your father, and I really think we will have a nice life with him."

"Maybe I am missing something. But how can you plan to marry someone I have never even met? How do you know he will like me and if he does not like me, what will happen?"

"We have discussed this and he has agreed that you will live with us and you will have your own room. Originally, he wanted to send you to boarding school, but you were so against the idea when we talked about it and I do not want to force you to live away from home."

"My God, isn't that big of you. First you tell me that you are going to marry a man I have never met, and then you tell me he really does not want me to live with you but has made a major concession and will allow that. Now you expect me to feel good about this whole thing."

"Look, you are young. Eventually you will have a life of your own. Hopefully, you will find someone who will love you and take care of you. I am no longer young, nor am I beautiful. This is my chance to have a good life and to not be alone. All I am asking is that you make the best of the situation and accept Morris and his generosity. I discussed this with Estelle and she is prepared to allow you to continue to spend weekends at her house if you do not want to stay with Morris and me. That way you can be with the children. But before you decide anything, I want you to meet Morris and to see the beautiful apartment where we will live. Just think, we will not have to have the ladies live with us any longer."

"Now we are moving! What is going to happen to all of our things?"

"Morris' apartment is completely furnished. We will sell the things that are here and just take our personal belongings."

"This explains why you have gotten rid of so many of my father's things."

"Your father is gone. I cannot live in a shrine to his memory and neither can you. Now we must move forward."

"I will never forget my father and all the things he stood for. You cannot force me to do that."

"No one is forcing you to forget your father. I am just moving on with my life and I want you to do the same. Let's face reality, you will grow up and have your own friends, and eventually you will marry. I am the one who will be left alone. I have the chance to have someone with whom I can do things and go places. It would be extremely selfish of you to deny me this opportunity. It is probably the last time I will be able to attract a man."

And so Ann learned of Cel's plans. There was nothing she could do but accept what was happening and try to make the best of the situation. Right there and then she decided that she would get away from them as much as possible.

That June Cel and Morris Atman were married by the Justice of the Peace in City Hall. It was a simple ceremony with Ann, Estelle, Larry and Sadie present. Morris' son Jerry and his wife Faye were supposed to be there, but they did not appear and no explanation was given. After the ceremony, everyone went to a nearby restaurant for dinner and then Morris and Cel left for their honeymoon, leaving Ann to stay with Estelle. Ann remained exceptionally quiet throughout the day and refused to discuss her feelings when Estelle attempted to speak to her that evening. It was during the course of this day that Ann learned she would be going to camp in one week and that she would be spending the summer there while Cel completed the move from the only real home she had ever known to Morris' apartment on Bennett Avenue and 187th Street, just eight blocks away and a totally different world for the twelve-year-old child.

Before leaving for camp, Ann carefully packed her own belongings that were to be moved. Included were the porcelain cat she had salvaged when the Jersey house was sold, the few things she had hidden that were her father's, including his prayer shawl bag, bible, his favorite sweater, and the menorah he had used to celebrate Chanukah. In the box went the last dress he had designed. Her father had said that one day soon she would be big enough to wear it, but she knew she would never do so. She would always keep it in her memory box. Also in the box went the pictures of Skippy, the dog she so loved, and the one Cel conveniently allowed to be hurt and then put to sleep so she would not have to deal with its care. Ann could not help but feel that Cel would get rid of her if she could.

Camp that summer was horrible. Ann felt totally out of place. The other girls called home but she felt she had no home to call. Mail call was always a disappointment, so she stopped going and on visiting day, she just spent the entire day in her bunk. Food and sleep became her best friends, and soon her clothes were too tight and she was ashamed to even attempt to participate in the activities. However, the worst part of that summer was the day she returned to the city. Cel met her at the bus on Fordham Road and looked at her with disgust.

"You have to weigh over one hundred and fifty pounds. What in hell's name were you eating all summer?"

"What difference does it make to you? You don't care about me. You never even bothered to write to me all summer."

"I was very busy getting things together and making a life for us."

"You were making a life for yourself. I know I am excess baggage that you are stuck with. Let's try to be honest with each other."

"You are an ungrateful, spoiled brat."

"You are an unfit mother. I will never forgive you for the way you treated me this summer."

When they arrived at the apartment Ann walked into the entrance hall and saw Morris sitting in a chair in front of the window in the living room. He never acknowledged her. Cel continued showing her around the apartment, which was much smaller than the one she had grown up in. There were two bedrooms, one bathroom, a living room, a hallway that served as a dining room, and a small kitchen with a table in it. The bedroom that was to be her room was so small that there was little available floor space. In it were a bed, a small desk and a half dresser. There was a free-standing closet that contained her clothes, most of which would not nearly fit her anymore. She was relieved to find her memory box on the floor of the closet. At least she had that. On top of the dresser was the television her father had purchased. Luckily there was a window in the room or else she knew she would go crazy in the tight quarters.

"Put your stuff away and when you are ready we will have dinner. I made your favorite chicken for dinner and we can all eat together tonight."

"What does that mean?"

"Well, Morris and I have decided that you will eat in your room some nights so that we can have dinner alone."

"I'll eat in my room tonight as well. The last thing I want to do is to intrude on you and your wonderful husband."

"Your sister was never this mean and impossible."

"My father never made her feel like an intruder! He has made it perfectly clear that he does not want any part of me. He did not even acknowledge me when I came into this horrible place. You can rest assured that I will have as little as possible to say to him. You sold out your own daughter."

"Don't you speak to me in that tone, young lady."

"The truth hurts. I've had all summer to get used to the idea."

With that, Cel turned her back and walked out of the room, leaving Ann to crumble in tears on the bed. She made sure to muffle her tears into the pillow, as she did not want Cel to know she was not as tough as she wanted to appear. She was now a homeless orphan, but she knew she had to get hold of herself if she were going to survive, and survive she would. She owed that much to her father's memory.

In the days and weeks ahead, Cel continued to cut Ann off from all of her father's family. She made it clear to them that she did not want them to have any contact with her or Ann. Estelle tried to give Ann some stability and even started talking to her about her weight and appearance. On weekends, Ann would go to Estelle's house, which was now in Norwalk, Connecticut. There Ann would play with Paul and Jeannie, Estelle's children. Laundry and ironing were also Ann's responsibility when she was there and she was happy to help out because she was away from Cel and Morris. And so life developed a routine where time was filled with school and Estelle's family, and no one even seemed to notice that the child was developing into a young woman. Ann's figure was filling out in just the right places and the excess weight was coming off, though it was hard to see this as she continued wearing baggy clothes and seemed totally unconcerned with her appearance. It wasn't until one evening when Ann was returning from babysitting for a neighbor that Estelle realized she had a young woman in her charge. Estelle had been asleep on the couch when she was awoken by Ann's screams. She ran to the front door and in the dim light she was horrified to see her neighbor with his penis out, trying to get Ann to touch him.

"What the hell are you doing? This is my baby sister. Get out of here, but mark my words, if you come near her again, I will tell your wife! Ann, go inside this minute."

"I don't understand why he tried to make me touch him."

"Come. It is time we discuss how horrible men are."

And so, Ann learned that men only want one thing from girls and that if they get their way, they keep pestering for more. Estelle coached her sister to never allow a man to touch her and to never touch his private parts.

"Always remember men are disgusting creatures and do dirty things to a woman. The whole thing is horrible and filthy."

"Even if you love someone?"

"Love is a relative term. There is a pure love that can exist as long as there is no sex. As soon as a man starts poking his thing around it is all filthy dirty."

"Are you saying you don't love Larry?"

"Larry is my husband. I have to do things with him because it is my duty but, believe me, I keep those things to a minimum. It is easy to do because after he has those martinis, he usually just falls asleep and leaves me alone. Unlike Cel, I don't like sex, and if you are smart you will not start doing it. You are becoming a pretty young woman and men will try to get you to do things. You have to be tough and not give in. Am I making myself clear?"

"I didn't do anything tonight. Jack said he wanted to bring me home and the next thing I knew he was trying to force me to touch him."

"If he ever tries that again, I'll have his head. You just make sure you are never alone with him. That is your best defense. But remember, he is just like all the men out there. They only have one thing on their minds and you must make sure you are above that. If you give in, they will not respect you and they will continue to take advantage of you. You are vulnerable because they know you are unhappy and they think you are looking for love and attention. Added to that, you are young and pretty."

"Cel keeps telling me that I am ugly and have no sex appeal. In fact, she keeps telling me that I have as much sex appeal as a wet noodle. I'm confused."

"Don't listen to her. She is old and very jealous of your looks and youth. She used to do the same thing to me. It is her way of keeping you from her husband."

"Believe me; she has nothing to fear in that department. I hate Morris and if he even as much as touches me, I'd punch him."

"Keep that thought, but apply it to all men."

CHAPTER 21

Time is such a relative entity. It passes sometimes quickly and sometimes all too slowly. The time Ann had to spend in the apartment always seemed like an eternity. She would read and watch television, always with the bedroom door closed and the dresser pulled in front of it so neither Cel nor Morris could open the door. Most weekends when she did not go to Estelle, she would babysit for the children in the building. That way she earned money for things she needed. Morris continued to take her social security check and Cel refused to give her an allowance, so she was anxiously awaiting her fourteenth birthday so she could get a real job and be able to buy lunch with the other girls at school. Ann vowed to herself that she would never have to rely on anyone but herself for money and would never answer to anyone about how she would spend her money.

Summer came and Ann refused to return to camp. It was decided that she would spend the majority of the summer with Estelle, as Cel and Morris were going to Europe. For Ann, Europe was not far enough away. There were days during that summer that would be defined as blissful. Larry and Ann would spend hours together listening to music in his study. He patiently explained the differences between modern jazz and regular jazz. The Modern Jazz Quartet became Ann's all-time favorite record, and she would sit and listen while Larry drank martini after martini and eventually fall asleep on the couch. Sometimes he would take Ann and the children to the beach. Norwalk had a lovely public beach where on a clear day you could see all the way across the Sound. The waves were never too high, and Ann loved swimming and playing with the children. Sometimes she and Larry would sit together on the blanket and just talk. Ann came to realize that he was an extremely intelligent man but, deep down, also an extremely unhappy person.

"Why do you drink so many martinis every night?"

"They help me escape the realities."

"What realities do you need to escape from? You have a good home, two really great kids and you love Estelle."

"Don't get me wrong, I do love Estelle. She is a good person and no one can deny that she is beautiful, but she is cold and it is really hard to get close to her."

"You mean sex, right?"

"Sex is only part of it. She is a person who wants a set lifestyle. It has to be her way or no way. The house, the job, our friends – I just have to go along with it all."

"I thought you really liked your job. It is rather impressive to be the controller for a large company. What type of job would you prefer?"

"I always wanted to teach, preferably at the college level. I like academics but academics do not pay enough for the lifestyle Estelle wants. Hell, we would still be in an apartment in the city if I had become a college professor."

"I hope I never do that to someone I love. I would like to think that I would encourage someone to do his own thing. But then again, I know I will never be just a housewife. I will always work and earn my own money so that I can control how I spend it. I hate having to account to Cel if I spend money."

"Estelle never liked working. That is why we had Paul so quickly. She wanted to be able to stay home with a baby."

"I am going to go to college, no matter what. I really think that I want to be a doctor and help people who have cancer. Maybe someday we will be able to save someone so that they will not die like my dad. It would be really great if I can help prevent some other girl from losing her father."

"Hold onto your dream and don't let anyone come between you and your realizing your dream. You are smart enough to be a doctor or anything else that you set your mind on being. I promise you, I will help you. You can count on me."

"That's really nice. But I don't think that I will need to count on anyone. I looked into the city college system and I can go there for fifteen dollars a semester. If I continue living with Cel and I get a job, I will be able to afford the books and all. I am planning on looking for a job after school come this winter, and hopefully I will be able to save some of the money."

"Here you are, just a kid, and you are already planning for something four years away. What type of job are you going to look for?"

"Anything that pays. Don't worry, I am not planning on doing anything wrong and I will not compromise myself. Estelle keeps telling me how men are after young girls and how I have to be careful."

"There she is right! You are fourteen going on forty. I wish I knew someone in the city who would hire you."

"Something will turn up. I just know it. I also know that I will never tell Morris how much money I make. He will probably demand a percentage as room and board. Do you know that bastard takes my whole social security check? He is supposed to be such a rich man. Why does he need my eighty dollars a month?"

"People can be strange."

"I just wish you could be happier. You are a real special person and I cannot believe that all those martinis can be good for you."

"I made my bed, so to speak. I have no choices. Our lifestyle is expensive and you know how Estelle loves to shop. There is no way I could earn less and keep her happy. But don't you worry about me. I can control my drinking and it will not interfere with anything."

Ann hoped with all of her heart that Larry would prove to be right, but she had her doubts. His behavior was deteriorating and he would get angry at the smallest thing after he had been drinking. She also noticed that different people were coming to parties at Larry and Estelle's house. Sometimes, at the end of the party, Ann would notice that the couples leaving were not the same as the ones who came to the party. She had asked Estelle about it but was never given a straight answer. She would just say that these were business associates of Larry's and she had to entertain them. It was important for Larry's job. Ann believed that was part of the explanation but it did not answer her question. She really hated it when Estelle would treat her like a child. But, then again, it was none of her business, so she just stayed away from all of the people at the parties.

Survival is a basic instinct for all of us. Ann came to realize that her only way out of her life was to get a decent education so that she could earn enough money not to have to depend on anyone. School was the focus of her attention and she really loved it there. Luckily, she had some really good teachers who took a personal interest in her and encouraged her. After school she would babysit to earn spending money and her evenings were spent doing her homework, reading and watching the television that her father had purchased. Every night she had dinner in her room because Morris still did not want her to eat with them in the kitchen. After dinner, Ann would close her bedroom door and move her dresser in front of it so that neither Morris nor Cel could get into the room. This really infuriated Morris and most nights he would bang on the closed door when he got up to go the bathroom. Ann would just pretend that she did not hear him, and eventually he would tire of doing it and go back to sleep. What Ann could not understand was that Cel also pretended not to hear the banging and never did or said anything to make him stop. Ann never did discuss this with Cel because there was just no point to it. Ann knew her mother would never be there to defend her and in any argument Cel would choose Morris' side over Ann's.

The best times in the apartment on Bennett Avenue were when Cel and Morris would go on trips. Despite Ann being just fourteen years old, they would leave her alone in the apartment. Ann learned how to fix simple meals and take care of herself. It was great eating at the kitchen table, watching television in the living room and sleeping with her door wide open. Margie, the neighbor for whom Ann babysat, would check on her, and every once in a while Sadie would call just to make sure there were no friends in the apartment, as if Ann would ever consider bringing a friend there. Ann still had a few friends who lived up on Bennett Avenue across from the building where she had lived before. There were Joanie, Helen and Debbie, and they all knew Ann's story and would include her whenever possible. Joanie's mother would also invite Ann for dinner and tried to make her feel as if she was part of their family. But the best thing was being able to laugh and joke with the girls and giggle about boys. Joanie was as shy as Ann because she had had polio and had a deformed arm and leg, but despite that she kept up with the other girls and no one ever seemed aware of her deformity. She was a constant reminder of the terrible polio epidemic of '54 and she would carry the scars for life. Amazingly, Joanie continued to consider herself lucky. Others who had her type of polio, which crossed the body, had their lungs affected and were locked into iron lungs for the remainder of their lives. Newspapers continually showed pictures of those poor young people who would not have any opportunity to enjoy life. For Ann, Joanie was not only a friend but an inspiration. If she could overcome her problems, than surely Ann could survive living with Morris and Cel.

There were other friends who influenced Ann. Marian and Evelyn were sisters who had also lost their father and their mother had remarried. The difference was that their stepfather treated them as if they were his daughters and, together with their mother, did everything possible to make a good life for the girls. Ann was welcomed into this environment and would often find comfort in their apartment. It would be Marian who would start high school with Ann the following fall, as all of her other friends were older and ahead of her in school. High school was a frightening thought for both girls. Leaving Junior High School 115, where Ann had established good relationships with such teachers as Mr. Shapiro and Mr. Shore, and having to face all new teachers and new programs in a much less personal environment was scary and at the same time exciting. Once in George Washington High School, Ann knew she would be able to get a real job after school and further reduce her dependency on Cel.

Life fell into its own routine and the school year passed quickly. Before she knew it, it was time for the junior high school prom. Unfortunately, George asked Ann to go to the prom with him and that was impossible for her. She had promised her father that she would never date anyone outside of the Jewish religion and George was Greek. Rather than hurt his feelings, Ann told him she would not be able to attend the prom as she had to go out of town that weekend. It was a really hard decision for her to make, but she knew she would not be able to go against her promise to her father and

George was such a nice person that she could not bear to hurt his feelings by going with someone else.

Solace came from eating and sleeping. Sleeping was the greatest escape and Ann came to realize that her dreams were a far better place to be than the reality of her life. Even spending the weekends with Estelle were no longer a happy time for her. She was beginning to feel like a maid, taking care of the children, doing the laundry and cleaning up after the children finished playing. Larry was becoming more and more withdrawn. He was drinking more and more, often not even coming out of his den for dinner and then stumbling up the stairs to bed. Ann could hear Estelle and Larry arguing almost every night, and the arguments were usually about his being drunk and not giving the children any attention. Some mornings he would not even get up to go to work and Estelle would call his office and tell them that he was sick. Ann felt sorry for him and was frustrated that she could do nothing to help. He still considered her a mere child and he would not discuss his drinking or anything with her or anyone else. That summer Larry drank and Ann ate, and by the start of school her weight had gone over one hundred and sixty pounds and none of her school clothes even remotely fit. Cel was once again appalled by Ann's appearance when she came home from Europe.

"Look at you. You look like a fat pig. No one will want to have anything to do with you. Do you realize you have the sex appeal of a wet noodle?" she yelled at Ann.

"I don't need to have sex appeal. I have no interest in doing those dirty things. I am not like you."

"Don't be stupid. You have to start thinking of marriage and security. You will need someone to take care of you, you stupid girl."

"I plan on taking care of myself. I never want to have to have a man or anyone take care of me. I don't want to be like you and sell myself."

With that Cel slapped her across the face.

"Don't you ever speak to me like that again. I have had to make choices, first to take care of your sister and then to take care of you. You are an ungrateful child. Without me marrying Morris we would still have boarders in our apartment and there would be no money for anything. Your father's illness used up a lot of the money and more was lost when the factory went bankrupt."

"You could have gotten a job. Lots of mothers work."

"I do not have the skills to earn enough money. Someday you will appreciate what I have done to provide you with a decent home."

"This is not a decent home for me. You have provided yourself with what you wanted but you have never considered me. You married a man who cannot stand me and does everything in his power to make me miserable and you do nothing to prevent it. What kind of mother are you? Where are you when he bangs on my door in the middle of night? Are you going to tell me that you do not hear the commotion? You have not even stood up to him to allow me to eat at the kitchen table. You are a horrible excuse for a mother. Don't you even think about slapping me again. The next time you raise your hand to me I will respond in kind. I am not afraid of you and don't you forget that for one minute."

"You are an ungrateful, selfish child. Why can't you be more like your sister? She would never speak to me the way you just did."

"Yeah – look at my sister. She is in a loveless marriage to a drunk. She is almost as pathetic as you are. Maybe if she were a little bit more independent, her life would be better. I know one thing, I will get the best possible education I can get and I will have a career so that I never need to have anyone take care of me. If I ever marry, it will be because I love the man, not because he will take care of me. There is no way I will be a whore like you."

With those words, Ann ran into her room and slammed the door. She quickly pushed the bureau in front of the door so that Cel could not open it, and stood there trembling. She did not know what possessed her to say the things she said, but deep down she was relieved to have them out in the open. Love for her mother was not something she would ever be able to feel and she knew she was totally alone. Estelle had her hands full and could not offer any support. In many ways she was even more needy, what with two children and a big house to support. Somehow, Ann knew she would get through high school and into college despite her family. One thing she would do immediately was look for a job after school so that she would have more money than she could earn babysitting. If she did not have to go to Cel for money, it would be one more way to limit her contact with her mother.

Many years later, Ann would look back on her decisions and realize that she had changed the direction of her life on that day. Yes, she did get a job for the summer and for after school during the winter. Being able to buy the clothes she needed and the necessary school supplies gave her confidence. As for college, she researched the city college system and knew she would qualify to go to City College, and there she could get a degree that would have value no matter what career objective she decided to follow. She no longer spent her time sleeping and eating, and the added pounds quickly evaporated so that she began to feel better about herself, though she still made no effort to date or to cultivate new friends at school. She always felt that she could not have a date pick her up at her apartment, nor could she have friends over to just hang out. When Cel and Morris were home, Ann would plan to go to the library on the days she was not at work so she could limit her contact with them. As for Morris, Ann refused to even speak to him. At night, when he continued to bang on her door, she would not even acknowledge him, but she continued to make sure there was no way Cel could deny that he was doing it. Cel refused to attempt to stop him and the resentment that Ann felt toward her mother was beyond any other emotion. Ann often wondered what Morris would do if he had been able to get into her room. During the day he never made any sexual advances and she wondered if he was disturbing her simply to upset her as he undoubtedly knew he was doing. Either way Ann was taking no chances. Every night the dresser was pulled in front of the door and all the books in the room were placed on top of it to increase its weight.

One other major change happened during the summer of Ann's senior year in high school. She was at work when a young man came to the office to study with the doctor for whom she was working. They became friends and took long walks together, often stopping at the Nicholas' Ice Cream Parlor to share a sundae. He came from a poor but close family, and Ann was hesitant to divulge her life to him because she was sure he would not understand, and since theirs was a friendship and nothing more, she saw no reason to tell him. Little did she know that the friendship would continue to develop into a very special love and that the two of them would marry when she was eighteen and he was twenty-one. He showed her his love and caring even though at times she was afraid to open up and let him know her feelings for fear that she would be rejected or that the love being offered would have a price to pay attached to it.

Despite being married, and being welcomed into a whole family of people, Ann pursued her college education and changed her objectives to become a teacher instead of a doctor, because she now knew that she wanted a family of her own and felt that being a doctor precluded her from ever having children. Dave was going to become a podiatrist, so it was essential that she complete college as quickly as possible so she could get a real paying job and help him to have time to complete his studies. He was working nights loading trucks for UPS and going to school by day. But despite it all, Ann was happier than she had been since her father died. She and Dave had a one-bedroom apartment in a walk-up building in Washington Heights. It was a second-floor apartment and it was so dark that you could not tell if it was sunny or raining, but that did not matter to them as it was their apartment, their own place and a place that the door to the bedroom did not have to be closed.

Once Ann was married, Cel attempted to reconstruct her relationship with her. She would call and visit the apartment, often bringing Morris with her. Dave encouraged Ann to try to have a relationship with her mother and to attempt to forgive her for all that had transpired. There was no way he could ever truly understand Ann's feelings as his family only showed unconditional love for each other. Slowly, Ann began to accept their love and to realize that there were no strings attached to that love. They did not want anything in return except to have her love them. In particular, his Dad was very gentle with Ann and slowly showed her his feelings were pure and kindly. He was always there to say the right thing, to make her laugh when she was sad, and to make her see the other side when she was upset with someone. Gradually, Ann began to feel as though she had another chance at having a father. It was then that she stopped addressing him as Al and started calling him Dad, a name she never thought she would be able to use for anyone. It took longer for her to be able to address Dave's Mom as Mom, but gradually that too happened. Dave's Mom always considered everyone else before herself. Ann was not used to this type of person and Gert took her time trying to cultivate their relationship.

Besides getting married, graduating from college was a major milestone for Ann. As she accepted her diploma she felt the weight of her entire family on her shoulders. She was the first to ever graduate from college and the first to take a job as a professional. She could feel her father smiling down on her and she knew she would forever cherish the moment. Dave, too, was all smiles. He knew how hard she had worked to achieve the degree in just three years instead of the usual four, and knew she did that so she could give him time to study for his medical boards and complete the last year of podiatry school. They were a team and, as he stood watching her accept her diploma, he vowed he would always do everything in his power to make her life better; to love and cherish her was an easy thing for him, as each day he saw another special part of her personality and grew to value her love as she had grown to value his and accept it. It had been such a battle to gain her trust, but he was so happy he had. All he could think was how lucky he was to have such a beautiful and independent woman as a wife and partner. Ann, in turn, knew how lucky she was to have someone who could accept her as she was and who could put up with the demons that still lived within her. As independent as she was during the day, she still refused to sleep without a light on, hated ever having the door to the bedroom closed, and became inconsolable on the fifteenth of January every year.

Ann's transformation from student to teacher was a rapid one. Since she graduated in January, three days after graduation from college she began teaching in the south Bronx. It was a very poor neighborhood, where crime was rampant and where the majority of the children were from single-parent homes and were on welfare. Being the newest teacher meant that she would have the worst class. Ann was assigned to the second lowest class in the grade. The children were non-readers and most of them had police records. Ann had been hired to teach math, even though she had graduated with a degree as an English teacher, but jobs were few and hard to find and she gratefully accepted the position. It did not take her long to realize that she would not be teaching math as she had always known it to be taught; instead she would attempt to teach math as it applied to the lives of her students. How to calculate the cost of something and determine if you could afford to buy it; how to count the change you were given or to even count the money in your pocket; these were the concepts she wanted to get across to the children. To know how much the subway cost was important and she soon found out that many of the children would sneak onto the train, not because they did not have the money, but because they did not know how to count it out. Middle-class values had to be left behind and the needs of these special children had to be addressed. It did not take Ann long to realize that she could make a positive contribution and that the rewards outweighed everything else.

With Ann working full-time, Dave was able to quit his job at UPS and they were actually able to spend time together in the evenings. For Ann, it was just peaceful to sit in the same room as Dave and watch him studying. They did not need costly entertainment. On weekends they would go to Al and Gert's for dinner and there were always care packages to take home. Often they would have enough food for several dinners, and Ann would be profoundly grateful as her cooking prowess was definitely a lacking skill.

Dave graduated that June, and Ann encouraged him to take a fellowship under his uncle and to study at Jewish Memorial Hospital. She continued teaching, except she was now offered a position as an English teacher in the same school. The only difference was that she was now trying to teach the students how to read necessary signs instead of how to count change. She could never understand how children could be allowed to reach junior high school and be totally unable to read. It was not uncommon for her to arrive at school early and to stay until six in the evening, and for several of the children to stay with her getting extra help. The rewards were ample; the reading scores for the majority of the class went from zero to third grade. Even more than the academic aspect, Ann was rewarded by the love these children returned to her. They would protect her in the halls, escort her to Dave's car when he picked her up after school, and even buy her little gifts, which she discouraged because she really did not want them to spend money on her when every penny was needed by them. Of course, it became a family joke when she would buy winter coats for students who did not have any and make sure there were always extra ties in the closet in case boys came to school without one, as ties were required under the school's dress code. Here she was, earning fifty-four hundred dollars a year and attempting to support herself and her husband, and yet no child would be permitted to go hungry or to miss school because of not having a winter coat. Ann knew that welfare checks were being misspent on drugs and alcohol, but she could not make the children suffer. She always remembered how important teachers had been to her when she needed help. It made her feel good to be able to help her students and in a way felt like it was payback time.

The black cloud once again came over Ann's world when she learned that she was pregnant. This was not in the plans. She and Dave had to work to establish a practice, and having a baby would only be an impediment.

"Don't worry, it will all work out. My family will help babysit and we will find a way to manage. You always say you want a family – maybe it is starting a little early but it will work out," Dave continually told Ann.

"I do not see how we can manage. We need my salary."

"You can work the rest of this year, and by then, I will have completed the fellowship and I will be able to get a job working for someone in his office."

"You always said you wanted to start your own practice."

"I will, but I will work for someone else for now so that there will be money coming in immediately."

"That sounds like it will be hard to do."

"Not really; a new practice does not require six days a week. I will work elsewhere two or three days a week and the rest of the time I can devote to our own office. I was planning on doing that anyway."

"I will want to go back to work once the baby is born."

"Depending where we decide to settle, we can try to work that out. If we are close to my folks, I am sure my mother will babysit for us. I don't think you would want a stranger to take care of our child."

"I am still sorry this happened."

"It's not your fault; there is nothing to be sorry about. We will work it out."

And so Ann began to feel good about being pregnant and even started to look forward to having a baby of her own. As her little belly began to grow, she shared the news with her colleagues and each time became more excited. Everyone told her she was glowing and, most importantly, Dave kept telling her how beautiful she looked. Instead of finding her less sexy, he kept telling her that he found her more sexy and it was as though a new dimension came to their relationship.

The happiness began to unravel one day in school. Ann went to the ladies' room and watched in horror as the bowl filled with blood. Dave was immediately called and rushed her to the hospital where their fears were confirmed. Ann had miscarried and needed a D&C. Having no health insurance, and fearing the expense, Ann refused the procedure, saying that women had miscarriages all the time and nature would take care of it. She was warned to go home and stay in bed, and if the bleeding became more intense to return to the hospital immediately. When they arrived back at the apartment they were surprised to find Gert there, bags packed, telling them they were going to her apartment to stay with them until Ann was better. There were no excuses accepted; she was not going to leave Ann in the apartment alone while Dave was at work. Since her place was bigger, they were coming and that was that.

"How did you hear about all of this in the first place?" Dave asked his mother.

"Susan called me from school to find out how Ann was when she did not hear from her. When she told me what was going on, I came right over, let myself in and packed Ann's bag. Now you get whatever you need and let's go."

"How unlike you to take over!"

"Go, enough talk. Daddy will be home soon and he will be worried."

And so it was that Ann went home with Gert and was fussed over by the entire family. If she ever doubted their love, she could no longer do so. They were just totally unselfish. Gert made Dave's younger brother give up his room and sleep on the couch and she moved the young couple into his quarters, put Ann to bed and told her, in no uncertain terms, that she was to remain there. It took two weeks for Ann to stop bleeding and start feeling like herself. It surprised her that she felt so depressed about losing the baby, but Gert would not tolerate the depression and encouraged her to get on with life.

"There'll be another pregnancy. This is not that unusual. Many women have multiple miscarriages before actually having a baby. You are young and healthy and you will become pregnant again."

"I know you are right. I also know now was not a perfect time for us to have a child. It is just that I feel like I lost something precious and it makes me sad. I was already thinking of names so that I could name it after my father and he would finally have a name."

"Don't let anyone diminish your feelings. Everything you feel is real and justified. But there is no going back and there is nothing we can do except pick up and move forward. Dwelling on what happened is not good for you or for Dave."

With that, Ann got herself out of bed, put on makeup and was ready when Dave came back from the hospital to go home and pick up life where it had been left off. It was good getting back to the apartment and she knew it would be good for her to go back to school.

"This is just another chapter that has ended and a new one begun," she told Dave that night. "Together we will get through it all."

"You're right, but I cannot help but be amazed that Cel never even got in touch with us during this whole time."

"Is she even in New York?"

"Who knows? She definitely is missing in action."

"How like my mother!" Ann replied laughing. "She has always been MIA where I am concerned."

CHAPTER 22

Life can prove to be totally amazing. Just when everything seems to be going wrong, things turn around and start to improve. So it was during the weeks following the miscarriage. Dave found an office where he felt he could afford to open and start a practice. He had originally wanted to move to Florida to be near his cousin, but his Dad had become very upset at the idea of Dave moving so far away. Dave decided to remain in the New York area. His feeling was that if he could not make a go of a practice in the New York area, he could then move to Florida and his father could not object. He chose an area in suburban Nassau County where he could sublet an office from an established dentist at a rent that seemed affordable. The office was small with just room for one treatment room, a small reception area and an even smaller consultation room. They had enough money to outfit the office without taking expensive loans, so they could be set to open right after his fellowship was completed. Whether they would actually see patients remained a major question, since neither Dave nor Ann knew anyone in the area and he certainly did not have a referral base. Ann was able to secure a teaching position in a neighboring town, so they had her salary to help keep them afloat and they did find an affordable apartment not far from Ann's school, so they would not need a second car, another expense that was saved. They were both excited about the new adventure. The unhappiness that had clouded their lives soon became a distant memory as they both dedicated themselves to trying to make Dave's professional dreams a reality. He did take a position at his uncle's office in Manhattan, where he would work two days a week to help bring some immediate money in, and Ann did go to the office with him when she was off from school so she could answer the phone, which rarely rang. Years later, they would remember playing hangman while waiting for the occasional telephone call requesting an appointment or for a patient to come into the reception room. They would always remember the very first patient seen in the embryonic office. Her name was Mrs. Ahern. She lived in the apartment directly behind the office and had fallen and injured her foot. She had come out of her apartment and met Ann, who was walking the dog, and the two women started talking. Before long, Ann had learned of her injury and was able to suggest that Dave might be able to help alleviate her pain. It turned out that Mrs. Ahern had fractured her foot and the fracture had not been diagnosed at the local hospital. Dave was able to help her and she, in turn, told her friends about the young doctor, and so a practice was born.

Ann was never happier than during this time of her life. She and Dave would go to the park and cook hamburgers and hot dogs on the grills or play horseshoes. Sometimes Gert and Al would come and join them on a Sunday afternoon. There were also the long walks at Jones Beach and the joy of just being together. It was amazing how little money they would spend on entertainment and yet how much was available to them.

Teaching was very different in the new school. The classes were not homogenously grouped, so there were students who could not read in the same class as extremely advanced students. The general goal was to teach to the middle of the class and to allow the chips to fall where they might. This was not part of Ann's psyche, so she would encourage the students at either end of the spectrum to come in after school for additional help. Ann made it her policy to stay in her classroom until the last student left and most of the students seemed to appreciate her efforts. The additional reward was that Ann really got to know the students, and it was especially gratifying to see the underprivileged children make progress and learn to read and write.

No matter how happy Ann was, her relationship with Cel remained a thorn in her side. She rarely spoke with her mother, and Cel and her husband made no attempt to come and see where or how Ann was living. Cel basically remained missing in action and there was a small part of Ann's being that missed having her mother as part of her life. Gert did everything possible to fill the void, but she was not Ann's mother and there was always some reserve in their relationship. That reserve did not extend to Al. He always seemed to know just what to say and what to do to make Ann feel extra-special, just as she imagined her own father would have done. It was easy to call him Dad.

Happiness is always interrupted, and for Ann the ceiling came crashing down when she went to the gynecologist and was told that she would never be able to become pregnant. There were too many adhesions from miscarriage which the doctor suspected was a tubal pregnancy, and it was the doctor's opinion that conception would be impossible. At first, Ann and Dave were devastated by the news, but then they came to accept it and to continue to find enjoyment being together. Ann began to make plans to further her career. She started taking courses at Hofstra University for her Masters degree and began planning to go into administrative positions in the school system. For Dave, things were going better. His practice was showing signs of growth and he was feeling the reward of being able to help people. But just as that was happening, so was the war in Vietnam escalating. President Johnson announced plans to start drafting married men who were exempt from the draft under President Kennedy's administration. It did not take long for Dave to receive his notice to report for his pre-induction physical. Here was a war that both Ann and Dave intellectually opposed and now it was going to ruin their lives. The infant practice would not be able to be sustained and the rent would not be able to be paid, but worse than anything, they would be separated.

Gert was also reacting to the news. She kept telling Ann that it was worse for her to face having her son go to war than it was for Ann to see her husband go off. After all, if anything happened to Dave, Ann would be able to get another husband, but she would never be able to have another son.

"I know what you are saying, but this is not a competition. We will both be profoundly affected if Dave is actually drafted. We both love him, so please let us stop trying to argue as to who loves him more. You are his mother and I am his wife. We love him differently, but one does not outweigh the other."

"You're young. Your whole life is ahead of you. My life is coming toward the twilight and I cannot face losing my son."

"I cannot face losing my husband!" With that, Ann walked out of the room, knowing that Gert would probably never understand the depth of her relationship with Dave and not really caring if she understood it or not. One thing she did know was that she was going to do everything possible to keep him from being drafted.

Ann contacted patients, the hospital and even their Congressman and Senator to try to get letters explaining Dave's role in the community's health needs. Dave placed little value in the campaign, but decided it made Ann feel better to be doing something so he went along with it. It was not until after he had actually gone for his army physical that they received word that he was being placed in a non-draft status. The news came just before New Year's Eve in 1966 and to say it was the happiest New Year ever was an understatement.

The year 1966 was forever the year of the most pleasant surprises and the year of the impossibles coming true. In March, Ann learned that she was not dying from some mysterious illness, but was actually suffering from morning sickness. When she told the doctor that it was impossible for her to be pregnant, he laughed and said, "There are lots of impossible babies out there."

At first both Dave and Ann were overjoyed by the news. They had buried their feelings about actually having a family when they thought it was an impossibility, but now they both felt a little fear. They knew their lives would be forever changed by a child. Plans made would have to be changed and, of course, there was the financial aspect of Ann not working any longer. Would the practice be able to sustain them? Would they ever be able to buy their own home? Dave was insistent that Ann not return to school after the baby was born.

"We will just have to manage on what I bring home. I do not want my child being raised by a stranger."

"I agree with you in principle, but if we need the money..."

"We'll just have to make do with what I bring home and that's it. We've done without in the past and we can do it again. The practice is growing."

"I know you're right, but it just frightens me. I've always worked and it will be really strange not going back to school when September comes. Do you realize that school seems to always have been a part of my life?"

"You'll be so busy; you probably will not even miss the classroom."

"You know, what really worries me is the thought of what type of a mother I will be. I really am afraid of being like Cel. All the books say that we tend to mimic our parents in our relationships with our own children. I would hate to become an abusive parent."

"You are too smart to let that happen. You know that she was both mentally and physically abusive, and I have confidence that you will stop yourself before allowing yourself to mimic her. I cannot image you hitting any living thing or playing mind games with anyone."

"God, I hope you're right. I know my sister has tried to not be the type of mother Cel was, but she is so cold to her kids that they must wonder if she really loves them. I always think of how she turns her face when they come over to kiss her so that they actually kiss her hair. It always gives me an eerie feeling. And it is funny, but I doubt she really knows she is doing it."

"Your sister is frigid. She cannot help but keep everyone at arm's distance. Look at her relationship with her husband. My God, she did everything in her power to drive him to drink."

"I know you're right. I always liked Larry, but he always seemed like a very unhappy man. Now that I know what it means to really love someone, I realize that he never had warmth or love in his relationship and possibly never had fulfilling sex either."

With that, Dave took Ann into his arms and held her really close. There was such strength there that Ann began to relax and to feel that he was indeed right and everything would just work out for them.

CHAPTER 23

True, many things had happened during the ensuing years from when Mark was born to the day that Cel was buried. While Morris was alive, Cel continued to live her life without any attempt at being a part of Ann's life or really caring about the children; Ann now had two sons. She never got to know her grandchildren; they were either too noisy or too active for her to be able to enjoy them. After Morris had his stroke and was left unable to speak or walk, Cel's life changed. She did manage to transfer many of Morris' stocks to her own account and to secure an ample amount of his cash before she put him into a nursing home, claiming she was not strong enough to care for an invalid. She could not find a man who would be interested in her and she became angry with the world. Friends were not around anymore and Cel was really alone. The television became her only contact with the world. Only Estelle seemed to be interested in giving her time. But it was only in later years that Ann would understand why her sister was so interested in Cel; she was able to secure much of the money Cel had taken from Morris and use it for herself. Ann did not know about the money until she broke up Cel's apartment and found the documents hidden in her dresser. There were sale reports for IBM and General Electric, along with transfer slips to a bank in Connecticut.

It all became clear. Estelle had actually called Ann nine years ago and told her that she could not take care of Cel anymore, that she could not "handle it" and was changing her phone number. Copies of Cel's bank accounts were then sent to Ann and Cel was virtually penniless. Since it was beyond a possibility to have Cel come and live with them, Ann and

Dave decided to hire a caretaker to stay with Cel during the day. Dave never complained about the expense and Ann was grateful that someone other than herself was looking after Cel. Whenever Ann would come to visit, Cel would tell her how much she hated her and how much she loved Estelle. How ironic that the "hated one" remained there to take care of her. Ann knew in her heart that if the tables had been turned, neither Cel nor Estelle would be there to take care of her. But Dave kept telling Ann that if she had found a dog in the street, she would take care of it, and there was no way she would be able to live with herself if she did not do the "right thing" and take care of Cel. Being honest about her feelings was the only salvation for Ann and she never missed a chance to let Cel know that she was fully aware of her hatred.

"I know it will never change. I am sorry you hate me so much and hopefully one day you will realize how much you have missed," Ann told her mother on the last visit to her apartment.

"I have missed nothing from you. I am only sorry you were ever born."

Little did Ann know these would be the last words she would ever hear her mother utter. One week after that visit, Cel suffered a massive internal bleed. Ann had her taken to Dave's hospital where the doctors did what they could for her, but she ended up having a stroke and lapsing into a coma. Ann saw her in the hospital bed: a little, shriveled-up old lady who had nothing to live for or anyone who cared about her. Ann's only hope was that Cel would die and she would, at last, be free of her.

As the rain pelted the window, Ann came to understand that Cel was a failure as a person, a mother and a grandmother. She allowed her selfishness to control her at the expense of those that she should have cared about. In the end, she was a great loser in the game of life. It was ironic, but she even lost out with her courtship of the money god.

The rain was still coming down, but night had set. Ann realized she had been sitting in the room for hours, but she was grateful that the family realized she needed the time to put all her emotions into place. One thing she knew, she would never allow herself to become a "Cel" or to allow money to be her god.